The Perfect Crime:
Unmasking the Isabella Stewart Gardner Heist

A Theo Perdoux Mystery

Books by Larry Maness

Jake Eaton Mysteries
Nantucket Revenge
A Once Perfect Place
Strangler

A Theo Perdoux Mystery
The Last Perdoux
The Perfect Crime

Novels
The Voice of God

The Perfect Crime:
Unmasking the Isabella Stewart Gardner Heist

A Theo Perdoux Mystery

Larry Maness

SPEAKING VOLUMES, LLC
NAPLES, FLORIDA
2023

The Perfect Crime: Unmasking the Isabella Stewart Gardner Heist

ISBN 978-1-64540-997-7

For my partner in crime, Marianne.

Chapter One

In the early morning hours of March 18, 1990, robbers entered Boston's Isabella Stewart Gardner Museum and stole 11 paintings, a Chinese vase, and a Corsican eagle finial collectively worth millions of dollars. On June 1st, 1990, museum director, Clair Bowman walked into my Charles Street office 20 minutes late for her appointment. It was a warm, spring like morning, sunny with a slight breeze.

I had been on the telephone talking with my business partner in Spain. For the past thirteen years, Gina Ponte and I had honed our skills negotiating disputes between auction houses, private parties, museums, and insurance companies all claiming questionable ownership of the artwork in dispute. Gina's home base was Barcelona where she ran Sala Ponte, a combination art gallery and art theft recovery business. My office, set up exclusively for research and investigation, was in Boston where I'd taken early retirement from Boston's Tactical Patrol Force.

My conversation with Gina related to a Matisse stolen from a private collector in London. I'd traced the painting to a gang of thieves in Nice who wanted to flip it for cash. The owner was willing to pay the ransom on the condition that the thieves provide him information on his family's art collection stolen by the Nazis during World War II. The loot from that war period was Gina's and my niche, primarily because my family's art collection was one of the hundreds packed up and carried off to Germany. Like the London collector, my mother spent her life tracking down her family's collection. When she died, I took over.

I hadn't started out with a passion for hunting down stolen masterpieces. In fact, all through the police academy, I never gave much thought to what a thief took. The fact that a law was broken, that someone was bending the rules, taking advantage of those of us who abided by the rules was enough. That I wanted a level playing field was, no doubt, the result of being raised by the couple who adopted me, Helen and Arthur Zachary. Arthur was a journalist, and Helen was an attorney.

Truth and justice.

I knew nothing of my biological parents until thirteen years ago. Just shy of my forty-fifth birthday and a member of Boston's Tactical Patrol Force, someone threw a rock the size of a grapefruit from the roof of an apartment building. The side of my face was no match for what felt like a boulder when it struck. I was blind in my right eye for two months and after several reconstructive surgeries, regained partial use of that eye. I could have stayed on the desk at Boston PD when I got out of the hospital but decided instead to take a medically induced early retirement.

I bought a house on the beach in Provincetown, walked the dunes, did some fishing, and generally took the time to smell the roses. I'd even reconnected by phone with my ex-wife in what can only be described as cool yet cordial chatter. She was then a nurse in Vermont and had called to see if the slow pace of retirement had yet driven me crazy. After I hung up, I wondered if that was wishful thinking on her part.

All was going well in retirement until I was rousted from my sleep at three in the morning by a heavy fist pounding on my front door. I slipped into my robe and walked cautiously downstairs. With the security chain latched, I eased the door open a few inches. A short, well-dressed man stood before me with urgent news. My mother had recently died in Spain. It was her last wish that I come to Barcelona and continue her life's work. She was a Perdoux, daughter of Claude

Perdoux, an art gallery owner in Paris whose collection was stripped by the Nazis. Simone Perdoux had spent her life hunting for her family's collection. As the last Perdoux, the job was being offered to me from her grave.

That I wasn't looking for a job didn't seem to matter.

I let the little man in, convinced that he had the wrong house. My name was Theo Zachary. My adopted parents were killed years before in a sightseeing airplane crash in Hawaii. I knew no one named Perdoux and knew nothing of any family art collection stolen by the Nazis.

It was then that the little man produced a black and white photograph of a young woman standing in front of a grand French chateaux, holding a newborn in her arms.

"You with your mother. Your father was called back to Berlin and could not stand for the picture. He would not have been welcome, of course. Everyone in Paris hated him," the little man said. "Your father is Wilhelm Barr, the German officer charged with stealing the soul of Paris, one art collection at a time."

How people absorb startling news is unpredictable, especially when the information borders on horrific. I remembered the cold glare from the eyes of a man I'd once informed that his daughter hadn't survived a shooting. He didn't want to believe it. And how could he? An hour before, his daughter was leaving work just as the holdup unfolded. I think I held the identical cold stare when the little man from Spain told me about my biological parents. I was forty-five years old and learning for the first time about my European parents, parents I'd often wondered about but now wanted no more of this unsettling news.

I remember my jangled nerves vibrating like a tuning fork. "My father was a Nazi?" I'd said. "I don't believe it."

"Then focus on your mother and the art collection she has left you in her will," he advised. "All you need do is find where your father hid it. Like hundreds of other collections stolen during the war, it's missing. That is something you will discover about your past, Theo. That which disappears is a theme. Paintings go missing, and so did a child."

"What are you talking about?" I'd demanded. "What child?"

"You," the little man said. "I'm talking about how your mother pronounced you dead, and how you have sprung back to life. For how long is the question."

"Don't talk in riddles," I snapped.

"I talk the truth, Mr. Perdoux. When your father learns you are alive, he will come after you. Simone kept your life a secret all these years, because she feared what he might do. That's why all those years ago in Paris she told Wilhelm you had died when the bombs fell. You and other children all killed. It was the only way she could think to protect you, to keep you from the man she learned to despise."

I stubbornly resisted what I was hearing. I was Theo Zachary, firmly in the middle of the middle class. Retired. Reasonably content if not happy. It made no sense that a man I'd never met, a man who the Spaniard claimed was my father, wanted to kill me after all these years.

"Why would Wilhelm Barr want to see me dead? It doesn't make any sense."

"Your death will end their war, Theo. Simone and Wilhelm fought over you from the day you were born."

"But Simone is dead."

"And Wilhelm plans on being the last man standing. That's who he is."

"You told me the who, now tell me the where."

"I don't know where your father is. He fled Germany like the other officers who managed to get out. Simone would not now ask for you to take up her work if she didn't think you could succeed. You have the training. You were a police officer. You can stand up to your father. You might even survive. Simone's business partner, Gina Ponte, will welcome you should you accept the challenge."

I had every intention of tossing the little man out in the street and would have if I could have thrown out with him the idea that I was the man he called Perdoux. How do you take such an accusation back? How do you deny it? How do you make it disappear like the family's art collection?

The answer is you don't. You move on. In my case, moving on meant a new career with a new partner and a new focus on finding looted art. Some of that stolen art belonged to the London collector with the missing Matisse. Some of it belonged to the Perdouxs, a family I never knew I had but had grown to admire. As for my father, we'd met once many years ago in an Italian hilltown. The encounter was strained and brief and violent. Two men died; others left injured.

As I thought of that frightening moment, I remembered diving to the ground when Wilhelm fired his rifle aimed at me. The Spaniard's warning that Wilhelm wanted to see me dead again raced through my mind as I lay there like Gulliver snared by the Lilliputians. That my father let me live was one more puzzle that I wanted to solve. Why not shoot to kill? And where are the stolen collections you have so cleverly hidden?

My hope was that my dealings with the London collector would help answer the last question. On the telephone, I passed along to Gina the terms the collector demanded before he'd pay the ransom for the Matisse and had just ended the call when Clair Bowman stepped into my office.

Clair Bowman was in her early forties, medium height and weight with light brown hair bordering on dirty blond cut short. Her expression was serious like a banker who was about to tell you that your loan had been denied. She wore a light blue suit over a white turtleneck and carried a leather briefcase.

We'd crossed paths before at a Christie's art auction. She was there looking to buy a piece for her private collection, and I was there making sure the auction house had pulled a canvas from the sale that proved to have a questionable provenance. One of my clients raised the red flag, claiming the painting had been stolen years ago from her parent's summer house on Martha's Vineyard. I raised the issue with Christie's too late to have the picture's listing removed from the sale's catalogue, so I sat in the back row making sure my client's interests were protected.

The Gardner Museum's heist was front page news with police spokesmen saying little about the investigation and Miss Bowman saying less. There were, however, leads. A witness saw two men in a car about the time of the break-in. There may have been two cars, he wasn't sure. The witness was also a little vague on descriptions. One man was taller than the other. One was thin. Hair color? He wasn't sure of that either. Make of car or cars? Foreign. Maybe. He didn't get the color other than dark. It was after midnight, and he'd been drinking with friends.

The two security guards inside the museum couldn't offer much either. The one downstairs behind a bank of motion detector monitors had opened the service entrance door and let the robbers, dressed as Boston Police, inside. Yes, he knew that was a breach of protocol, but the thieves said they were in the area checking on a robbery. They wanted to confirm that the museum was secure. To make sure, they called the second guard to the first floor and proceeded to handcuff them both. The guards were then led to the basement, their mouths wrapped in duct tape before tying them to heating pipes. Ninety minutes later, the robbers were gone, and the museum was out thirteen prized pieces of art.

I walked around my desk when Clair came in and shook her hand. "Good to see you," I said. "You're a fixture now on the nightly news. How are you holding up?"

She sat in the leather chair near the windows. "All right, I guess. Everybody wants a statement, and I can't offer much. In fact, there's not much to say. It's like the pieces walked out on their own and disappeared. I feel terrible about it, just dreadful. The board is furious with me, and I don't think the public is too happy either. How could this have happened?"

"Smart crooks," I said.

"Smarter than our security guards, that's for sure." Clair inhaled a quick breath and let it out as she leaned back in her chair. "I need your help, Theo. The board and I met last night and decided that we had to do something on our own to get those paintings back. We want to hire you."

I put one hand up to stop her. "The Boston police will have no patience with a private investigator poking around in their business. Even one of their own, retired, wouldn't be welcome. I'm afraid I'll have to decline."

"Hear me out, Theo. I've spoken to the police about this, and they seem to think that it's not relevant, not connected to the robbery. Maybe they're right, but the board and I want to track every possible option to the end. What if our suspicion has merit?"

I could see the quicksand ahead and knew if I asked Clair to say more, I'd be stepping in it. Still, I was curious.

"What suspicion have you got?" I asked.

For the first time, Clair seemed to relax. "Six months ago, a freelance writer in the magazine *Art World* published an article on the

Gardner's Cavelli guitar, one of only two known to exist in private collections." She pulled a copy of the magazine from her valise and handed it across my desk. "Page forty-two," she said.

I opened it on a multi-picture spread of a darkly varnished guitar decorated with ivory inlay and swirls across the body. The text below one of the pictures identified bone and mother of pearl as the decorative materials.

"Nice," I said without reading the article.

"More than nice, Theo. It's extraordinary but in need of repair. The neck has come loose from the body, and there is a significant crack across the back panel. Not bad really for an instrument made in 1720 by the famous maker Jacopo Mosca Cavelli. We feel blessed to have it as part of the museum's collection."

I handed the magazine back. "I didn't know Mrs. Gardner had interest in guitars."

"She had an interest in beauty," Clair said. "When she saw something she thought beautiful, she bought it, often with the encouragement of Bernard Berenson."

"Berenson had a tremendous influence on Mrs. Gardner, didn't he?"

"Yes, her and many other wealthy collectors interested in the Italian Renaissance. Most of those collectors had money but not much knowledge of what they were buying. People like Berenson bridged that gap and pointed out possible additions to their collections. It was very competitive, and Mrs. Gardner liked winning as much as she liked collecting. Like many pieces in the museum that are now priceless, the Cavelli guitar's value has risen significantly. Expert repairs would make it more so." She returned the magazine to her valise. "A few weeks after the article appeared, I got a letter from Aldo Conte identifying himself as someone interested in making those repairs. Being

Italian and from a long line of violin makers, he believed that he could bring the Cavelli back to nearly new condition."

"A unique way of introducing himself," I said.

"Yes, it was."

"You checked him out, of course."

"Of course," she said and pulled a printout from her valise. Handing it over, she said, "It's all there. Aldo Conte's family goes back several generations and has a reputation for making beautiful string instruments and repairing and refurbishing old ones. His instruments are said to be of the quality made by Stradivarius. Musicians from all over the world seek him out. He doesn't advertise. His website has a few photos of violins. He doesn't list prices and posts no photographs of himself."

I flipped to the second page of the printout and scanned a list of awards Conte had earned, most of which I'd never heard of. "Impressive," I admitted.

"We thought so."

"His shop's in Rome. You could do a road trip," I quipped.

"Better yet, Mr. Conte was going to be in Boston on other business and offered to visit the museum and evaluate the guitar's damage. Once schedules matched, we agreed to meet and see if we should move ahead with the repairs. Mr. Conte came to the Gardner this past January with his assistant, a pleasant young woman who helped conduct the evaluation."

"Which amounted to what?" I asked.

"Visual observation, of course. Conte took detailed measurements and photographs. He had one of those laser measuring devices and the camera on his cell phone. His assistant made notes, but all in all, I thought it a rather simple yet thorough analysis."

"How long did all of that take?"

"Just short of an hour, including the time we spoke to get a sense of one another. Then, I went about getting the museum ready to open for the morning and left him under the supervision of the security guard I'd asked to come in early. I wanted someone to watch the process."

"You mean you didn't fully trust Mr. Conte," I offered.

Clair cracked a knowing smile. "I mean we wouldn't permit anyone free access to the Gardner's collection without some staff on hand. Conte came in early before we opened. I'd made arrangements for security to come in early as well."

"One guard?" I asked.

"Yes. Aldo Conte is a well-respected maker of world class instruments. I had no reason to think he came to the museum for motives other than his interest in repairing the Cavelli. That is what I thought then. I have since changed my mind."

"What happened after he made his evaluation?" I asked.

"I finished up a few things in my office and then took him and his assistant to an early lunch."

"What made you change your mind about him?"

"I don't know, really. I thought his approach to the repairs was reasonable. Instead of shipping such a fragile piece to his Rome shop, I asked him if he might work with the curatorial staff at the Museum of Fine Arts and do the work at their shop here in Boston. Their conservatory shop is only a few blocks away and much more complete than what we have at the Gardner. The members of the board agreed that Mr. Conte should do the repairs here in Boston. Besides, we could then keep an eye on his progress."

"Meaning some board members were also suspicious of Mr. Conte?"

"Meaning one can never be too careful when pieces of extreme value are left in another's care. If that were not the case, Theo, you would be out of business. We at the Gardner know only too well that thieves are everywhere."

"What did you do next?"

"I wrote a letter of introduction to the MFA for Mr. Conte and sent it via e-mail to the conservatory shop along with a copy of the *Art World* article and Conte's resume. I followed up with a phone call saying they should expect a visit from him soon." Clair pulled in a quick breath and slowly let it out. "I thought there must have been a breakdown in communication between Mr. Conte and me, because he never made it to the Museum of Fine Arts. I waited a week or so and tried to contact him in Rome. I left a message on his cell phone and an e-mail message. No response from either."

"Maybe he just changed his mind. Flying back to Boston, working at the MFA," I shrugged. "Maybe when he added it all up, he decided it wasn't worth it."

"Fine," Clair said. "Why doesn't he say so? We're all adults."

I leaned forward on my desk and said, "All right, I'll bite. What do you think is really going on with Aldo Conte?"

"Maybe it's just because of the robbery. Or maybe it's just because the past two weeks have been a living hell that's left me exhausted, but I can't help thinking there's a connection between his visit and the break in."

"There is such a thing as coincidence," I reminded her. "He read the article about a special guitar, he had an interest in taking a look, he . . ."

"He used the Cavelli guitar to plan something. I'm sure of it." Clair shook her head. "I don't know what I'm saying, really. The police said I'm clutching at straws. They said it sounded like Aldo Conte read an article in *Art World* and wanted to play big shot. I reminded them that in the world of crafting beautiful violins, he *is* a big shot. They said I should stop clutching at theories that don't add up and stop bothering them. Some on the board think the same thing. Others on the board agree with me. Those that do and I want to find out if Aldo Conte was playing big shot here in Boston, or if there is more to it. I know your business is in finding stolen art, Theo. I also know you're not in the business of tracking down missing people, but I'm not clutching at straws like the police believe. Aldo Conte is involved somehow in the robbery, and I want to know how."

"As in Aldo Conte cased the joint, then came back and stole thirteen pieces." I shook my head. "Sounds like a reach to me, Clair, and like you say, I'm not in the business of tracking down missing persons." Clair's disappointment sailed across my desk. "I can recommend . . ."

"No, Theo. You have connections across the European art scene. You've tracked down masterpieces all over the world. You can't recommend anyone who has your qualifications. All I ask is that you look into it before you say no. Please."

I pulled in a deep breath and pushed it out, thinking of a graceful way to stay out of what I knew would be a tedious case. But Clair Bowman was not a frivolous woman. She was dedicated, smart, and in trouble. The Matisse case was nearing its end, and I did have some free time.

Like a planet doomed to its orbit, I said, "Men don't disappear without a trace. Credit cards, car rentals." I shrugged. "Unless someone was helping Mr. Conte vanish, he's left a trace somewhere."

Clair Bowman brightened. "You mean you'll look into it?"

"No promises," I cautioned. "But, yes, if you really want me to dig around."

She cracked a slight smile. "I really want. Thank you, Theo."

I pick up a pen and paper. "I'll start with the security guard who watched over Conte and his assistant. What's his name?"

"Charles Raskin. He's on in the afternoons. Weekdays."

I made a note. "And all you have on Aldo Conte. Maybe you ought to give me back that printout. Anything in it about his assistant?"

Clair shook her head. "A name, that's all. Angela Ricci."

When Clair put the printout on my desk, I asked if she had a photograph of Mr. Conte.

"Security takes a photo of anyone who works on any of Mrs. Gardner's pieces. I'll have Chuck Raskin make sure you get a copy."

I made another note. "I might have to chase your violin maker all the way to Rome. Answers won't come cheap."

"We're already looking at millions of dollars in stolen art. Getting all or some of those pieces back will be worth the cost. You and Sala Ponte have an excellent reputation, Theo. What do you think are the chances of success?" Her question carried mild concern.

"It's hard to say. Thieves come in all shapes and sizes with motives of all shapes and sizes. Finding out who they are is one thing, catching them another, retrieving the stolen objects something else again. But keep in mind," I reminded her, "you're hiring me to find Aldo Conte. I'm not bumping heads with Boston PD looking for the artwork."

"I understand," she said. "I just thought . . ."

"I know what you thought," I said. "Conte leads me to the stolen pieces, and I solve the case. You don't want to get your hopes up, Clair. I know who's running the investigation in Boston. Brody Flynn's solid. Let him do his job, and I'll do mine. Now, what can you tell me about the robbery that wasn't in the newspaper?"

Clair thought a moment. "The police have kept quiet about the motion detectors; I suppose so the robbers will believe that their every movement inside the museum was captured on tape. But that is not the case. The motion detectors on most of the first floor and some of the second did not work. We have partial recordings of their movements inside the museum, but certainly not on every minute of the nearly ninety minutes they were inside."

"That's a long time for thieves to be on the loose. Smash-and-grab robbers are in and out in five minutes, maybe less."

"What does that tell you about our situation?"

"That they might have been looking for particular pieces. That they had to spend time searching. It's hard to say, Clair. But it might indicate that Aldo Conte had nothing to do with the robbery."

"Why do you say that?"

"He was in the museum. He looked around, or his assistant did the looking. If he's your robber, he would have entered, tied up the guards and gone directly to the pieces he wanted. In and out in a flash." I saw another wave of disappointment cross her face. "But we can't be sure. He may have gotten inside and acted like a kid in a candy shop. First one thing, then another. Before you know it, an hour and a half is almost gone."

"And so are our priceless gems. Find him, Theo. Get the truth. Who knows where it will lead?"

"I'll see what I can do, Clair," I said and stood.

We stopped at my office door. "I want to be kept informed. Even if it's bad news."

"Duly noted," I said and opened the door. "You can tell Charles Raskin to expect a visit."

Wrecked lives have many causes: Bad marriage, bad health, bad career. Clair Bowman felt her career in jeopardy, because, on her watch, thieves carted off thirteen pieces, including a priceless Rembrandt and Vermeer. Clair Bowman's name would forever be linked to the most expensive art heist ever. I sympathized with her wanting to make amends, to do something, anything to help get the artwork returned. I wasn't confident that spending the time and money on connections between the Gardner, an antique guitar and Aldo Conte would produce results, but that was what I was being paid to do.

I decided to start earning my pay with a visit to the museum.

Chapter Two

It was a beautiful day, so I decided to ride the T to Huntington Avenue, then walk over the Fens to the Gardner Museum, which was built as a replica of a 15th Century Venetian style palazzo. Mrs. Gardner lived on the top floor and used the floors below as display rooms for her art collection. Upon her death, the Isabella Stewart Gardner Museum formally opened to the public.

When I walked inside and announced that I was there to talk with Charles Raskin, I was told to wait. In a few minutes, a tall man of about sixty wearing a blue pinstriped suit and polka dot red bow tie came around the corner. His thick gray hair was razor cut, and his polished shoes gleamed. His total presentation made me feel underdressed in my blue button down unpressed cotton shirt, blue blazer, chinos and unpolished leather boat shoes. I traded fashion for comfort when I turned fifty, six years ago. The man introduced himself as Stanford J. Brothers, Chairman of the Board of Directors at the Gardner.

"May I have a minute?" he asked, more as a demand than a question.

I nodded and followed him into the courtyard garden at the center of the museum's ground floor. The air was warm and humid, the flowers beautiful and sweet. I'd been to the Gardner on many occasions over the years but never spent much time in the garden. I wished I'd done so sooner.

"I will get directly to the point, Mr. Perdoux. All of us in an official capacity at the museum are deeply concerned, distraught even, over this dreadful situation. I mean a robbery and the needless destruction." He shook his head as if he still couldn't believe that thieves had sacked the place. "All of us want the crooks arrested, and the paintings returned as soon as possible."

"I can imagine," I said.

"We are also not very pleased that Clair, Director Bowman, sought you out and drew your attention to this business with the Cavelli guitar. Looking into any connection between that published article and Aldo Conte is not worth anyone's time. It's a meaningless diversion," Brothers said bluntly.

"Why do you say that?"

"The police considered it for one thing, and they rejected it. I spoke personally with the detective in charge of the investigation. Quinn is it?"

"Flynn," I corrected. "Brody Flynn."

"Yes, Flynn. Regardless, he agrees with me that the timing of this absurd speculation doesn't fit. An article comes out about the Cavelli in November, Aldo Conte shows up in January, and the museum is broken into in March. Where's the connection?"

"I don't know yet. Maybe there isn't one."

"And another thing. Why would a man who makes violins for a lucrative living in Rome come to Boston to steal eleven paintings and two other minor pieces?"

"I don't know that either," I admitted. "But why does it bother you to investigate Aldo Conte?"

Brothers stiffened. "Because your investigation won't stop there. You people start digging in one corner and pretty soon the entire garden is one dark hole after another. You will turn this into an unsightly mess, that's what will happen, and I don't want any part of it. Let me make myself clear, Mr. Perdoux. It's nothing personal, you understand. It's not you or anyone on the Boston police force. It's that this museum is a special place." He gestured at the garden courtyard with the sweep on one arm. "Look at it. A gem right out of Venice. If you use your imagination, you can almost see a gondola floating toward us. Mrs. Gardner created this out of her own vision. It was to be a palace for her own art. Art she wanted to share, not in a glass and steel cold building but in her home. That's the way to look at the Gardner Museum, Mr. Perdoux. Not as a public building with art on the walls, but as a woman's home with an open invitation for all to enter."

"That's certainly what the thieves did," I reminded him.

Brothers glared at me, his dark eyes narrowing. "I am painfully aware of that," he said. "But running off to Italy looking for a violin maker will only waste time and money. Neither of which the museum has in abundance, I'm afraid. Our low cash reserves are not all Miss Bowman's fault, I can assure you, but like the captain of the ship, she is in charge."

"You sound like you don't care much for Miss Bowman," I said.

"Do I?" Brothers blanched. "I don't mean to be so obvious, but I will tell you that Miss Bowman was not my first choice for director. I was on the search committee and had gone up to Vermont for the weekend to tap the maple trees for the spring sap run." Brothers must have caught my quizzical look. "Maple syrup. It's a hobby of mine as it was with my father and grandfather before me. We have a small farm of a few hundred acres in the North Country with a grass air strip so as to make quick trips up and back possible on short notice. I flew up Friday afternoon after the stock market closed to get an early start on the taps Saturday morning. As sometimes happens, a late spring snowstorm dropped nearly a foot of snow Sunday. I couldn't fly out as the runway was covered in ice. I missed the vote, and Miss Bowman was offered the position."

"When was that?"

"About five years ago."

"The board must be pleased. She's still here," I offered.

"And she's done some fine things, I admit that. Not always to my liking to be sure, but that's the natural conflict between a board that pays attention and a responsible director. There is always a bit of tension as there was last night when this business of Aldo Conte came up. Miss Bowman wanted the board's opinion regarding hiring you to look into the matter. A few members and I were against it for the simple reason that the answer to who stole those paintings lies right here in this very building," Brothers said, studying me with an intense look.

That got my interest. "You're saying you know who's behind the theft?"

"Yes," Brothers blurted. "I mean, no. Not specifically."

"Who unspecifically?" I pressed.

"You need to understand something, Mr. Perdoux." We stepped around a large iron urn with white cotton top flowers cascading over the sides. "About one year ago, Miss Bowman, at the recommendation of the board's committee on security, hired a consultant to review and update the museum's security status. We knew the possibility of a robbery existed. We also knew that our security guards were inadequate to protect the remarkable holdings Mrs. Gardner had collected. We wanted to increase our insurance exposure and to modernize the building to prevent theft."

"Seems like a sound idea," I offered.

"Yes, well, we didn't follow through with the consultant's recommendations," Brothers admitted sheepishly. "You have to understand that Mrs. Gardner left very specific instructions in her will relating to how the museum was to be managed, how her collection was to be dealt with, and how much money could be spent yearly to maintain the building. If any of the conditions of her will were not followed to the letter, the museum was to be closed and her collection given to Harvard University."

"I heard she was a stickler for details. Once a painting was hung to her liking, it could never be moved. That sort of thing."

"Exactly. The consultant took those restrictions into consideration when he returned with his recommendations. To rewire the building without causing much of a disturbance, to alarm all the rooms, and to create a secure control space to monitor it all would be cost prohibitive. Even if the board members added substantially to the capital resources, Mrs. Gardner's endowment would be depleted, breaking the budget and resulting in the museum's closure. None of us wanted to be responsible for that. The Gardner is a true gem, Mr. Perdoux. We want to see that it survives."

"Not easy if you don't have the funds to run it," I said.

"Not easy, but we could manage, if, at the consultant's suggestion, we did two things. The first was to evaluate how we insured the collection. Some pieces are insured at full value, others for damage only." Brothers paused, then said, "Unfortunately, the pieces that were stolen two weeks ago were insured only for damage."

"Ouch."

"Yes. Very painful, indeed. At least no one can accuse the board of robbing the museum to collect the insurance money." He tried to laugh and failed. "There won't be any insurance payout. I'm afraid if that little item got into the press, we'd all look like fools. How can you not insure a Rembrandt or a Vermeer worth millions for its full value, for god's sake? The museum doesn't need any more bad publicity, Mr. Perdoux. Not after the largest art theft in the world happened right under our noses. We're already a laughingstock."

I didn't disagree. "You mentioned two things, Mr. Brothers. What is the second?"

"Replace our current staff of security guards with fewer, yet more professionally trained watchmen. Currently, we rely on part-time employees who are retired or college students. Neither group is particularly efficient."

"How many guards do you currently hire?"

"I'll have to get you the exact number. It's not large. Regardless, the consultant recommended cutting that number in half and supplementing the newly hired guards with a few well-placed cameras and additional motion detectors. A control room separate from the first-floor entrance would also be added. If we went ahead with those recommendations, we would save money in the long run and have greater protection from theft. The board agreed, and Miss Bowman held a meeting with the current security personnel explaining that they might be let go. Needless to say, they were not happy."

"And you think . . .?"

"I think security turned a blind eye and let the robbers in, because the robbers were, in fact, our own security guards. Not all of them, of course. Some of the malcontents. An act of spite, Mr. Perdoux. An act of revenge for possibly being removed from what I consider to be a very cushy job," Brothers said with his chin jutting out.

"Inside jobs are frequent in cases such as this," I admitted, "but the pieces are usually held as ransom. Amateur thieves want the money, not the art. They're not collectors. They want the cash fast. Have any demands been made?"

Brothers shook his head. "Not yet."

"It could still happen. It's only been a couple of weeks," I said. "They might want you good and anxious hoping you'll agree to anything. I'm sure the police have already interviewed security."

"Yes. Security. The board members. Volunteers. Every man and woman with anything remotely connected to this marvelous place has been interrogated. What they learned, I don't know. The police tell us nothing."

"Might be nothing to tell," I said, adding, "Maybe I should talk to Charles Raskin now. See what I can find out. Is he on your list as one of the possible robbers?"

"Raskin is a former salesman. Men's wear over in a specialty shop in Cambridge, if memory serves. His shop went out of business, and he wanted to try something else. I wouldn't put him at the top of my list as a thief."

"How old is he?"

"Mid-fifties, maybe."

"Any sort of trouble since he's worked here?"

"None that I can think of. He shows up. He does his job. He's been here the longest of any of our security staff. That's why he was selected to watch over Aldo Conte when he came to inspect the Cavelli. I think I would rule him out of any involvement in the robbery," Brothers said.

"A man above suspicion is the perfect candidate to mastermind the robbery. Where can I find him?"

"Upstairs," Brothers said, coolly. "I trust you'll see the folly in perusing this matter once you speak with him."

"One way to find out," I said and headed for the stairs.

Charles Raskin stood guard in the Dutch Room as a woman led a small, fussing child out into the hall leaving me alone with him. Raskin was heavy for his frame, about six feet tall with thinning hair. His flat expression gave nothing away except maybe a hint of boredom.

"Charles Raskin?" I asked.

"Chuck, but yes, I'm Raskin."

I introduced myself. "Miss Bowman suggested I talk with you about the day Aldo Conte examined the guitar in need of repair."

"The Cavelli, yes. Miss Bowman said you would be wanting this." Raskin reached inside his suitcoat pocket and removed an envelope. "Conte's picture and some other bits about him are in there."

I opened the flap and peered inside. The black and white photograph looked identical to a grainy passport picture. The man stood stiffly in front of a security camera. He appeared to be in his late forties with shallow eyes, a thin mouth, and slim nose. Nothing in his expression cried out thief or crook or beware. He looked ordinary. The picture of the woman on the next page revealed someone in her mid-thirties with medium dark hair, large dark eyes, and an inviting smile.

"I take it the female is Conte's assistant?"

"That's right."

"These the only pictures you've got?"

"The only ones. We're not exactly high tech here at the museum. Miss Bowman may have told you that security improvements were one of her priorities." Raskin shifted on his feet. "She even hired a consultant."

"So I heard. Big changes coming your way, if his recommendations were followed."

"Big promises is more like it," Raskin said, not hiding his disdain. "I've been with the museum for about six years. Miss Bowman came after I did. That's when all this consultant business started. Change the plantings in the courtyard garden? Hire a consultant. Change the humidity settings for the artwork? Hire a consultant. Upgrade security?"

"Hire a consultant," I chimed in.

"You got it. Nothing ever comes of it."

"Why is that?" I asked as a man entered and began the slow slog around the room, known to all museum goers. "Why does nothing ever come of the consultations?"

"Money," Raskin said confidently. "Looking around at all this wealth, you'd never guess the museum is broke—or close to it. The board is made up of old Boston money. They're not like the new Boston money who buy million-dollar condos in one of those new highrises. Old Boston money doesn't like to spend, that's why they're still flying around in their little airplanes, tapping their trees in Vermont." As though it were obvious, Raskin said, "I haven't had a meaningful raise in over two years. None of us has."

"Why do you stay on?" I asked.

"I ask myself that from time to time. Every now and then, I check out the want ads, brush up my resume. Lots of sales opportunities out there, but I don't want to go back into sales. Sales is a dying profession. The people in those million-dollar condos buy everything online. A computer takes their measurements and style preferences, and every week a box shows up with everything from designer underwear to silk sweaters. No, sales is out. I've had enough of that to last me a lifetime."

The man on the slog approached us and stopped. "Sorry to bother you," he said, pointing. Over Raskin's left shoulder hung the empty frame of Rembrandt's *Christ in the Storm of Galilee*, over his right the equally empty frame of Vermeer's *The Concert*. "The paintings used to be there, right? The ones stolen?"

"That is correct, sir," said Raskin, his voice friendly and helpful. "Cut from their frames as you can see. We rehung the frames thinking Mrs. Gardner would want it that way. A reminder for us all of the loss, you might say."

The man shook his head. "Terrible, isn't it? Who would do such a thing?"

"The police are asking that very thing, sir. And, yes, it is terrible."

"Worth a lot of money, I'll bet."

"Millions."

The man shook his head, amazed at the number. "And somebody just walked in and carted them off. I mean, I could have walked in and carted them off. Imagine," the man said and moved along, his head still shaking.

"Any ideas about the robbery?" I asked Raskin when we were again alone.

"None that I haven't already told the police. Security on duty that night broke protocol and let two men inside. That's not supposed to happen. Then again, security here is not top shelf. Guards on the night shift have been known to let friends in to smoke a little weed out in the courtyard. But you're not here to talk about the robbery, are you? Miss Bowman said you wanted to know what happened with the Aldo Conte visit."

"That's right," I said. "What do you think connects it to the robbery?"

"Nothing," Raskin said quickly. "How could there be a connection? Conte's focus was on the old guitar. Nothing else."

"You stayed with him the entire time?"

"Every minute."

"What about his assistant, Angela Ricci? She always right here with you?"

Raskin hesitated with a nearly imperceptible movement like a boxer's feint, then said, "Yes. She was right here taking notes. Conte would call out a measurement, and she'd make a note." I listened as Raskin talked me through how an expert measures and photographs a guitar in need of repair. When he finished his description, he said, "Pretty boring when you come right down to it. He took a measurement. His assistant wrote it down. He took another. She wrote that one down. His focus was always on the guitar and hers was on making notes."

"They never walked around the museum? Never explored other rooms?" I asked.

Raskin shook his head. "He came in the front door. Because they were going to be examining one of our pieces, we took both their pictures. Miss Bowman brought them right to the Cavelli. Conte got right to it, carefully picking it up and holding it like it was so fragile it would fall apart at any minute. He did nothing for the longest time but look."

"What did his assistant do during that time?" I asked. "You're sure she was always with the two of you?"

"Mostly," Rasking said with a shrug. "If she ducked out, it was only for a second or two. Had to go to the bathroom once. Stretched her legs, that sort of thing. I didn't blame her. I wish I could have walked around and stretched mine. When Conte was done and Miss Ricci had taken all the notes, Miss Bowman took them to lunch. That was it."

"What was your impression of Aldo Conte?"

Raskin thought a moment, then said, "Professional. Thorough. Focused. He never said two words to me. Not that he was nasty. He was just locked into that guitar. I mean, it's got a crack in the back and a few other problems. How long does it take to figure that out?"

"Were you surprised that Conte didn't follow through with the repairs?" I asked. "Or at least keep in contact?"

"I was surprised at first, yes; but then I got to thinking about it and figured that it fit a pattern, know what I mean? Consultants. Fix the crack on the Cavelli guitar? Hire a consultant."

"And then, nothing happens," I said.

"You got it. Miss Bowman and the board mean well, but, like I said, they're Blue Bloods, old family money and all that off tapping their trees. They don't want to spend a dime if they don't have to. Being associated with the Gardner is like a trophy for them, a badge of honor. Their excuse for not doing anything is Mrs. Gardner's will. She didn't want any changes made to her pride and joy. So, when they're confronted with a problem, the board members wring their hands and make no changes. Everybody's got a clear conscience while the museum falls to ruin."

"That's quite an indictment."

"But true. You might say someone did those thirteen pieces a favor by getting them out of here."

"Someone like a security guard, maybe?"

"Maybe," Raskin said. "Not every security member is a dedicated professional, Mr. Perdoux. Take me for example. I came over from sales. Some guys, the ones younger than me, are part-time college students. Like I said before, once in a while they let friends in to sip a glass of wine or smoke a little weed. It doesn't happen every night, but you know, it happens. The older guys are retired, and instead of signing on at Home Depot to sell weed whackers, they do security work here. When we took the job, we got a week of training, and that was it. Most of us stay on, because it's a nice place to work, and there's not any heavy lifting. But what's any of that have to do with Aldo Conte?"

"I wish I knew," I admitted.

"You want my opinion?"

"Shoot," I said.

"I'd say Aldo Conte has nothing to do with the robbery. Further, if I can speak for the guards, none of us had anything to do with it either. The two on duty the night of the robbery are clean as a whistle. Not a crooked bone in either one of them. What there is in them is fear. When they went to the basement, they thought they'd never come back up. They thought they were going to be shot."

"You spoke to them?"

"The very next day, right after Sanford J. Brothers grilled them. The guy is no friend of the working man. He thinks the cleaning staff steals from the supplies closet. As for security, we have orgies after midnight in the courtyard." Raskin shrugged. "No amount of evidence will ever convince Sanford J. Brothers that one of us didn't commit the robbery. It's not in his nature to believe in the world occupied by the little people below his station in life. To him, we're all crooks."

My read on Sanford J. Brothers was that Raskin was right. I thanked him for his time and headed for the exit. I thought about sticking my head in Clair Bowman's office on the way out but wanted to do more thinking first. To help with that thinking, I took out my cellphone and put in a call to Keith Lazard.

Chapter Three

Boston's Museum of Fine Arts was a fifteen-minute walk from the Gardner. Keith Lazard, an old friend of mine, had been head of security at the MFA for several years. His official title was Operations Commander in charge of the Operations Center, a sophisticated surveillance network that protected the people and contents inside the vast building's nearly 617,000 square feet. Keith had just finished conducting a meeting with his security personnel and was looking forward to a break. I met him for coffee in the café reserved for staff.

Keith looked like a cross between a computer nerd and a CEO in his neatly cut dark brown suit, crew cut and wire rimmed glasses that kept sliding down his nose. He was about fifty, looked thirty-five and ready to box ten rounds without breaking a sweat. He and I met at a now closed Gold's Gym. Over the years, we'd shared a few moments in the ring and at a few bars. We picked up two black coffees in white styrofoam cups and sat at a table in the corner away from foot traffic.

"I figured I'd see you sooner or later," Keith said. "That Gardner business brings out all kinds. You on the case?"

I shook my head. "Not really. Although it might morph into that. I'm technically looking for a missing person."

"Who's the guy?"

"Aldo Conte."

Keith sipped his coffee. "Never heard of him. How can I help?"

"Listen to my rambling. See what I don't. I've been hired by the museum to learn if there's any connection between the repair of an antique guitar, a missing repairman, and the robbery. In addition to talking to the museum's director, I've spoken to a security guard and the chairman of the board who thinks it was an inside job."

"The guards did it," Keith chimed. "It's like one of those Agatha Christie novels when one of the British coppers says, 'The butler did it!' Museum thefts are often inside jobs. You know that."

"Why is there no ransom demand?"

"Maybe they got cold feet. It happens. It's like buyer's remorse, only for thieves. They did it but wish they hadn't. The idea of going to the slammer can be a heavy weight, especially for a security guard."

"Cold feet is a possibility," I admitted. "Any other ideas?"

"The guards are waiting for the right moment to reveal their demands."

"The guards over at the Gardner are either retired or college kids. Even if they did pull the job, I'm not sure they're capable of thinking too far down the line."

"Ok. Put security guards on the back burner." Keith pushed his glasses higher on his nose.

I nodded agreement. "Who's left?"

Keith sipped more coffee. "You know the police have asked my opinion about that. The security operation here at the MFA is second to none. We do surveillance inside the building and outside along the perimeter. We record every movement and monitor it on closed circuit TV. The Gardner has very little of that. My staff rehearses and prepares for all manner of attack, not unlike the military. We listen to the rumors."

"Were there rumors that the Gardner was going to be hit?" I asked.

"A few. You know how it is when your job is to listen. You hear things."

"Like?"

"Like Whitey Bulger's Winter Hill Gang was looking to ship guns overseas. Whitey needed cash and had a buyer for some art. That's why there's no ransom demand. The pieces went from the museum to

30

the buyer. Whitey got the cash. The guns were bought and loaded onto a container ship. Nice and neat."

"Goodbye artwork," I said. "That theory won't make Clair Bowman very happy."

"No, but rumor number two might. In this version a crime family in the North End hit the Gardner and is waiting for the museum to offer both a reward and a promise of no prosecution."

"Easy work if you can get it," I quipped. "Which family?"

"Vincent Garcetti's mob."

"I thought Vincent was doing time."

"He is and none too happy about it. Him being pissed off is what set this whole thing in motion. Part of rumor number two is that when the art is returned, Vincent gets released from prison. Him getting out will be part of the negotiation."

"Quite a swap," I said. "They get money, no threat of prosecution, and daddy gets out of the slammer."

"Assuming he can pull it off," Keith said. "Deals like that have been made before. It all depends on how much the Gardner wants their stolen items returned."

"And how open the authorities are to negotiation," I added. "The museum can't cut a deal like that on their own. The Feds will have to be involved if Garcetti is to walk."

"They're involved up to their neck, Theo. They're taking over the investigating and your buddy, Brody Flynn, is none too happy about it. Turf wars leave a rotten taste. Glad I don't have to pick a side because I like Brody, but he can't win with the Feds calling the shots and taking all the credit when they solve the case. Which could be bad news for some of the top dogs over at the Gardner."

"What are you suggesting?" I asked. "An inside job starting from the top?"

Keith shrugged. "That's rumor number three." He leaned forward across the table and lowered his voice. "This one I don't want to believe, Theo, but here it is. You know the Gardner is burning through its endowment."

"I heard it was short of cash, yes."

"They're hamstrung over there. The collection they have in that beautiful old building is it. Nothing new is allowed to come in. No new exhibits. Nothing. Unfortunately, that adds up to no new memberships. It's the way Mrs. Gardner wanted her museum run with no changes. So, what does the board do to remedy this? They approve a proposal from Director Bowman and some of her consultants to build a new art space in a brand new building next to the original building. The new space will have a restaurant, a gallery space for new, exciting exhibits, a bookshop—all the things that bring in new members and make money. And, with none of the restrictions Mrs. Gardner set forth in her will."

"I thought the Gardner was broke. How could they afford such an undertaking?" I asked and sipped my coffee as a menacing thought struck me. "Someone planned the robbery to save the museum? Hard to swallow, Keith."

"That's rumor three, Theo. Someone high up at the Gardner planned the hit to lay the groundwork for the new building. A buyer wanted certain pieces. He got them. He paid. The money will be held in an overseas account for a while, then mysteriously find its way into the construction budget for the new building. The money wouldn't pay for the entire building, but it's a very good down payment."

I leaned back in my chair, thinking. "Any names attached to rumor number three?"

"Anybody and everybody." Keith scrunched his shoulders. "Who knows? But I can tell you this, I know most of the people over there,

Theo. The board members and Director Bowman. All good people. I wouldn't think any one of them capable of such a scheme, but you asked for theories, and those are the ones I've heard. Of course, there is always the one involving your father."

"Always," I said without rancor. "He's the poster boy for unsolved, high-end art robberies. When all else fails, blame the heist on the man no one has seen in years. Rumor is he's still in South America, but no one knows for sure. In addition to his success as a thief, he's also expert in keeping his whereabouts a secret. Is he the official rumor number four?"

"Not really," Keith said. "We keep special tabs on known criminals with an interest in art theft. Wilhelm is at the top of the list, but he wasn't a blip on the radar screen concerning the Gardner heist. He's a quick hitter. He goes after the most expensive pieces and takes off. He wouldn't hang around for over an hour."

"Plus, he's not a collector. He steals to maintain his very expensive lifestyle. A client wants a Vermeer, he delivers one at the agreed upon price. He would never destroy the value by cutting a masterpiece from its frame."

"Bad for business," Keith said, adding, "Still, there's always the possibility that he's got his hand in."

"That's what I told Brody Flynn when he quizzed me about my father's possible involvement. All very polite stuff handled professionally by Flynn and his minions. No one accused me of holding the door open for my old man while he carted off the prizes. Still, it's possible he was involved."

"We'll put him on the back burner next to the security guards," Keith said. "I'm afraid none of my rumors gets you any closer to finding your missing man. What was his name again?"

"Conte," I said. "Aldo Conte. He was going to repair a rare guitar." I explained about the *Art World* article and Conte's later visit to the Gardner. "He was going to make arrangements to repair the Cavelli in your shop here at the MFA."

Keith's brows rose in surprise. "In our conservatory? We certainly welcome outside experts, but it's not an every day occurrence. If he applied to use our facilities, I'm sure we have a record."

I followed Keith back to his office and stood looking at his framed citations for excellence hanging on the walls while he picked up the phone. When he got an answer, he explained who I was and that I was looking for information about Aldo Conte's request to work on an antique guitar in the MFA's workshop. He waited for a response.

"You're in luck," he said, handing the phone to me. "Shelly O'Brian manages the conservation center. She has news for you."

I took the receiver and listened. Clair Bowman had forwarded an e-mail introduction regarding Aldo Conte to the conservation center's office on January 9. The e-mail referenced the Cavelli guitar and Aldo Conte's interest in making the necessary repairs using the facilities at the MFA.

"I sent an e-mail back to Clair saying that I would very much like to meet Mr. Conte," Miss O'Brian said. "We are always looking for expert specialists, especially those involving musical instruments. We have a large collection as you may be aware," she said pleasantly. "Unfortunately, Mr. Conte never contacted this office."

"You're sure?"

"Positive. I'm looking at my notes on the matter. Like I said, I was eager to meet him. He did not phone, e-mail, or show up here in January or at any other time. I just assumed he and Clair did not agree on the details, and the matter was dropped. That happens. Undertaking the restoration of a valuable item presents a large economic as well as emotional commitment for all involved. Complicated restorations do not always succeed, you understand."

"I do," I said.

"I'm sure Clair was very disappointed."

"Yes, she was." I thanked Miss O'Brian for her time and put down the receiver. To Keith I said, "A guy flies from Rome to Boston, goes to all the trouble of examining the object, takes measurements, takes pictures, spends an hour of his time screwing around in the museum, and then doesn't follow through. What's that sound like to you?"

"A hidden agenda," Keith said, again working on his glasses. "The man never wanted to fix the guitar. He wanted something else."

"Access to the nearly empty Gardner," I said, thinking. "He pretended to study a crack in the guitar while his assistant poked around elsewhere."

"Did they take anything?"

"He took pictures and measurements," I said.

"He wouldn't need a special appointment to do that. Paying guests can shoot all the pictures they want in the Gardner. Why go to all the trouble taking measurements?"

"Buying time. You measure, you measure again. The security guard tries to figure out what the hell you're doing with all the measurements while the assistant roams around. Pretty soon the bored security guard trails off with the assistant."

"That makes sense," Keith said. "But roaming around doing what?"

"That I don't know," I admitted. "But there's an answer there somewhere, and I'm going to find it."

I thanked Keith for the coffee and left.

Chapter Four

The Heath Street trolley on the Green Line is notoriously slow, so I hopped a cab on Huntington Avenue and took the material regarding Aldo Conte out of my jacket pocket for something to read while weaving through traffic. I hadn't paid much attention to the papers Charles Raskin added to what Clair Bowman had given me earlier regarding Mr. Conte, and I wanted to learn more about him.

Conte looked good on paper. His ancestors were famous luthiers. Marco Conte, the craftsman who started the family tradition, apprenticed under Stradivarius beginning in 1687 in Cremona, Italy. According to my reading, Nicola Amati trained Stradivarius in the art of violin making and Stradivarius trained Marco Conte who, after years as an apprentice, went on to open his own shop. Marco's son sought greater exposure and moved the family to Rome. Since 1780, the Contes have been making, repairing, and selling violins in their small shop on Via di Montoro in Rome's Centro Storico.

Aldo Conte became master of the shop in 1963 after his father retired. Aldo is a member of the European Federation of Violin Makers and the Society of Italian Violin Makers who, two years ago, awarded him their Certificate of Merit and their Medal for Tone. His violins, selling for six figures, are played by the top soloists in the world of classical music. The wait for one of his instruments is two years. So, why would a very busy and successful violin maker care about a Cavelli guitar? How could he afford to take time away from his shop not only to travel to Boston but also to make the time-consuming repairs? As I thought of an answer, I turned the photo of Angela Ricci over, looking for information about her. Nothing. Like my mind, the back of her picture was blank.

I scanned the personal information on the printout and learned that Conte was divorced and living in Villa Conte, the family's Rome palazzo, with two grown children. Under the Villa Conte address were two phone numbers. I punched in both. Neither ring was answered. I put the printout back in my pocket and wondered what sort of game Aldo Conte was really playing. Or was he genuinely interested in restoring a three-hundred-year-old guitar?

One of my favorite neighborhoods in Boston is the North End, a congested section of the city famous for its lack of parking, high rents, and good Italian restaurants. The Irish settled the North End a hundred plus years ago. Once they prospered and moved out, the Italians took over and have held the fort ever since.

Sony Tommaso tended bar in a place called Judy's tucked away in a crowded alley off of Union Street. Fruit and vegetable vendors from the old Haymarket jammed the place after covering their pushcarts with tarps for the night. During the day, they popped in for a drink and a quick lunch. Judy's was working class devoid of noisy college students and confused tourists. Sony had bushy eyebrows that framed a jagged scar on his forehead caused by a drunk who hit Sony with a beer bottle. Sony took bets on all the games and served an honest drink. He was also a sponge, a man who absorbed all the news unfit to print.

While I waited for him to pour my drink, I weighted the theories Keith Lazard had posed. Not that I was jumping into the ocean and swimming after the Gardner paintings. My investigation had boundaries, and I planned on staying within the lines. But I wanted to explore how Aldo Conte might fit into any of the rumors. The Winter Hill Gang had a reputation as a ruthless and efficient mob capable of pulling off any crime at any time. Could they romp through the Gardner stealing Old Masters to buy guns? Certainly. Would a man with Aldo Conte's violin-making background fit in? Sure, if I wanted to imagine Aldo stashing machine guns in violin cases and blasting his way past gray haired security guards. No, I thought. Not a match.

Sanford J. Brothers suggested I was wasting my time tracking down Aldo Conte. Was Sanford J. putting me off the scent by protecting some Gardner board members and their involvement with Conte's plan to steal the museum blind? White collar crime in any museum robbery had to be considered a real possibility, but I had a hard time picturing members of the board trading their bow ties for false mustaches and wrapping frightened security guards in duct tape. How Aldo Conte would fit into such a scheme, I couldn't imagine. On paper, he didn't seem the bow tie type.

As far as the rumor of my father's involvement, I couldn't dismiss it so easily. Wilhelm Barr possessed a brilliant criminal mind that he combined with an astute knowledge of military tactics. During the war, he was responsible for looting thousands of pieces of art and shipping the cargo by truck and train to Berlin. Since the war, he stole to survive. Hiding out in high-end villas and constantly on the move was expensive. He was certainly capable of masterminding the Gardner robbery, but as Keith Lazard said, Wilhelm would not ruin the value by cutting a masterpiece from its frame. What Keith didn't say was that not all of the artwork was cut. Some of the pieces, including Rembrandt's self-portrait, were intact. I kept Wilhelm's involvement a possibility.

As for the rumor that the Garcettis were involved, I came to Judy's to ask Sony what he'd heard about that. The Garcetti family was famous in the North End neighborhood. For many, Vincent and his son Peter, held the North End together, making sure the best traditions remained, and the new, unwanted incursions were kept at bay. Nothing happened in the North End that the Garcettis didn't know about from the threatened eviction of an elderly widow to someone selling drugs.

And once the Garcettis became aware, they acted, keeping drug dealers out and the elderly safely in their apartments.

Sony wiped the bar with a wet cloth. The noon news played on the television bolted to the wall behind him. The sound was down, but Clair Bowman was again being interviewed.

Sony said, "That lady ought to have her own TV show. She's on every day. When she's not, your buddy, Brody Flynn is hogging the screen."

"Brody been in?" I asked.

"Sure. Asking questions like everybody. You know what I think? Like I says to Brody, Brody I says, nobody really gives a rat's ass about them pictures. Why not go down to the lower end of Washington Street and bust them guys with the backseat full of coke. That's what's ruining the city. Get the drugs off the streets, and half the robberies and muggings and shootings will vanish like them paintings. That's what I think," Sony said, his voice the voice of a man convinced he was right.

"How did Detective Flynn take your opinion?" I asked.

"The man has no sense of humor," Sony said. "Always serious. Always in a hurry."

"It's a big job finding out who robbed the Gardner. He's got to be serious."

"I guess," Sony said as he poured a draft beer for a customer a few seats down. When he came back, I asked what he'd been hearing.

"Nothing. You know how it is, a whisper here, a whisper there." He shrugged his thick shoulders. "Not much to any of it as far as I can tell."

"Nothing? Not like you, Sony." I put fifty dollars on the bar. "Who are the Red Sox playing tonight?"

"Cleveland."

"Fifty on the Sox," I said as Sony pocketed the cash. "There must be some rumblings you've picked up."

"Quiet as the grave," Sony said. "That's a sign, Theo. When nobody's talking, that's a sign something happened, you can bet on it."

"I just did with my fifty. Go Sox."

Sony cracked a weary smile. "Guys that talk, don't do a thing. The quiet ones, that's different. Everything's quiet about the Garcetti camp if that tells you anything. The boys are real touchy about blabbing what they shouldn't. Keep it quiet, you know? Safer that way."

"Quiet about anything in particular?"

Sony put my scotch on a napkin in front of me. "The museum heist. Guys in here mouthing opinions all of a sudden got no opinions. Who pulled the job? No idea. Who's got the paintings? No idea. Why didn't they just rob a bank? No idea. You can't fool me. They got ideas. More than that, they got answers, but they ain't saying."

"Did you tell all this to Brody Flynn?"

"Tell what?" Sony asked. "That the guys ain't talking? That's not much to tell. So, you tell me something, Theo. I'm serious about this. We know some of the heavy lifters in Garcetti's camp would rob their mothers if ordered. So, why didn't Vincent or Peter or somebody just tell the boys to stick up a bank? An armored car even. Why screw around with a bunch of pictures?"

"They don't want the money. They want something else," I said and sipped my cocktail.

"Like what?"

"A bargaining chip." I drank more scotch. "Are you giving odds that the Garcettis did the job?"

"No way. That was just a question. An honest question, Theo. And one I wouldn't ask to just anybody who might rat me out. I'm not looking for trouble."

"Understood," I said and swirled the ice in my glass as Sony headed to the other end of the bar. He was down there long enough for me to finish my drink and to think about having another. But it soon became clear Sony was too busy to chat, so I left ten on the counter and headed for my office on the other side of Beacon Hill.

The afternoon breeze had cranked into a stiff wind; still it was nice to be out. I walked past Faneuil Hall, crossed Cambridge Street and jogged up the steps toward City Hall. The gold dome of the State House behind me, I eased down Mt. Vernon Street to Charles. My office was in three-story brick building I had the good fortune to buy about ten years ago.

I made the purchase after Gina Ponte and I located a Renior that was part of the stolen Perdoux Collection. During the course of their partnership, my mother and Gina had located five pieces of the collection. Their agreement was that if mother didn't want to keep any of what was found and eventually returned to her, Gina would sell the paintings through Sala Ponte. Gina and I kept that arrangement once I became her partner, and the Renior brought a significant sum that Gina and I shared.

Since my retirement from the police force, I had been living in Provincetown in a beach house I bought as retirement present to myself. I kept the house and acquired the Charles Street property, which had my office on floor number one and my condo on floors two and three. Many of my clients found travel to Provincetown inconvenient so the Charles Street location made meeting them easier. After late meetings, I didn't often feel like driving the three and one-half hours to P-town even in my Porsche 911, so staying in the intown condo made good sense.

The previous owner was an architect with a minimalist's flair. His downstairs office, now mine, was simply furnished with a sleek wooden desk, two red leather chairs, a file cabinet, and a sideboard with a coffee maker and cocktail bar. The upstairs living quarters had a full bathroom on each of the two floors along with a bedroom on each. The second-floor kitchen was professional grade, which suited the previous owner more than me since I rarely cook. The living room off the kitchen had a wood burning fireplace framed by built-in bookcases. A camelback sofa covered in a solid light gray color matched two over-stuffed chairs. In addition to the bath and bedroom on the third floor were two large closets and an exercise room complete with stationary bike and rowing machine. I bought the property furnished, had it professionally cleaned, and moved in.

Once in my office, I checked my phone messages. One call was from Clair Bowman. She left a number, so I rang her back.

"How did your conversation with Chuck Raskin go?" she wanted to know.

I told her all went well, then said, "I also had a chat with Stanford Brothers."

"I knew he would track you down, once I let everyone know you were stopping by today. Stanford likes to stick his nose in. I'm sure he told you not to be bothered with Aldo Conte and that the robbers were likely on our payroll."

"That's what he said," I admitted, then told Clair about my talk with Keith Lazard.

"You've been very busy."

"Maybe not all that productive but busy. Keith has heard rumors about the robbery. One had an interesting take on it connected to a proposal to build a new building."

"You mean the theory that I planned the robbery to finance a new, separate building for the museum?" Clair said with a terse laugh. "That would be funny if it weren't so pathetic. Regardless, some people believe it."

"Keith didn't," I said. "He was simply passing along rumors. But I wouldn't be doing my job if I didn't ask, did you?"

"I don't know how this relates to finding Aldo Conte, but I will say for the record that I didn't plan the robbery. Neither did anyone I know on the board. The police brought that absurd notion up, and I thought I'd shot it down. Guess not if you heard about it."

"It's Keith's job to pay attention to the scuttle. Nothing personal."

"It is personal when it deals with one's reputation. But in one respect, I take after Mrs. Gardner. I've developed a rather thick skin when it comes to what others think. It comes from having a vision and carrying it out. That's what Mrs. Gardner did with her collecting and building her museum. Many thought she was out of her mind buying all that art and building a palace to put it in, but she did not waiver. My vision for the museum is equally unwaivering. In order to grow and prosper while maintaining the conditions of Mrs. Gardner's will, we need to think creatively. As I told the search committee and board when I interviewed for this job, building a new art space is one way of achieving that. Not the only way, but certainly something worth exploring. I did not say that we should plan a robbery to finance it, however."

"When you proposed the new building, did the board go along with it?"

"Not unanimously. It's never healthy to have a board that rubber stamps every proposal. I encourage robust debate." Clair hesitated a moment, then said, "Why do you ask?"

"Something Raskin said about consultants and proposals and nothing ever coming of any of it."

"'Nothing' is a bit strong, but you need to understand how the Gardner functions, Theo. I was hired to direct the museum toward the future. I am following through on the vision that I laid out. The board is more conservative in its thinking and acts cautiously. They evaluate proposals, consider the budgets for each, then offer their recommendations. I have no problem with that. I'm not a dictator, nor should I be. If I were, I would have told the police no more on-camera statements from me."

"I saw you on the tube this afternoon."

"What did you think?"

"The bartender had the sound off, but my cocktail was just fine."

Clair laughed. "Maybe I should have a drink before I make my next appearance, but I felt strongly that I should say something. Those paintings are delicate. Cutting them from their frames likely did untold damage. Hauling them around, not treating them with the care they deserve . . ." She trailed off. "I wanted to make a plea for whoever has them to be mindful of the treasures in their possession. They're priceless and should be returned immediately."

"Would the museum be willing to pay a ransom to get them back?" I asked.

"Do you have a spy in our board meetings?" Clair quipped. "We are currently discussing that very issue. We would give something for their safe return, certainly. How much remains to be seen. Additional funds would have to come from private sources who see the value of the Gardner as a prized Boston institution. We are looking at our available cash on hand and contacting interested parties on the outside to see what we can reasonably offer as a reward for their return."

"It's a good idea to plan for a ransom demand."

"I can't take credit for that," Clair admitted. "Detective Flynn told us that might be the robber's next step. It's encouraging to learn that all you professionals are thinking along the same track," she said as a beep on my phone announced another call.

"I'll be in touch, Clair. Someone's trying to reach me." I switched to the other line and heard bar noises and Sony Tommaso's husky voice.

"Something that may interest you, Theo," Sony said. "I was feeling kind of guilty not working very hard for that fifty on the Sox."

"What have you got?"

"Not a lot of meat on the bone, but a nice scrap. Peter Garcetti threw a party a few days after the robbery in a private dining room at the Capital Grille. Big celebration. All the top brass was invited. The chair at the head of the table was empty. According to my source, Peter offered a toast saying that he hoped soon his father, Vincent, would be sitting in it."

"The wheels are grinding to get him out?"

"So it would seem."

"Any idea who Garcetti fingered to do the job?"

"Nobody's offering that, Theo, but Nick Bianchi is Peter's go-to guy. He's a good bet."

"Where's Nick hang out these days?" I asked.

"He's a creature of habit, Theo. Try Sully's, his old stomping ground."

Chapter Five

Sully's was a Broadway Street bar in South Boston made famous when two armed men stormed the place and shot dead three members of the Angiulo brothers' mob. I was still a cop then and worked the investigation with the Tactical Patrol Force. An eyewitness said he saw Nicolo Bianchi fire the first of a dozen shots before running to the back of the bar and out into the alley with his accomplice. We brought Nick in for questioning as well as a handful of other young toughs trying to make a name for themselves in the Vincent Garcetti crime family.

Nick admitted nothing. The eyewitness lost his memory, and, like other Mafia hits, no one was ever brought to trial for the Sully's murders.

I drove over the Summer Street Bridge to Broadway Street and parked in the lot behind Sully's, a working man's bar and the joy of the locals who'd had their fill of trendy watering holes opening in the area. Sully's served no drinks with pink umbrellas floating on top.

The Red Sox and Cleveland were playing ball on television. Ten or so men sat at the bar sipping beer from bottles and looking up at the screen. Nick wasn't one of them. I checked the booths along one side of the bar, then stepped around a chest high wooden divider into the dimly lit dining room. Nick Bianchi and a woman I thought I recognized sat in the far corner near the back door. Her medium length dark hair was pulled back behind her ears making her inviting eyes the center of attention.

"Haven't I seen you somewhere before?" I asked her.

"Nice try," she said dismissively.

Two of Nick's mates sat at the next table. JoJo Weems and Ronnie Torres made sure no one caused Nick any grief. Not that Nick needed much help getting out of trouble that he usually caused. Nick wore a checkered sport coat with a dark green shirt open at the collar. I could see the top of the grip of what looked like an automatic pistol tucked in a clip holster on his hip. The smile dropped from his rugged face when he saw me approach.

"Mind if I join you?" I asked and pulled out the chair that Nick pointed to beside the woman. I held my gaze on her longer than usual, but still couldn't place her. "Care to introduce me?"

"Sugar," Nick said, "this is a retired cop who must have gotten lost to come all the way over here. This isn't what you'd call his stomping ground."

"Pleased to meet you," the lady said dully and reached for her nearly empty wine glass. "If you two have business, I'll get myself a refill."

Nick pushed his glass toward her. "Make it two," he said, and she left. "What can I do for you Zachary? Check that. You've got a new name now, right? Like witness protection, right? You go in one door Theo Zachary and come out another Theo Purdy."

"That's old news, Nick. But just to refresh your memory, it's Perdoux," I corrected. "I changed names ten years ago. You need to keep up with the times."

"Purdy, Perdoux. Who cares? You're still out of your element over here."

"Over here as in the scene of the crime? Bring back fond memories for you, does it, Nick? You storm in, guns blazing?"

"That's old news too, but, yeah, very fond memories. Besides, I like this place. Mostly good people come. Present company excluded. But these folks always treated me with the greatest respect. Not like some cops I know. But you're out of that racket, right? You're private. I can confess to anything I want, and you can't touch me. Not that I have anything to say. I've done nothing and never did. You can't prove otherwise."

"Like when you stormed this place? Maybe they treat you nice, Nick, because they're afraid you're going to whip out a gun and shoot all the customers if they don't."

"Or maybe I'm a big tipper."

"You'd have to be at the Capital Grille. I understand you and some friends had a celebration there recently."

"Offended you didn't get an invite?"

"Broken hearted," I said.

"Just goes to show Peter Garcetti has good taste. He didn't want to smell up the joint with riffraff. That leaves you out."

"I was thinking the party might be a little premature."

"Why's that?"

"Vincent's still doing time in Danbury. He's not likely to get out any time soon."

"I wouldn't know," Nick said.

"Of course, you could speed things up if you swapped an armful of paintings for time served."

"I don't know nothing about that either."

"What'd you do with the paintings, Nick? You must still have them since you want to trade them for your boss. Were you one of the guys dressed up like Boston cops? Or did you leave that to JoJo and Ronnie?"

Nick cocked his head to one side as if his hearing had failed. "I think I hear a fly buzzing around my ear. Annoying as hell," he said as his lady friend put two glasses of wine on the table and retook her seat. "You know something, Purdy, you're interrupting my evening with my lady friend. You can go back to wherever you came from any time." When I didn't move, Nick said, "This guy, Sugar, me and him go way back. He couldn't take the heat as a cop, see, so he retires after some guy bounced a rock off his head. See that saggy eye and scar? Nearly lost his sight in that eye. But he found something more important. He finds out all the time he called himself Theo Zachary, he's really a Purdy. Theo Purdy."

"Perdoux," I said calmly, wondering how far Nick was going to push.

"And he finds out another thing. He's got family overseas. See, Sugar, this was once big news in all the local papers. An adopted kid, a Boston cop at that, finally learns as an adult who his real parents are. It's a story full of life's ironies, you know? Full of twists and turns and tragedy. Like a real soap opera with Purdy resurfacing this very day as a private cop slumming in South Boston looking up his old friends."

I looked around the room, catching the stony glare from JoJo and Ronnie. "I don't see anybody here that qualifies," I said.

There was heat behind Nick's forced smile. "This guy, Sugar, comes from a long line of art dealers in France. Claude Perdoux being the last, right?"

"It's your story."

"And like a lot of art dealers at the time, the Nazis ripped off Claude. Stripped his gallery walls clean. Right again?"

I nodded.

"This, Sugar, is one of the twists. Purdy's old man is now one of the world's most famous art thieves. He plans the heist, trains someone to carry it out and swaps the loot for cash before he goes back into hiding. Imagine that," he said letting the moment build.

Sugar's eyes slid toward me. "Really? Your father?"

"Afraid so."

"That must be horrible, you being a cop and all."

49

"My father is like back pain. You learn to live with it." I glanced at Nick. "How is it Wilhelm's on your mind, Nick? You studying the moves of an expert to learn how to rob a museum?"

"Filling in Sugar on your glorious past is all. You're one of a kind, ain't that right, boys?"

JoJo Weems and Ronnie Torres nodded.

"Besides," Nick said, "you broke up our little party. Me and the little lady was having a fine time until you show up. Ain't that right, Sugar?"

"Whatever you say."

Nick's eyes narrowed. "No, no, Sugar. You have to put some feeling into it. We were having a good time. Am I right?" Nick reached for her wrist and squeezed. "Am I?"

From the frightened look that fell across her expression, it was clear she knew better than to pull away. "You're always right, Nick," she said as her gaze fell into the red liquid as she lifted her glass with her free hand and took a sip.

"That's better. Now, where was I? Oh, yeah, Purdy's father . . ."

"I think that's about enough, Nick," I warned. "Your date and I are both bored. Why don't we talk about something else like your involvement in the Gardner robbery?"

Nick pushed back from the table, a look of mock surprise on his face. "Me? I thought it was just your face that got busted up from that rock. Maybe it was your hearing, too. I don't know nothing about anybody's interest in any paintings. You got that? Nothing as in zero." He leaned toward me across the table, a storm brewing behind his eyes. "Now, why don't you get the hell out of here?"

"After you answer one more question. Aldo Conte. You ever heard of him?"

"No," he snapped, his gaze catching the slight shift in Sugar's expression.

I saw it, too, and came back to its cause. "Aldo Conte," I said again. "He traveled all the way from Rome to examine an antique guitar. Soon after, he disappeared. Vincent Garcetti knows something about making people disappear, doesn't he, Nick? He had it in for the Angiulo brothers that you took out right here in this very restaurant."

Nick's fist slammed the table knocking his wine glass to the floor. JoJo Weems and Ronnie Torres jumped to their feet. JoJo, the taller of the two, pointed what looked like a Sig Sauer at my chest while Ronnie stepped around the table toward me, his fist pounding into the palm of his open hand.

I felt a charge of adrenaline kick in followed by a calm confidence as my eyes flicked from one man to the other. What passed between us was an unspoken challenge that I would accept when the odds were not three against one, with one of the three pointing a gun in my direction.

"A little nervous, aren't you Nick? Afraid of . . ."

"Afraid of nothing, Purdy. Mark that down. Afraid of nothing."

"Then you won't mind me reaching inside my pocket."

"Go ahead," he said, glancing at his bodyguards to make sure they remained ready.

Slowly, I pulled out my business card and flipped it on the table. "Perdoux. Theo R. Repeat that ten times, Nick, so next time you'll get it right. Perdoux."

"There won't be a next time. Purdy."

The two thugs kept their eyes locked on me as I stood. The moment called for a reasoned retreat. I pointed to my card. "My number's on there, Sugar. When you want to tell the truth, call."

Nick scooped the card from the table and crumpled it in his fist. He threw it to the floor as I turned to leave.

Chapter Six

The ride back to my office was a blur. My thoughts kept bouncing from trying to remember where I'd seen Nick's girlfriend before to Nick's annoying jabs about my past. I knew I'd seen Sugar somewhere, but where alluded me. It wasn't with Nick, I knew that, the sleazy bastard, calling me Purdy. Dragging up bits about my father. Why was all that history about my past so fresh in his mind?

I parked behind my building and unlocked my office. I ignored the blinking red light on the desk phone announcing messages and poured myself a scotch over ice. I sat at my desk, punched in a telephone number and sipped my drink while waiting for an answer. On the seventh ring, Gina Ponte answered with her usual soft but firm Italian accented voice.

"Sala Ponte," she said. "How can we be of help?"

"It's Theo," I said. "You can help by locating a missing person."

"Missing paintings? Yes. Missing people? Maybe not. Theo, what are you doing joking around? Are you here in Barcelona?"

"Still in Boston," I said. "I accepted a new client today. It's a little out of our primary focus, but I think we can make it work."

"Then, you're not joking about hunting for a missing person?" Gina asked cautiously. "A famous art collector, no doubt? Or maybe an artist? How about a painting by a famous artist that was recently stolen from a London collector?"

"You have more information about the Matisse?" I asked, hopeful of good news.

"I have news, and it's not all bad. The thieves with the Matisse are complicating matters. The good news is they made contact again. The bad news is they're not dealing with Niles Huygens, meaning they made contact directly. Huygens is out of the picture, no pun intended."

"An amateur's mistake," I said, smiling at the joke. "Huygens has never been formally accused of any crime, but every thief in Europe knows he's the man to deal with."

"He's the man you *must* deal with," Gina corrected. "That is if you demand a smooth, no fuss swap. The Matisse thieves disagree. We'll have to deal with that, Theo. There's no other way."

"What's the plan?" I asked.

"Half the ransom upfront. The rest in five days when they hand over the paintings. I told them that was unacceptable. We need to see that the canvas is undamaged and original before they get any cash."

"And their response?"

"They're thinking about a neutral location where we can meet. They'll get back to us."

"Niles Huygens would have had those ducks in order."

"Agreed," Gina said. "But we'll make this work while protecting the interests of our client. Which brings me back to your call, Theo. Who is the missing man we're supposed to find?"

"Aldo Conte. He's got a shop in Rome where he makes prized violins."

"I know the name," Gina said. "You can't be Italian and not know of Aldo Conte. The man's a legend in the music world. Some say the beauty of his craftsmanship is surpassed only by the sound of his instruments. I'd like to meet him."

"We'd have to find him first," I said and explained about the Cavelli guitar and Clair Bowman's invitation for Conte to visit the museum. "The visit was a ruse, Gina. A way for him to get inside without suspicion. The security guard assigned to watch him fell in love with his attractive assistant and followed her around with his tongue hanging out."

"While Conte hauled the pieces out the door? Not likely," Gina scoffed.

"No. The robbery took place three months after his visit."

"Then, I'd say there was no connection," Gina said. "A robber cases the locale right before he makes his move. He doesn't wait."

"I thought of that," I said. "A lot of it doesn't make sense, Gina, I admit. But if Conte has nothing to hide, why did he disappear? Clair Bowman is an intelligent woman. It could be she's simply humiliated that she was taken in by a hoax, or maybe she's trying to save face with her board by grasping at anything that might produce results. Besides, finding Conte might lead to who really robbed the Gardner."

"There are lots of rumors," Gina said. "Middle eastern oil money, Russian billionaires, on and on. Nothing's really gained traction. And nothing has circulated with Aldo Conte's name attached to it. I would have picked up on that."

"How about my father?" I asked. "Has his name crossed the pond?"

I could almost see Gina's eyes pop wide. "Is that the real reason you took this case? You think your father has a hand in?"

"No."

"Of course, you do. You're just like your mother in that regard. Any chance at all to track Wilhelm down, Simone jumped at. You're the same, Theo. Admit it."

"I said no."

"Hard to believe when you accept a missing person case. Upfront, if that missing person was the most infamous Nazi looter of all time, I could see you eager to sign on. But Aldo Conte three months removed from the actual robbery? A man who simply doesn't return calls from Clair Bowman? A man who more than likely had a simple change of heart and decided he didn't want to work on a guitar? Tell your partner the truth, Theo. We're after Wilhelm Barr. Like I told Simone when she veered in that direction, Sala Ponte and our art recovery business would be put on the map if we turned Wilhelm over to the authorities. He's been in hiding since the war like other war criminals only he's never been close to being captured. So, tell me, why do you think he was involved in the Gardner heist?" Gina asked eagerly.

"I'm not saying he is; I'm suggesting a connection. Do you remember the details of the Stedelijk Museum robbery of a few years back?" I asked referring to the theft of Amsterdam's modern art museum.

"Of course," Gina said. "The Mondrian and Chagall have never been found. So?"

"So that theft began with a so-called expert being welcomed into the museum under the false pretense of examining a rare porcelain clock in need of repair."

"I remember that," Gina said, adding, "And I also remember that the robbers hit the museum the day after the repairman cased the place. End of similarities."

"Perhaps not," I said. "The repairman was invited to the museum after presenting credentials that proved false. He wasn't an expert in clock repair. He was someone who gained access to the museum who later disappeared. Was he one of the two thieves who carted off the Mondrian and Chagall? We don't know. What we do know is that the robbery was well-planned, well executed with those involved free to strike again because they've never been apprehended."

"And you think they came back and hit the Gardner," Gina mused.

"I think it's possible," I admitted, adding, "Wilhelm is an expert at planning. The Amsterdam authorities are almost certain he was the mastermind of the Stedelijk robbery. If something works once, he may repeat the pattern with necessary variations. He adds a magazine article about a special guitar and has an expert follow through. Only like the clock repairman, the expert's credentials are false."

"All right, say I buy into that, where does that get us? Wilhelm is still the master at staying in the shadows."

"True," I said, "but now we have a thread to tug on in the name of Aldo Conte. He may not answer Clair Bowman's calls, but if I'm pounding on the door of his shop, he can't ignore me."

"You're heading to Rome, then. One of your favorite cities. Another reason for taking on this missing persons case. What would you like me to do, Theo?"

"Same as always. Exhaust your contacts. See what Alicia can dig up," I said, referring to Gina's lovely wife who was also an expert researcher.

"Glad you mentioned Alicia, Theo. Since you are headed to Rome, you may find this tidbit Alicia dug up useful. Seems a well-placed Italian family has picked a fight with Niles Huygens about the value of a significant canvas. I don't know who the family is or whether they are buying or selling. Alicia is sorting out those details. In the meantime, I'll see what I can learn about Aldo Conte."

"Good. I'll work this end. If we're lucky, we might both end up at the same place."

"At Wilhelm Barr's front door?" Gina quipped.

"Maybe," I admitted. "Or maybe we'll find those thirteen stolen pieces."

"Both would be a boost for Sala Ponte," Gina admitted and ended the call.

After Gina rang off, I was about to go over once again the material Charles Raskin had given me on Conte's background when my phone rang. I picked it up. "Yes?"

"Theo Perdoux?"

"Speaking," I said, trying to remember where I'd heard that voice.

"This is Angela." Her voice was muffled as if she were speaking through gauze. "We don't need last names, do we?"

"It would help?"

"Sugar to you."

As I tossed down Raskin's notes, Angela Ricci's black and white photograph flipped into view. The simple picture sent a charge through me. Sugar and Angela were one and the same.

"So, you do know Aldo Conte," I said, recalling her denial when I'd asked that question at Sully's. "What can I do for you, Sugar?"

"Meet me at the Five Horses Tavern in Davis Square. D'you know it?"

"Somerville on Highland," I said. "What time?"

"Nine o'clock."

"What's the occasion?"

"I want to sell you something."

"Some paintings?" I tossed out.

"Some information."

"You're not coming through loud and clear," I said. "Why not help me out? Information about what?"

"Tonight at nine. The Five Horses," she said and hung up.

I checked my watch. I had a few hours before my meeting with Angela and decided to do what I always did when seeking clarity, I sought out Brody Flynn. Boston Police Detective Brody Flynn was working the Gardner investigation and someone I knew well as we'd both risen through the ranks of the Tactical Patrol Force. After my accident, he came to the hospital a time or two to check on my progress. When I retired, I kept in contact with Brody, congratulating him on his promotions and inviting him to Provincetown to do a little fishing.

I walked through the Public Garden and over to Berkeley Street where Brody had his office on the third floor of the Boston Police Department Division-4 building. I checked in with the duty officer and climbed the stairs. Brody stood up from behind his desk when he saw me at the door. He was about my age, mid-fifties, stocky, strong, and straightforward. We shook hands and sat across the desk from each other.

"Theo." Brody seemed glad to see me. "I figured you'd be making contact before now. Thanks for staying out of the Gardner business. I've got my hands full, what with every damn reporter and private eye offering their two cents. No offense."

"None taken."

"Has Clair Bowman been in touch?" Brody asked.

"She has. Did you put her on my tail?"

"I might have. You sign on to track down the missing guitar repairman?"

"So, I have you to thank for that."

"Just trying to do an old friend a favor," Brody said with a wry smile. "Besides, I wanted to get Miss Bowman out of my hair. She likes daily updates even when there's nothing to update. I figured you could handle her better than me. My patience is a little thin since the FBI took over the Gardner investigation. Taking orders in my own backyard doesn't sit well."

"Maybe this will make you feel better. The missing repairman had a female assistant with him when he visited the Gardner to look at the Cavelli guitar. I haven't found him, but I did find her."

"You don't say?"

"I do say. She's Nick Bianchi's girlfriend, Angela Ricci."

"Now, how would you know anything about Nick's girl?" Brody asked, the friendliness gone from his voice.

"I paid Nick a social call. Nothing more to it than that. Angela Ricci was with him. She wants to meet tonight. She's selling information."

"About what?" Brody asked.

"She didn't say."

Brody leaned forward on his desk; his fingers entwined forming a steeple. "Just so you know we're doing our job since you retired, we'd already run a background check on Garcetti's known associates, including your Angela, last name Ricci. Age 31. Went to college out west, dropped out after a semester abroad and hitchhiked around Europe for a year. Married once. Divorced. No kids. Came back to the States and worked as a dancer in strip clubs. Arrested twice for shoplifting. Otherwise, clean except for her poor taste in male companions, such as Nick Bianchi."

"Very thorough."

"We try."

"How long have Nick and Angela been an item?"

"About a year. A little longer. Why?"

I shrugged. "I was just wondering if Aldo Conte and Angela arrived on the scene at the same time. He showed at the Gardner in January. But she's been a fixture with Nick long before that."

"Which leads you to believe?"

"I'm not sure, but it does seem convenient that she knows both men."

"I'll give you that," Brody admitted. "I'll also give you a little tip about a Capital Grille meeting Peter Garcetti called for all his lieutenants. Peter was not happy and ordered everyone to shut up about the robbery. Zip it. We don't know who did it. We don't know why. We don't know where the paintings are. We don't know nothing."

"Why such a tight lid?"

"He's planning his next move, and he doesn't want his underlings to screw it up. Best way to insure that is to cancel all the chatter."

"Makes Angela's call to me pretty risky for her, don't you think? Especially if what she's peddling implicates the Garcettis."

"Or it could be a trap," Brody said. "The one person willing to talk is going to reel you in so Nick and his pals can stomp on you. As I recall, you and Nick are not the best of friends. I think maybe I ought to tag along to make sure you don't get in any trouble."

"Three's a crowd, Brody. I don't want to scare off Angela."

"So, I'll show up a little late. Where's the meeting?"

I told him the time and the place. I pushed myself up from my chair. "Dinner's on me if you're interested."

"Busy," Brody said. "Another time."

Eating alone and enjoying the experience is both a skill and an art that I exercised at Artu's, a small restaurant in the basement of a mixed-use building on Charles Street a few blocks from my office. When I finished, I hopped the Red Line for an outbound train to David Square. The Five Horses was a leisurely ten-minute walk from the T stop. I like to arrive early for all appointments, and this was no exception. I took a seat at the bar and ordered espresso with a brandy on the side. It was fifteen minutes to nine. At a quarter to ten, Brody walked in.

"Did I miss the party?" he asked.

"She didn't show," I said. "Maybe she changed her mind."

"Someone calls a meeting is usually the first to arrive."

"That's what I mean," I said. "Maybe she figured calling me was a mistake. Maybe she figured it was best to follow Peter Garcetti's warning and keep her mouth shut."

"Or maybe someone shut it for her." Brody turned to the door.

"What are you doing?"

"I'm going down the street. Angela Ricci has an apartment in a triple decker a few blocks from here down near Union Square. You stay here in case she shows," Brody said. "Call me, and I'll hustle right back."

I watched Brody cross the street and get into his unmarked car. I waited another fifteen minutes before ordering a second brandy. The after-movie crowd soon filled the bar, and at 10:30, I paid my bill and left. No word from Angela Ricci and no word from Brody Flynn.

A few cabs lined up in front of the Davis Square T stop, so I got in one and played a hunch. Brody said Angela Ricci had an apartment near Union Square. Highland Avenue connected Davis and Union squares. I told the driver I wanted to do a little sightseeing and off we went. It didn't take long before we slowed to a stop. A Somerville police cruiser, its blue lights flashing, blocked the street.

I handed the taxi driver a generous tip and got out.

"What's the trouble, officer?" I asked as the patrolman waved me along with a handful of other curious onlookers. "Detective Flynn inside? Brody Flynn, Boston PD?"

"What's your business with Flynn?"

"Angela Ricci," I said.

"You family?" the patrolman asked.

"Yes," I lied and hurried toward the gray triple decker with a cluster of uniformed police on the first level porch. The youngest of the group looked right out of the academy and a little pale around his mouth. I could only imagine what he'd seen inside as I opened the screen door and stepped into the hall.

The second door on the right led into the apartment with a rectangular living room decorated in light blues and greens. I stepped around an officer taking photographs and into the dining room where Brody Flynn spoke in quiet tones to a stunned woman of about sixty. She kept dabbing her forehead with a moist cloth before wiping away a gush of tears. When Brody tapped her gently on one shoulder, she sobbed her way out into the hall.

I took her place. "What happened?" I asked.

"Somebody shot Angela Ricci," Brody said as I looked at the body lying across the bed in the bedroom, what was left of her head lolled over to one side. "The landlady lives upstairs. She heard screams then one shot. She came downstairs and found the door open and Miss Ricci where you see her."

"She see anything else?" I asked.

"She said no. I didn't press, because this isn't Boston. It's Somerville and the investigation is in good hands with the locals. So, let's get out of their way."

I followed Brody outside and down the steps. When he opened the door to his car, he turned back to me. "Theo, murder doesn't open the door for you. In fact, it slams it shut."

"But she called me," I reminded him. "She wanted my help."

"And look where she ended up." He let the thought hang. "Look, Theo, we're not enemies. It's not good cop running off the bad cop. I've got my hands full with a million-dollar robbery and now a murder that might be connected. On top of that, I'm jumping through hoops held by the FBI. I don't need you poking around, getting in the way. I don't *want* you poking around, getting in the way. Take your client's money and go after your guitar player. That's your job, Theo. Go do it and leave this end of things alone."

Brody got behind the wheel and slammed the door. As he sped off, I thought about Angela Ricci and the cruel waste her death was. The one time I'd met her, she didn't strike me as naïve, timid, or shy. She was in her element with Nick Bianchi, enjoying life with a glass of wine, listening to Nick's stories about my past. Something he or I said must have hit a nerve because she picked up the phone and called my number.

She must have known the chance she was taking when she phoned me. She must have taken precautions to keep our upcoming meeting secret. Then she made the call and paid the ultimate price for wanting to talk. The obvious conclusion was that someone in Peter Garcetti's circle got wind that Angela was trying to sell some information and put a stop to it. It wasn't a stretch for me to imagine Nick Bianchi standing over the frightened woman and pulling the trigger. Yet sometimes chasing the obvious is a step backwards. It keeps you from studying the entire scene, looking in the darker corners for the real culprit.

Walking to where I hoped to find a taxi, I called Brody Flynn on his cell.

"Yeah?"

"What if Aldo Conte killed Angela Ricci?"

"I thought we agreed you were leaving this alone."

"Just tossing you an idea, giving you a good reason to start looking for him."

"I don't want a good reason. But if you really believe he killed her, Theo, it's all the more reason for you to find him," he said as my phone went silent.

Chapter Seven

I reserved a room in the Raphael Hotel near Piazza Navona. It was centrally located and provided a business center that Gina Ponte and I found useful when our art reclamation duties brought us to Rome. My first stay in the Raphael was years ago when my wife signed us up for one of those whirlwind guided tours to Venice, Florence, and the Eternal City. We were going through a rough patch in our relationship, and she thought a trip to Italy would bring back the romance. It didn't. After five days of riding buses and chasing our guide's twirling pink umbrella through one museum after another, I wanted nothing more than to get back to Boston. The highlight of the trip was the Raphael's rooftop terrace with spectacular views of the city including St. Peter's across the Tiber. It was on that terrace sipping a cold glass of prosecco that my wife and I decided that more than the trip was a disaster, our marriage was as well. We clinked glasses and agreed to divorce.

As I packed for my trip to search for Aldo Conte, I caught the latest news regarding the murder of Angela Ricci. No witnesses had come forward. No motive given for her execution-style killing. The police spokesman at Somerville PD said they were following all leads and questioning suspects; however it did not appear that the general public was in danger. It was the usual official statement meant to reassure the public that the sky was not falling.

I locked my apartment and headed to Logan Airport. The overnight flight was uneventful as was customs and the taxi to the Raphael where I checked in, unpacked my bag, and took a shower to freshen up. The hotel was about a 15-minute walk to Aldo Conte's violin shop. My plan was to start there, then play it by ear. Investigations often follow that pattern. Do something, then react to it. Doing something meant finding Aldo Conte's shop.

Rome is not an easy city. The cobblestoned streets fight with walkers, and walkers are everywhere. With each step, the elderly look for a safe landing to avoid the feared fall while children race around the crowded sidewalks blocked by rows of parked Vespas. I followed a leggy young lady in a tight skirt and stiletto heels as she cautiously selected each wobbly step, one hand pressed against the stone buildings for support. Fashion has its price. I didn't stay around to see if she made it to the end of the block without breaking an ankle as I was busy looking for any sign directing me to Via di Montoro.

Across Corso Vittorio Emanuele, a heavily trafficked street, I hurried through the Compo di Fiori, a large open air market selling fruits, vegetables, flowers, and dry goods from truck beds and pushcarts. On my previous visits, I'd jogged through here in the very early morning and watched as dozens of vendors arrived and set up, their hopeful voices of a profitable day selling ringing throughout the square. Outdoor cafes and more formal restaurants line the Compo. Behind them, grocers, butchers and wine shops provide the apartment dwellers living above those shops the necessities of life. A person could live his entire life in the Compo and never want, unless you were Giordano Bruno, who was accused of being a heretic in 1600 and burned alive. His stone monument rises from the Compo's center.

I left the Compo on Via Del Pellegrino, an ancient, curved street whose apartment building front doors open directly onto the street. I passed a fountain of plump cherubs spewing streams of water looking for a street sign directing me to Aldo Conte's shop. I thought how oddly wonderful it all was: The cobbled streets, the bustling open air market, the fountains and buildings crowding the streets, the cafes filled with coffee drinkers all of it crying out that Rome was not the product of an orderly mind, yet somehow everything fit. Even Aldo Conte's small violin shop with his name painted in gold letters on the glass window seemed a perfect fit.

I opened the front door and stepped in to a long and narrow space smelling of wood shavings and wet varnish. A man of about sixty, tall and thinly built, sat at his workbench, his concentration on the partially completed violin he held delicately in his hands. On the bench rested rows of tools, some of which I'd never seen before, all neatly positioned, their cleanliness gleaming in the overhead light. In time, the man gently put the instrument aside and turned to face me. It was then that I saw his almost radiant pride in his role as master violin maker. I also saw clearly that he looked nothing like the photograph Charles Raskin had given me of the man who visited the Gardner calling himself Aldo Conte.

When he stood, he swept back a lock of his nearly black hair speckled with bits of gray along the temples. His crisp features matched his thin build. As he approached, he cocked his head to one side as if trying to remember if he'd made an appointment he couldn't honestly remember.

I moved the moment along. "Mr. Conte?" I asked.

"I am Conte, yes." His curious eyes scanned me. "I don't recall . . ."

"I don't have an appointment," I reassured him. "And I'm not here to inquire about one of your beautiful violins." My gaze drifted to the framed photographs on the wall of Itzhak Perlman and Isaac Stern. In each picture, both musician and the beaming Aldo Conte held a prized instrument between them, broad smiles on all. Beside the photos were various plaques and awards recognizing the superior quality produced in this shop. "Would it be fair to say that you've never been to Boston?"

"Boston?" He pronounced it 'Boss-a-ton' with his thick Italian accent. "No, I've not been to Boston." Conte took a step back toward his workbench. "I have work, you understand, Mr. . . .?

"Theo Perdoux. I'm a private investigator looking into the whereabouts of this man," I said and handed over the printout and photograph of the man who impersonated Conte at the Gardner. "Do you know any reason that might explain why this man is passing himself off as you?" As the color drained from Conte's face, I said, "You recognize him, don't you."

"I . . ." He shook his head, thinking. "What has he done?"

"He may have been involved in a robbery."

Conte stiffened, his eyes as cold and dark as the sea boring in on me.

"The imposter worked with a woman named Angela Ricci," I said. "She was murdered. It's possible your impersonator killed her."

Conte's expression turned blank as he handed back the paper and photograph. "No," he finally said, unconvincingly. "I don't know this man."

He walked back to his workbench and sat; his eyes cast downward. For the longest time, he stubbornly resisted my presence.

"Maybe if you thought about it," I said and waited. "I've traveled a great distance to get some answers, Mr. Conte. I'm not going to leave Rome without them. I can come back a little later, and we can . . ."

"No," he said in a short burst. "A customer has an appointment. I have a responsibility with him, you understand. I need an hour with my customer, then an hour more to clean up. Come after lunch. Villa Conte is not far from here," he said and gave me the address. "We can talk there."

Most people can't get away with even the smallest lie, and Conte was one of them. I knew he recognized the man in the photograph, but

I didn't know why he denied it. What I did know was that if he lied once, he might do so again. Was he really expecting a client? I decided to hang around to make sure Conte wouldn't run off. I ducked in a nearby pharmacy and kept the violin shop in plain view. In half an hour, a man walked through Conte's door and immediately picked up an instrument. Convinced he was there to do business, I bought a toothbrush and went on my way.

I followed Conte's directions past the Palazzo Farnese where a clump of angry looking men and women crowded around a man with a bullhorn who worked the group like a Baptist minister works his congregation. I didn't understand what came out of the bullhorn, but judging by the approving shouts, he was hitting all the right notes. The scene wasn't threatening, more political theatre than much else. Italians were famous for calling strikes, and I thought this demonstration was a prelude to the next. I decided to take in more and sat at an outdoor café to watch. Besides, I hadn't had anything to eat since the flight. Killing time before meeting Aldo Conte, I ordered a glass of red wine and mushroom bruschetta. Both were delicious.

I ordered an espresso and leaned back to enjoy the warm sun. The waiter in his shiny black suit bobbed and smiled when he delivered the frothy cup. A picture of civility and kindness. Across the palazzo, a group of giggly school children pranced behind two nuns dressed in full habits. The young boys wore ties, the girls knee socks and skirts. They pranced single file into a church as the ringing belfry bells scattered pigeons. I could get used to this, I thought and finished my coffee.

Past the Farnese, I walked along the short, narrow Via del Mascherone toward the Tiber. Off to the left, a stone arch opened onto a walled garden that Conte told me was the rear entrance to Villa Conte. I could imagine that centuries ago, charioteers on their say to Circus Maximus housed their racehorses inside these walls.

I entered the beautifully kept grounds and walked past a fountain of bronzed nymphs that splashed water into a kidney-shaped swimming pool. At the far shallow end, a young boy, I guessed about ten, with what looked like rubber balloons strapped to his arms, enjoyed a swimming lesson. His instructor, a plump woman in a bathing suit and large floppy hat to protect her from the sun, coaxed strokes out of her young student. Both seemed to enjoy the moment as shouts of encouragement and joy skimmed across the water.

I moved along trying to identify delicious fragrances surrounding me, past trellised pink and white bougainvillea lining the walk which curved along toward the front of the house. A row of umbrella pines opened onto a courtyard and the villa, a grand, 3-storied stone fortress with a second-floor loggia set off by marble columns. When I climbed the stairs to the massive front door and looked behind me, I could see the river flowing by.

I was either in the wrong place or crafting and selling violins was more lucrative than I'd ever imagined. The round, weathered bronze knocker felt warm in my hand as I banged it home. The door opened a crack bathing me with the sounds of someone playing a Brahms concerto on a violin.

"Yes?" the woman in the housecoat asked.

I introduced myself. "Mr. Conte is expecting me."

The door fully opened, and I stepped in to a long, wide hallway lined on each side with bronze statues holding musical instruments. I followed the housecoat over the tiled floor, her soft rubber soles breaking the silence with an occasional squeak as it mixed with the captivating music. Before getting to its source, she motioned for me to enter the door on the left where Aldo Conte stood at an enormous and beautifully carved sideboard packing his pipe with tobacco. He'd changed out of his shop clothes and now dressed more formally in a summer suit open at the neck. Behind the sideboard hung an intricate tapestry of wildflowers and grazing unicorns. The paintings and marble busts made me feel like I was in a museum being serenaded by a skilled violinist. If I didn't know better, I would have thought I was at the Gardner Museum listening to one of their Sunday afternoon concerts.

Conte registered my fascination. "Beautiful, isn't it? The music? The space? The villa has been in the Conte family for over two centuries, two centuries during which the Conte name has been greatly respected. When you told me that our name had been abused, had been associated with crimes, I didn't know how to respond. I needed time to think, you understand?"

"Of course."

"I needed time to consider how to deal with you. A man who brings shocking news is not always welcome. But then, I thought, if you come to Villa Conte, if you see who we are, if you see how we live, it might provide context and help you understand the information you seek. Let's start with introductions. Follow me, please."

We walked to the end of the hall and looked in. The spacious room held a collection of musical instruments. Nearest the arched windows that looked out onto the beautifully inviting swimming pool stood a grand piano. In the far corner on a slightly raised stage was a harpsicord and beside it a harp. To the right, behind glass cases were lutes, guitars, and violins. At the end of the room stood a stylishly dressed, black-haired woman of about forty listening intently to the young man practicing Brahms. She tapped her finger on the music stand to stop the session. She took the instrument and bowed the strings. Sharp, crisp notes rang out. She returned the violin. The student played again as the woman looked on approvingly.

"My daughter, Lia," Conte whispered. "I build the instruments; she gives the lessons."

He motioned for me to move along. At the end of the hall, we stepped down a twisting flight of stairs and into a large workshop filled with young men and women, six in all, with small planes in their hands. Each stood behind their own workbenches as they shaved thin pieces of wood with their planes. At first glance, the space looked like a larger version of Conte's workshop without the master holding the tools. In front of the room, demonstrating proper technique, was a sturdily built man in his early thirties wearing a leather apron and a demanding demeanor. The students mimicked his every move.

"Silvio," Conte said so only I could hear. "My son offers instruction on how to work the wood. Who knows? An artist may emerge."

We walked outside. In back of the villa, the pale blue waters of the swimming pool stretched out before us as the child climbed out of the water, his lesson over. His swimming instructor wrapped him in a towel and hurried him toward us. Aldo put his pipe down on the glass-topped table and swept the boy up in both arms, kissing him on each cheek. The boy squealed with delight.

Conte spoke in Italian. The woman brought the tips of her fingers to her lips and kissed. "*Bellissimo, signor* Conte. *Molto bene.*"

The boy squirmed away and raced toward the house followed hurriedly by his swimming instructor.

"My grandson, Marcus, named after his famous ancestor. Marcus Conte was trained in the art of violin making by Stradivarius. I will teach Marcus myself how to make a wooden box sing." Conte picked up his pipe and examined it as if he'd never seen it before. "I wanted you to meet my family before we talk of anything more. Nothing else matters, you understand. After my divorce, I realized that. Some lessons are difficult to learn. Some are never learned. A house is not complete without the sound of children. We Italians live for beauty and family. Everywhere you look in this country, you see beauty and family. It's who we are." Conte offered me a seat at the table and poured two glasses before putting a match to his pipe. He watched the smoke rise and said, "You've met my family, Mr. Perdoux. Lia, her son Marcus, Silvio, and me. It is a house filled with children as all should be. Do you have many?"

I shook my head. "None."

"And your wife. She's fine with that? Most women need children to make them happy. That is what they are told by our church, you understand. Catholics need many children. I take it, you are not Catholic."

Again, I shook my head. "Not Catholic and not married. Divorced."

"Then, we have another thing in common in addition to a curiosity about a man who uses my identity," Conte said.

"Curious?" I asked. "I had the impression back in your shop that you recognized the man in the photograph."

"Perhaps I've selected the wrong word," Conte said apparently not interested in hunting for another as he raised his glass. "I make the Lemoncello myself. Salute."

I sipped my drink. The cool, lemony taste slid down like a buttery Popsicle. "Delicious."

"Perhaps I should add good wine and great food to beauty and family." Conte drank half of the contents of his glass, then said, "But like all things in life, there lives the opposite. Rome is a wonderful city, a living ruin really. One imagines at any moment, it could crumble from the weight of its own ineptitude. That's the politician's fault. They can't get anything done, you understand. Always fighting each other, bickering. One steals from the coffers, goes to prison, gets out and wins another election. Like many things in our country, it doesn't make sense, but it is the way it has been done for centuries. In the void, the

Mafia moves in and runs things. Most Italians think the Mafia does a better job of running the country than the politician ever could, so we leave them alone."

"Cynical view, isn't it?" I asked and sipped my drink. Lemonade with a bite.

"I am a realist, Mr. Perdoux. You learn to be when your family name is Conte."

"I'm not sure I follow."

"What name comes to mind when you think of fine violins?"

"Stradivarius."

"Yes, Stradivarius first, Amati second, Conte third," he said matter of factly. "All three families began making violins at about the same time in the early seventeen-hundreds in Cremona, south of Milan. Nicolo Amati taught Stradivarius, Stradivarius taught Marcus Conte, my ancestor who set the family off on this remarkable journey. My great-great-great grandfather wanted to be near the glorious music halls of Rome. He found this palazzo in need of repair after a wool merchant lost his way. My family bought the structure, making improvements as the Conte reputation grew."

"It is beautiful," I said admiringly.

"A family treasure but not without its drawbacks. The politicians tell us the reason they do nothing is that they haven't any money. So, they raise taxes on those of us with property." One arm swept toward his grand house. "Taxes and upkeep on the villa led to a mistake of mine, Mr. Perdoux. Something I am very sorry for, you understand, but responsible for nonetheless. The tradition in my family is that the son apprentices, learns to make the instruments, and when ready, helps his father continue the Conte quality. Without a seamless transition maintaining quality, the family name becomes worthless. No one would buy a violin that doesn't make the deep, rich Conte sound. That is what our violins are known for, you understand. That is why we have a waiting list of over two years for our instruments." Conte studied the pipe in his hand, thinking. Finally, he said, "Unfortunately, my son, is not capable of making such an instrument. It looks the same. It feels the same, you understand. But it does not sound like a Conte and cannot be sold as a Conte. I will not allow it. He was furious with me when I gave him that news, of course, but that is another matter. Without sales, we cannot continue. What was I to do? I did what I thought best for the family and took on a different apprentice. It was against my better judgement, but after consulting with my business manager I believed it had to be done. My instrument sales and repairs, Lia's lessons and Silvio's classes on making violins produce enough income to support us. Our manager said that, after Rome's most recent tax increase, we needed to increase our income or risk losing Villa Conte. It's been in our family for hundreds of years, and we don't intend to let it go." He relit his pipe and blew a line of smoke. "One of Silvio's students showed promise. He was good with the wood. Was he an artist? I decided to find out and took him on as an apprentice even though I knew he wasn't fully ready. All violins wearing the Conte label would still come mostly from my hand, but some of the more basic tasks— steaming the ribs, sanding the pegs—that sort of small element in the completion of the instrument would fall to him. If he showed appropriate skill, I would reward him with more responsibility. However, he did not stay. In one month, he was gone from my shop. He simply disappeared."

"When was this?" I asked.

"Late December, just before Christmas."

The timing fits, I thought. Early January was when the imposter appeared at the Gardner. "You're talking about the man in the photograph I showed you, aren't you?"

"Yes. I am talking about that man."

"What's his name?"

"Francesco Vega."

"He seems to be in the habit of showing up and then disappearing," I said. "What can you tell me about him?"

Conte shrugged. "Competent. Highly skilled in particular areas. A bit rough at the edges. A man with big ideas but lacking direction. He knew Silvio from the streets. Francesco is older, more experienced in the ways of street life. He and Silvio roamed with an unsavory crowd that I did not approve of. I warned Silvio that he was ruining his life. He didn't listen, you understand. Young men ignore their parents and lean toward the wild life. Eventually, Silvio came to his senses."

"And Vega?" I asked. "Did he come to his senses?"

"Francesco was a different sort," Conte said. "One of his strengths was that he'd packed a good amount of living into his life. His weakness was that he did not stay committed to anything. For a while he was a student studying art. From what I understand, he was a very good painter when it came to copying the old masters, but he lacked creative initiative. His originals were flat, boring. In a way, he had that in common with my son. Silvio could make beautiful looking instruments, but they lacked the artistic element that made them sing. Their sound had no passion. You can't teach instilling that certain quality. It's not possible. You either have the ability to make instruments sing or you don't. But you can teach how to make a beautiful *looking* instrument. Silvio does that and does it well. Apparently, Francesco suffered the same flaw with his brushes. He could copy an old master's technique but not their passion. Frustrated, Francesco eventually dropped out of art school. He traveled a bit. Came back to Rome and enrolled in one of Silvio's violin making classes. Silvio is an excellent teacher, you understand. Excellent. Francesco excelled in his classes, so with some urging, I accepted him as an apprentice." Conte waved a stream of smoke into the air, his gaze fixed on me. "There is one other thing, Mr. Perdoux. Something I thought best to speak of here without the worry of intrusions. Francesco Vega was once married to Angela Ricci."

I felt the hairs prickle across my neck. "You're sure? When?"

"Yes. Years ago. The lovers were both very young, very footloose. Angela was hitchhiking the country, and as Francesco told me, they fell madly for each other and took off together. It didn't take long to realize that they'd both made a hasty decision and had the marriage annulled before Angela returned to America."

"Where Francesco met up with her again in January," I murmured mostly to myself.

"So you say."

"How did they end up at the Gardner together?"

"I don't know. I was shocked when you told me. More so when you told me Angela had been killed."

"Where is Francesco Vega now?" I asked.

"I don't know," Conte said. "Lia might be able to answer that. She knows much more about the comings and goings of her friends than I do."

"She and Francesco were friends?" I asked.

"Yes," Conte said, turning his gaze back toward the house, as we both became aware that the violin lesson had ended, and silence filled the air.

Lia, a tall, striking looking woman with black hair swept back behind her ears walked confidently to where Aldo and I were sitting. She seemed relaxed, aware, and mysterious all at the same time. She filled a small glass from the table with Lemoncello and raised it to her lips.

"One of life's many pleasures," she said and sat across from me as her father made introductions.

"Mr. Perdoux is looking for Francesco," Mr. Conte informed her. "He's come all the way from Boston to find him."

"Really?" She held her glass delicately, like an astonished bird drinking with a cat who might pounce. I could tell as she narrowed her eyes that I was the cat. "You are friends with Francesco, is that it?"

"Not friends, no. I've been hired by the Gardner Museum to find him. Francesco visited there pretending to be your father," I said.

"Why would he do that?" she asked, suspiciously.

"That's what I'm trying to find out. Would you happen to know where I could find him?"

"No," she said. "He was around quite often when he took classes from Silvio, then he went off to work in father's shop for a short while. He left without a word to anyone as far as I know. But I wouldn't know, would I? We were never that close," she said.

"When did you see him last?" I asked.

"Sometime in March. The date I don't remember, the circumstances I do," Lia said. "We had planned a trip to his father's upholstery shop to pick up some fabric for lining new violin cases. At the last minute, Francesco cancelled. He was like that. He'd make a plan and then do something else. No discipline. No commitment. Francesco was one of those unfortunate souls who was someday going to change the world. Someday never came."

"I take it you didn't appreciate his fantasy."

"I didn't, no. I need order and reality in my life. Giving lessons and raising a son demands responsibility. Francesco was never very responsible."

"Then, it doesn't surprise you that he is a suspect in a Boston museum robbery?"

"The surprise would be that he actually carried it off. Like I said, he was not one to follow through with anything. Even his marriage to Angela was short lived."

"You knew Angela?" I asked.

"Not well." Lia thought a moment, then said, "How well do you know people who pass quickly through your life? Angela came to Europe as an exchange student, then quit school after a semester. Hitchhiking around, she found her way to Rome as many do. In those days, everyone congregated near Piazza di Spagna. She, Francesco, me, and Silvio were part of the crowd. I asked her once why she didn't go back home after quitting school. All she said was that she never wanted to go back. She was on her own and wanted to stay that way."

"Doesn't sound like the marrying type," I offered.

"It was a marriage of convenience," Lia said matter of factly. "They were attracted to each other, they wanted to see the world, to travel without commitments. Getting married seemed the thing to do, just like getting divorced seemed the thing to do a short time later."

"Do you think the same thinking might apply to robbing the Gardner? It seemed the thing to do at the time?"

Lia shook her head slightly. "I can't see that," she said. "No. I don't know what Francesco was doing there, but robbing a museum would not be something he would do."

"Even with Angela's help?" I prodded. "When he came to the museum pretending to be your father, Angela was with him."

"Really? I didn't know that."

"I suppose you didn't know that someone shot her to keep her quiet. She set up a meeting so she could tell me something. Before we could talk, she was killed."

The news seemed to deflate her. "Killed?" she repeated in a whisper as she put down her glass. "Who would do such a thing?"

"Someone who has something to hide. Her former husband, maybe?"

No one spoke for the longest time. Finally, Aldo Conte broke his silence. "Shouldn't you get ready for your next lesson, Lia? Lia?"

Lia stiffened at the sound of her name. She looked at her watch and nodded. Without saying another word, she walked slowly back to the house.

"When you are young, news of someone your age dying always shocks," Conte said, explaining his daughter's departure. "Especially when the death is murder. And I will answer your question, Mr. Perdoux: Francesco is many things, but I don't believe him capable of killing anyone. Silvio could probably confirm that, but he is busy with his workshop. And I have responsibilities that require my attention," Conte said and stood.

"Of course," I said and followed him to the front door. "I'd like to speak to Silvio when he has time."

"He's very busy. We all are, you understand. Haven't Lia and I answered all your questions?"

"You've been helpful, and I appreciate it, but . . ."

"Where is Francesco?" Conte said, anticipating my question.

"For starters," I said.

"I'm afraid it will also be the end. Francesco is out of our lives. None of us knows where he is. Frankly, none of us cares. Goodbye, Mr. Perdoux," Conte said and closed the door behind me.

Chapter Eight

Outside Villa Conte I saw one of the students from Silvio's workshop. He was easy to identify in his leather apron. He looked about twenty with medium length brown hair, weathered features, and a serious look. He lit a second cigarette from the first and crushed the butt with the toe of his boot while talking on his cellphone. I caught up with him pacing along the Tiber, gesturing wildly as if what he was hearing through his phone would forever change his life.

"Excuse me. Sorry to bother," I said, "but Silvio's father was giving me a tour. My son is interested in joining one of the workshops, and I wondered if you could give me a bit more information. You know, the unofficial version of what it's really like in there."

His call ended, the man glanced at his watch, then glared at me. "Our break is short, and my phone calls . . ." he said dismissing me.

"Just a few questions," I said. "I know you have to get back."

"I cannot say much," the man said, his Italian accent pleasant to my ear. "It is a workshop. You work with the wood and hope it sings when Lia plays."

"Is that the final measure of your success? Lia playing?"

"Success or failure," the man said. "Not all violins have the voice. They may look the same, but . . ." The man shook his head and filled his lungs with smoke. As he blew it out, he said, "Lia plays, then *signore* Conte passes judgement. If the instrument is good enough, *signore* Conte admits you into his shop. You work there, you learn more, you go off on your own. That is the way. Not an easy way, your son should know that. Years of practice may produce nothing. *Signore* Conte may not invite you in. He usually does not. You have to go elsewhere to learn more, and there are not many making instruments in Roma."

"You mean he may not accept you as his apprentice," I clarified.

"That's the word, yes. Silvio teaches how to make the instrument, Lia lets you hear its music, but *signore* Conte is the judge who matters. Few are invited to work in his shop. That is why we all work so hard; we want to be one of the few."

"*Signore* Conte mentioned Francesco Vega as one that he recently invited."

The man winced at the name. "Vega," he said contemptuously. "Genius with the wood. But no good with his life. He walks out on *signore* Conte and the Pamphilj. Very bad to turn away from one, but two?"

I didn't waste time asking about the Pamphilj as the man turned back toward the villa. I hurried to keep up. "Why did Vega leave Conte's apprenticeship?"

He shrugged. "Why does a man step in front of a moving train? His mind goes crazy is the only answer. I don't know for sure. Something happened to Francesco and Silvio. What? I don't know. They both grow serious over the past few months. Not so much fun in the workshop. More like the army. Your son like rules?"

"Not especially," I said.

"You follow rules here now. Not so much fun as before," he said and flipped away the last of his cigarette.

"Why do you stay with it?" I asked.

"I want to work with *signore* Conte. Apprentice with him makes for a good life."

"I think my son should speak to someone like Francesco Vega, someone who did not stay with the program to the end. Get his reasons for leaving the apprenticeship. Do you know where I might find him?" I asked.

"The antique shop on Via del Cappellari next to the corner trattoria. Vega work there some," the man said as church bells filled the air. "Four blocks." He pointed with one hand before hurrying back toward his workshop.

I worked my way back through the Compo, now in the late afternoon, mostly empty as the market vendors had packed up for the day. The outdoor cafes surrounding the square were full of people enjoying the warm sun. At the far end of the Compo, two bakeries framed the beginning of Via del Cappellari, a tiny street lined with art galleries, artists' studios, and at the end, an antique shop across the street from a news stand. A portly, middle-aged man dressed in a sport coat and tie stood outside the antique shop talking to an elderly woman seated in a chair. Even though the temperature was in the low seventies, the woman had a wool blanket draped over her legs. She and the man were conversing in animated Italian as I approached.

When they stopped, I said to the man, "I'm looking for Francesco Vega. I was told someone here might be able to tell me where I might find him."

"Franco?" The man looked at the woman in the chair and rattled off something I did not understand. She responded with a shake of her head. To me, the man said, "Franco Vega is no here."

"Does he work here?"

"He paint sometimes," the man said, waving one hand as if it held an artist's brush.

I followed the man inside the shop crammed with antique furniture, oriental rugs, Venetian chandeliers, lamps, and walls covered in old paintings. Moving through it all without banging into something was a challenge. In the back of the shop, the man stopped in front of a large canvas resting on an easel. The shattered streets of Pompeii were painted a brooding gray with Vesuvius rising above them, shrouded in clouds. The man pointed to a section of the canvas above the signature. I recognized the artist's name and considered him a journeyman, not a master. The canvas before me was painted in 1832.

"Francesco fix," the man said as I leaned in for a closer look.

After a minute, I saw the retouched street scene clearly done by someone with skill. I have viewed hundreds of paintings in my work with Sala Ponte and have seen paintings ruined from poor attempts to restore the work to its original condition. The restoration of this painting was good, not great. Francesco matched well the brush strokes, but the colors were slightly off and the craquelure uneven.

"Very goods, no?" the man asked.

"Very good, yes," I said not wanting to point out the flaws. Back outside, I said, "I would like to speak to Francesco. I'd like to talk to him."

The woman in the chair spoke in Italian. The man nodded and shuffled his feet. Finally, the woman stuck out one arm and pointed a pale hand twisted like a cripple's at a green door belonging to the building across the street. "Francesco there," she said.

The man held up four fingers. "He live four."

"Fourth floor?" I asked.

"Fourth floor," he repeated with a nod.

I thanked them both and crossed the street to number 9. The green wooden door opened onto a small, enclosed entryway containing a table stacked with uncollected mail and above it, five intercom buzzers beside five name plates. The plate across from number four read 'F. Vega'. I pressed the buzzer and waited. I pressed it again. Somewhere inside I heard children laughing. A door closed above followed by the clack and clang of an elevator. Through the glass of the security door,

I could see the elevator's lights as the door swung open and a woman got out, holding the hand of a small, prancing child. The child danced toward me and opened the security door.

I stepped aside as the woman came out and went through the mail. The child looked up at me with questioning eyes as the woman selected her letters.

"Francesco," I said, hoping for a positive response. "Francesco Vega. I believe he lives here."

"*Como?*" The woman cocked her head, clearly not understanding English.

I showed her the picture the Gardner security guard gave me of Vega. After glancing at it, she pointed to Vega's name plate.

"Have you seen him?" I asked as she stepped back into the hall, gripping tightly her child and mail as if I were about to attack. She pushed the security door closed leaving me locked out, then she hurried to the elevator's safety.

I flipped through the remaining mail and counted four pieces for Mr. Vega before stepping back into the street and entering the nearby trattoria. An available table for two provided a perfect spot to watch Francesco's apartment building. It was early, but I ordered a half carafe of house white and pasta vongole. One thing I learned from my previous trips to Italy was that finding a bad meal was nearly impossible. This small trattoria filled with locals was no exception. The broth, clams, and pasta were all cooked to perfection. The wine cold, sharp with a hint of citrus. It was just after 5 o'clock when I sat down and 6:30 when I finished my espresso. I ordered a second along with the bill.

Outside, the street was filling up with families, lovers, and beggars. One stooped beggar entered the restaurant and stopped at each table, offering white roses for sale. She made a sale at a nearby table before

I waved her away. I followed her with my eyes, focusing on the sooty-yellow building housing Francesco Vega's apartment. Lights were beginning to come on in the building, including one in the window on the fourth floor. No one came or went using the front door. There must be a back entrance.

I paid my bill and crossed the street. I checked the mail and saw that Vega's letters were gone. I was about to push the buzzer to his apartment, when a young couple having a lover's quarrel yanked open the security door and rushed outside. My foot kept it from closing.

Once inside, I took the stairs up, thinking the elevator noise might announce my arrival. The dimly lit stairway led to a landing containing a metal fire door. I opened the door on floors two and three. In each case, a white tile floor led to an apartment door to the right and the elevator door to the left. Children could be heard on the second floor and a barking dog on the third. I climbed to the fourth and listened before opening the fire door.

Television voices filtered down from the floor above, mixing in the stairwell with the sounds of children playing and the barking dog. Nothing from the fourth floor added to the mix. Slowly, I pushed open the fire door and stopped as Vega's apartment door swung open. An attractive woman who looked to be in her early thirties, dressed casually, stepped out, holding the door partially open. She bent at the waist and spoke softly in that unmistakable tone and cadence that one uses when addressing a pet. She then closed the door, locked it, and put the key under the mat.

I closed the fire door and listened for the elevator to grind to a stop and the door to clang open. When I was certain it was on its way down, I entered the empty hall. I picked up the key from under Vega's mat and unlocked the door. A Siamese cat looked up from its nearly full food bowl in the kitchen then ignoring me, continued to eat. I closed the door behind me and went to the living room window. I could see the trattoria and bustle on the street. In a short while, the casually dressed woman walked past the antique shop and turned the corner.

I switched on the desk lamp and had a quick look around the tiny one-bedroom apartment. Francesco Vega kept a neat space. His double bed was made, the kitchen spotless and the living room clean. I opened the refrigerator and peeked inside. Other than white wine, cheese, and eggs, it was unoccupied. I looked for signs of life in the bathroom. A razor, toothbrush, deodorant and medicine bottles were missing. In the bedroom closet hung a jacket, sport coat, shirts, and a few pairs of pants. A pair of Nikes and work shoes sat on the floor. His chest of drawers contained the usual assortment of socks, underwear, and folded shirts. Nothing out of the ordinary jumped out.

I went back into the living room furnished with a sofa and two chairs with end tables on which sat shaded lamps. Bookshelves lined one wall. I couldn't translate many of the titles, but some were unmistakable art books containing the works of old masters. An English dictionary and various travel books rounded out his library. A copy of a book detailing walks around Boston was well worn.

On the desk, a framed photograph of an elderly couple looked directly into the camera. Their dress and expressions both looked forced, like people not used to putting on their finery to have their pictures taken. An anniversary picture of Francesco's parents? A birthday photograph?

I sat at the desk and opened the top drawer where a photograph of a young Angela Ricci looked back at me. Her wide, genuine smile seemed bursting with happiness. In the background, the Spanish Steps rose above the boat-shaped fountain in the center of the piazza. Angela sat on the edge of the fountain, beaming. I put the photo back and was about to work my way through the rest of the contents when the apartment buzzer sounded.

My heart clutched, and I held my breath, listening for other sounds. In seconds, the buzzer again filled the apartment. I pulled back the window curtain and looked out. A delivery man holding bags of groceries stood in the street looking up, searchingly at the apartment windows. I heard the elevator rattle down and watched the delivery man enter the building. Shouts of anxious joy echoed in the halls. Soon, I heard footfall in the apartment above me followed by muffled voices. The apartment building was coming to life, and I wanted to get out and come back during the quiet of the day.

I closed the drawer and took a quick look through the mail on the desk. A plastic wrapped newest edition of *Art World* magazine and a magazine focused on woodworking sat at the top of the pile. A stack of letters two inches high remained unopened. Most letters appeared to be bills or flyers announcing local store sales. I searched the stack looking for something personal, something that gave me insight into Francesco Vega. Toward the bottom of the pile was a postcard written in Italian from Galleria Doria Pamphilj. I remember the man from the workshop telling me that Vega had walked out on the Pamphilj. Now I had an address. I put the postcard in my pocket and along with another card announcing a fabric sale at Vega Fine Leathers. I turned out the lamp.

I locked the apartment door and put the key back under the mat, then headed for my hotel.

Chapter Nine

I didn't try to fight the jet lag that set in later. Or maybe it was the wine that made me feel listless and heavy. Regardless, I slept soundly and awoke with the bright sun glistening through my window over the dome of Santa Maria della Pace. I stood on my terrace, the railings of which were covered in yellow bougainvillea, and looked down at the piazza below. Waiters in white jackets stood at attention as the morning café crowd trickled in and sat at the many round tables.

The thought of a double espresso sent me hunting for my room key. In addition to spacious rooms, a fine breakfast, and wonderful location near the Piazza Navona, the Raphael Hotel provides excellent information at the front desk for tourists and private detectives alike. I presented the Galleria Doria Pamphilj postcard to the clerk who beamed with what amounted to civic pride.

"*Allora*! *Magnifico*! Beautiful! A grand palace not far from here," she gushed. "I took my sister when she visit. Pope Innocent the tenth, he collect most of the art." She made the sign of the cross. "He fine pope, no?"

"I'm sure," I said directing her attention to the handwritten note on the card. I asked her to translate the Italian into English.

She crinkled her brow, searching for the right words. Finally she said, "'God has promised forgiveness to your repentance, but He has not promised tomorrow to your procrastination.' St. Augustine of Hippo."

I took back the postcard. "Odd note, don't you think?"

"Odd, yes. What's it meaning?"

"I'm not entirely sure," I said and asked for directions.

The Pamphilj art collection was housed in the Palazzo Doria Pamphilj on Via del Corso, one of Rome's few wide streets. From my hotel, it took a little more than half an hour to walk there. The morning sun was bright, the streets already clogged with car and bus traffic turning onto the Corso. When I stepped off the curb, a Vespa sped by so closely it rustled the hairs on my arms. After a few blocks of not being run over, I spotted a sign for my destination.

Approaching the entrance, the awareness struck me that in Rome you don't have to work for your pleasures. A turn here, a turn there, and something beautiful surprises like the Palazzo Doria Pamphilj, a grand family palace of over 100 rooms that admits guests for a fee. It is massive and beautiful and inviting all at the same time. I bought a ticket and stepped inside not really knowing how to proceed. I'm here because of a postcard sent to Francesco Vega. I don't know who sent it or why. I don't even know if someone in this building sent it. All I know is that the postcard was printed for the Galleria, so here I am flying blind and calling the control tower for help.

When the last person in line bought her ticket, I handed the postcard to the attendant who glanced at it and said without a second thought, "James Alberts."

"James Alberts?" I repeated. "American?"

She did not answer but handed back the postcard. "Around the corner and down the stairs," she said as behind me the line for tickets grew.

Around the corner led to a door marked 'No Admittance'. I opened it and climbed down the worn stone steps into a brightly lit repair shop complete with workbenches, band saws, a paint station, stacked lumber, and an overweight and gruff looking man staring back at me. Behind him a delicate operation on an old canvas was underway. I couldn't tell if the technician was cleaning an old master's painting or restoring a damaged portion. Regardless, her intense focus impressed.

"You didn't see the sign?" the man barked in perfect English, clearly someone who appreciated the sound of his own loud voice. "The conservatory is off limits to tourists."

"Are you James Alberts?" I asked.

"Who else?" he said and attended a second employee at the back of the shop who called out a question. When Alberts finished providing detailed instructions, he turned back to me.

I handed him the postcard. He looked, then gave it back.

"Tell Francesco that horse has left the barn. I already hired somebody."

"He was in line for a job here?" I asked.

"Was," Alberts spit out. "That's what the quote's about: procrastination. Vega needed to get off his duff. He didn't, so I filled the position." He bobbed his head in the direction of the employee in the back who appeared to be regilding an ornate mirror. "I look for people with many talents who show up on time every day. That's a good start in my book. Francesco needs to learn that."

"Are you in the habit of quoting St. Augustine to possible employees?" I asked.

"St. Augustine, Kipling, Thoreau, Pope John. You name it. I try to be neither predictable nor boring. If it fits on a postcard, I use it. Besides, I'm good with my hands, not my brain. Others have said what I want to better than I ever could, so I put a line or two on a postcard and drop it in the mail."

"That explains why I was sent down here. Your postcard mailings are famous. Mind if I ask you a few questions?"

"Depends on who's asking those questions?"

I told him and added, "I don't think Francesco ever got your card. I found it on his desk along with a stack of unopened mail, which makes me wonder why you didn't offer him the job in person."

"I would have, but when I stopped by, he was never home. He was supposed to come to the shop as part of his trial to see if he was going to fit in. It's policy. Before you get a permanent position, you're more or less in training for three months. Only Mr. Vega set his own rules and only made an appearance for two weeks. The guy has talent. I sent him the postcard to give him one last chance before I hired somebody else."

"When was this?"

"Late January. Somewhere in there. I haven't seen him since." Alberts shifted his feet as if suddenly irritated. "Why is this important?" he asked. "As you can see, we're not wasting our time here."

"Francesco may have been involved in a Boston art robbery," I told him. "If you gave him access to the Pamphilj, he may have been planning to steal from you, too."

Alberts faced sagged. "The Gardner heist, right? I've been following it in the papers, since I used to live in Boston. Terrible business. Do you really think Vega was involved?"

"I'm leaning that way," I said. "It would help clear things up if I could find him."

"Good luck on that count," James Alberts said, a look of worry crinkling his brows. "Do you really think he might try something here at the Pamphilj? I love the place. If I thought I welcomed a thief inside . . ."

I cut him off. "Let's start there," I said. "How did Francesco end up here? For that matter, how did you, a fellow Bostonian end up working in a marvelous place like this?"

"Some skill mixed with luck. Isn't that how most things in life work out?" he said and walked down a narrow hallway. He closed the door to his office and sat behind his cluttered desk. I sat opposite. "I taught at the Bennet School for three years teaching shop. A priest from the parish burned that St. Augustine quote on a wooden plank and nailed it over the front door. You couldn't miss it. He didn't want the students or the staff to waste their time. And we didn't. We turned out fine craftsmen in woodworking, jewelry making, and antique restoration. Everything."

I knew the well-respected North Bennet Street School in Boston's North End by reputation. It had been around for nearly 150 years refining skills of the talented.

"Why'd you leave?" I asked.

"I dropped out of college my junior year, thinking that I'd rather work with my hands. One job led to another, and I soon realized that if I wanted more out of life than pounding nails, I needed more education. I went back to school and got a degree in management. Summers, I worked with a furniture maker who taught part-time at Bennet. He got me a job there. I liked the school, the North End, Boston. I liked all of it, but decided to see the world before I settled down. When you work with your hands, you can get a job most anywhere, so I came to Italy. My first employer's family owned an export business here in Rome specializing in antiquities. I learned how to do everything— paint, build, repair. Combined with my managing ability, I became valuable to places like this. I've been with the Pamphilj gallery for over ten years. As you can imagine in a palace such as this that's been here since fourteen hundred and fifty, there is always something that needs to be cleaned, refinished, or repaired. It's a special place and a perfect fit for a guy like me, but I can't do the work alone. I put the word out that I was looking for someone to help restore a damaged canvas, and Silvio Conte recommend Francesco."

I sat a little straighter in my chair. "You know Silvio?"

"I know them all, Aldo, Lia, and Silvio. The Pamphiljs had a lute that needed new pegs. Aldo found a hairline crack when he examined it. Silvio fixed it for us."

"Tell me about him," I said.

"What's there to know? He's not good enough to carry on the Conte name. His instruments look fine, but they don't project the right tone, they sound flat, slightly off. What is it they say? Those who can do, those who can't teach. That's Silvio. He tried to make a name for himself making harpsicords, but that didn't work out either."

I recalled seeing a harpsicord in the music room of Villa Conte. "Why didn't it work out?" I asked.

"Because it ended up on the wall of shame. Have you been to Villa Conte's music room?"

I said I had.

"Then you've seen the wall of shame: a grand piano, a harp, and Silvio's harpsicord. All placed there by Aldo to commemorate Contes who over the years have tried to make their mark by striking out on their own. None have been successful," James Alberts said.

"Doesn't sound like Aldo offered Silvio any encouragement," I offered.

"The Contes make violins. There isn't room for anything else, certainly not a harpsicord. Aldo is the last of the great Conte violin makers and that fact drives him mad. Aldo lives the legacy. He wants desperately to pass the skills and the Conte name on to his children, but they're not up to the task. It's like a slow death for him. The end of an era unless his grandson can make a worthy violin."

"What about Lia?"

"Lovely. Vivacious. Willing to try most anything once. Since Marcus came along, she's settled down and has little interest in anything except offering a few lessons and living the good life in Villa Conte. If I weren't happily married, I might make a run at her. Lots of men have."

"Her husband might object," I offered.

"Since when did she marry?"

"I just assumed she had a husband."

"Wrong assumption. Even in Italy, much to the chagrin of the Pope, single women start families," Alberts said. "Marcus is a love child. Lia's clock was ticking. She wanted a child about as badly as Aldo wants someone to carry on the family name. The boy's even named after Marcus Conte, the patriarch of the clan. Quite a burden for the boy, don't you think? Everybody has great expectations for him. That's a lot to live up to."

"It is," I said, wondering how Alberts knew such details. "You sound like you know the Contes better than meeting over the repair of a lute."

"Maybe I do," Alberts admitted. "It was one of those periods when Aldo needed to talk to someone. Personal problems, you know? It's sometimes best to unburden yourself to someone you're not all that close to. We'd known each other casually as people circulating in Rome's art world. One thing led to another, and we began drinking wine and talking. I'm a good listener."

"What did you learn?" I asked.

"Turbulence inside Villa Conte," Alberts said. "It never occurred to me looking at Aldo, the consummate professional with the reputation to back it up, that his life was anything other than wonderful. On the professional side, that was true. But on the personal side, not so." I caught the sense of pity in Albert's voice as he continued. "What he said struck me as a man's ultimate anguish. He said he'd earned all the respect he could ever hope for when he worked in his shop, but in his own house, he felt irrelevant. Like he wasn't even there, bouncing from room to room looking for either his children or his wife to pay attention to him. Marianna, his wife, must have felt the same, because eventually she left him."

I remembered that Aldo Conte spoke of his divorce. "What do you know about the former Mrs. Conte?"

"Not much. I saw her a few times. She kept mostly to herself. I heard her perform once. Lovely woman and a fine musician. Seems like a great combination, don't you think? Aldo should have done more to keep her happy. I know I would have."

"What instrument?" I asked.

"A violin, of course."

"Of course," I said and asked if Francesco Vega ever spoke about his wife.

"I didn't know he'd been married," Alberts said. "We never talked much about his personal life. He wasn't around long enough to get into much of that. He came to work. Made notes on everything we did here, then took off to parts unknown."

"What was he working on that had him making notes?"

"Restoration of a Pamphilj family portrait. The house is filled with them, some life size, others smaller, all are beautiful. One of the portraits, one painted by Pietro da Cortona, the artist known mostly for his frescos, ended up with a few inches of flaked-off paint. How the scratch got there, we don't know. There are nearly a thousand paintings in this palace. Keeping track of all, all the time, is almost impossible. Regardless, we undertook to restore the Cortona. That's one of the reasons I had hoped Francesco would work out. He had substantial experience in art school and additional experience as a craftsman. I thought those skills would come in handy here, but he had a lot to learn. That's one of the things that I liked about him, he knew he had a lot to learn and that he could hone his skills here. You can't approach a canvas painted three hundred years ago and correct the damage by squeezing paint from a tube and smearing it on. You have to go back to the original methods working with pigments and oils. Then, you need to study the brush strokes on the canvas and match those before drying the repaired area, making sure the desired craquelure matches the tiny cracks in the overall portrait. Last, applying the finished coat of varnish. There are, of course, secrets to making it all come together. Secrets learned only by watching an expert. You watch, then you practice. Making an old canvas look like new requires tremendous skill. Francesco watched our seasoned pros and made notes about how we achieved that here. He sucked it all in like a giant vacuum."

"Seems odd someone that interested would simply walk away."

"I thought so. Of course, it could have had something to do with his father's accident. If so, he should have said something. I'm a reasonable guy."

"What happened to Francesco's father?" I asked.

"I don't know in reality if anything happened to his father. Francesco got a call on his cell and said his father had an accident in his leather shop, a fall or something. I said, of course, he could leave and ask if he wanted a ride to the hospital. He said it wasn't that serious but that he should go see how his father was doing."

"Seems like a normal response. Why does it stick in your mind?"

"Because of the way Francesco acted. He didn't act like someone concerned about a hurt parent. He answers the call, listens, makes notes in his book, never asks about his dad, how the accident happened, which hospital was he in, nothing. Instead, he acts like he just broke the family china, and the butler caught him sweeping it under the rug. Francesco was getting an ear full from somebody none too happy. I could hear the anger in the man's voice from the other end. I couldn't make out all the words, but the heat was obvious."

"Any idea who made the call?"

"Man by the name of Katzen. What his connection to Francesco is, I don't know. All I know is that Francesco said more than once not to worry. 'Katzen, don't worry,' he said and then he hung up. That was the last time I saw Francesco Vega."

Chapter Ten

It was mid-morning when I walked back to Francesco's apartment building. Most occupants, I hoped, would be out working or shopping at the Compo and less likely to notice me nosing about. It also meant fewer people for me to follow inside, but after about ten minutes, an elderly man carrying a laundry bag opened the outside door. I stepped in behind him, held the security door open for him, walked in, and climbed the stairs as he took up space in the elevator. Francesco's key was under the mat where I'd left it.

People who keep notebooks or journals or diaries are a varied and unpredictable breed. What they record can be as dry as the wind and weather report from a captain's log to a teenager gushing about a first love. What Francesco found interesting enough to jot down clearly had something to do with what he went to James Alberts to learn. Alberts said Francesco needed to sharpen his skills regarding painting restoration. I saw the same clumsiness in the painting Francesco worked on at the antique shop. Was he making note of techniques required to restore old canvases? If so, why? What did that have to do with the Gardner robbery? I was hoping to find the notebook to learn some answers.

James Alberts mentioned that Francesco stopped coming to his conservatory in late January. I flipped through the stack of unopened letters and read the postmarked dates to get a sense when Francesco last collected his mail. I read postmarks from *Febbraio, Marzo, Aprile* and *Maggio,* a total of four months. But Francesco owned a cat. Would he leave it for that amount of time in someone else's care? Cats are survivors, I thought. Francesco seemed to be one, too.

I opened the desk's top drawer and put aside Angela's picture. Under it were the typical contents of a catch-all drawer: paper clips, pencils, postage stamps, rubber bands and blank sheets of typing or printing paper. It was then I registered that nowhere in the apartment did I find a computer or printer. Francesco was becoming more intriguing by the minute. An art student, a wood craftsman, a painting restorer, an imposter, and all without a computer that connected him to the modern world. I checked the stack of mail again. No monthly statements from a bank, no credit card bills, no indication that he was connected to any official businesses trying to get in touch with him. A man so disconnected was difficult to find.

It was also nearly impossible to live without any of those connections. Someone had to be helping hide Francesco Vega. What was the name James Alberts heard blaring from Francesco's phone? Katzen? Was Katzen hiding him? Who the hell was Katzen?

I closed the top drawer and opened the first drawer on the right side of the desk. I took out the two books: *Rembrandt's Complete Paintings* and *Rembrandt: The Complete Works*. Both volumes had bookmarks on the chapters discussing the artist's color palate preferences, his skills in mixing his own paints, and the method he used for preparing the linen and wood surfaces on which he painted. One of the books had a paper clip holding the pages that focused on Rembrandt's nearly 80 self-portraits. One of the paintings stolen from the Gardner was a self-portrait of Rembrandt. What was Francesco's interest? I wondered and returned the two books.

With the cat purring and brushing against my ankles as it slinked by, I opened the next drawer and discovered a telephone book, some travel pamphlets on Boston, and a pad of paper with the Somerville address of Angela Ricci and a Boston area phone number that I assumed was hers. Below that was an international phone number beside the name of Katzen. I tore off the page and put it in my jacket pocket.

The last drawer contained envelopes, a dictionary, an empty case for eyeglasses, and two pages, front and back, of rough pencil sketches for what looked like designs for shipping or storage crates, a picture frame with no canvas attached, and a large sofa stripped down to the bare wood. The sketch of the sofa, even to my untrained eye, showed an unusual piece of furniture that certainly wasn't in Francesco's apartment. Neither were any storage containers or picture frames. What was Francesco's interest in these items? Near the bottom of one page were numbers and calculations made in neat columns that made no sense to me. I folded the two pages and added them to my pocket.

I had just closed the drawers when I heard the elevator door clang open. When the footsteps came closer, I hurried to a position behind the front door, listening. A jangle of keys prickled the hair at the back of my neck. Was Francesco about to come home? It certainly wasn't the cat lady; she used the key under the mat. I pulled in a deep breath and flattened my back against the wall as the sound of a key sliding into the lock turned the tumbler.

As if kicked, the door flew open with hard thrust that pinned me along the wall. I lunged forward to get free just as a meaty hand reached around the door's edge and gripped my throat. I clasped both hands together and slammed them down on the man's arm, breaking his chokehold and gaining a needed breath. I spun away from the wall gaining room to maneuver and see my attackers. Both were about my size at just over six feet, fit, strong and determined. The man with the meaty hands lunged and hit me with a right hand that felt like the rock that smashed my face years ago. My knees buckled and lights flashed behind my eyes.

I wobbled backwards and steadied myself against one arm of the couch. When I looked up, I saw the man with the beefy hands roaring toward me. I stepped to one side, using his momentum to my advantage, and threw my best punch along the side of his face as he stumbled past, knocking over a side chair and a table lamp. He dropped to one knee. I saw my chance for a drop-kick to his mid-section and wound up to deliver it when I caught a glimpse of the second man swinging something at me. I lifted my forearms to block the blow but was too late. The butt of a handgun smashed into the side of my head.

I could feel myself being dragged into the center of the room. I struggled to get to my feet when a massive blow landed across my back and drove me flat to the floor. I rolled to one side and saw the boot coming. I raised my hands for protection, but the kick knocked me into another world.

I wasn't certain how long I'd been out, but when I regained my senses the cat woman stood over me, iron pan in one hand ready to land another blow.

"What are you doing here?" Her accusing voice rode a harsh Italian sound wave, fading in and out. "How did you get in?"

I rolled slowly to a sitting position, focusing my good eye on the woman. My bad eye was still blurry from being hit with the gun. The woman was far prettier than my quick glance of her revealed yesterday when she put the key back under the mat. Her rectangular face was highlighted by large dark eyes, full lips and reddish-brown hair that hung to her shoulders. Her summer dress was a canvas for the blue flowers that swayed side to side when she moved. The dress showcased an inviting full figure that looked less inviting with the raised pan above my head. She took in short breaths as if getting ready to attack.

"I hope you're not going to use that pan," I said, reaching for my wallet whose contents were scattered across the floor. I grabbed my driver's license and the other identifying documents and offered them to her. She glanced at the pieces in my hand. She didn't seem impressed, so I stuffed them back in my wallet.

"Papers don't tell me anything," she finally said. "Who are you really?"

"Theo Perdoux," I said. "I'm a private investigator looking for Francesco Vega. Mind if I get up?" I asked, wondering if I could manage. My ribs ached along with my head. When she didn't object, I crawled to my knees and stood, my legs like jelly. I leaned against the desk chair for support. Starting with my face, I conducted a quick survey of my body parts. Everything seemed to be in working order except my bad eye. When I checked my pockets, I saw that the sketches and page with the phone numbers were missing. "How long have I been out?" I asked.

"I came a half an hour ago," the cat lady said and finally put the iron pan away. "You were breathing, so I didn't call for an ambulance. Should I?"

"No, but I appreciate the thought. Mind if I ask who you are?"

"Theresa Abutto. I care for Franco's cat when he's away. My cat, really. Pets are not allowed in my building, so I keep him here. I used to sneak the cat and Francesco into my apartment when Francesco was good." Her expression brightened for a moment, then turned dull. "Which was not very often. Like now when I haven't heard from him in weeks." She seemed to study me with a new sense of curiosity. "Why are you looking for Francesco Vega?" she asked, a new seriousness in her voice.

"A client wants to ask him some questions. I understand Francesco keeps things of importance in a notebook. I was looking for it when two very strong men knocked me out. When I hit the floor, they used their feet." I winced when I pressed harder on ribs three and four. "They were very thorough."

"You look like they were," she said. "Maybe I should call an ambulance. I'm not interested in playing nurse."

"No, no, really," I said and sat in the desk chair while Theresa Abutto took the sofa. "I'll be all right in a few minutes. Maybe you'd answer a few questions while I catch my breath?" When she didn't reject the idea, I asked her if she knew where Francesco kept any of his notebooks.

"He only has the one that he keeps with him. It's like the Holy Grail. You'd think he had the combination to the Vatican safe written in it the way he never lets it out of his sight." Out of nowhere, the cat shot toward her feet. She bent over and picked it up, cradling it in her arms. "Francesco has two weaknesses: his cat and his notebook. He used to have three when I was around, but that changed."

"What happened?" I asked. "How did he change?"

She shrugged and stroked the cat. "He became like an old man. Serious. No fun. I say, Francesco, you and me love the life. We play. We drink the wine. But he have no time to love the life. He has work to do. He study his notebook. He scowl when I come over. Now I come to see my cat, not the man. I can't be with Francesco when he wear the long face. He's now like Silvio, two old men."

"Silvio Conte?"

"His best friend, yes. Silvio Conte. Silvio wear the scowl, too. Not so long in the face as Francesco, but Francesco older. He have more to scowl about is what I think."

I asked, "When did Francesco begin to change?"

"Christmas, maybe," she said, putting the cat down on the seat beside her. "Should be a happy time, but no. Then, he go away. When he come back, work is all he have time for. Always work. No time for Theresa."

Always working didn't fit the procrastinating picture James Alberts painted of Francesco. "I thought Francesco walked away from a job at the Pamphilj Gallery. That doesn't sound like someone who works all the time."

Theresa waved one quick finger my way. "No, no. He not want to work there. He go to learn about brushes and making paint, and I don't know what. With the violins, the same. He go to Aldo Conte to learn how to behave like Aldo Conte. Francesco not care about making violins."

That makes sense, I thought. If you want to pass yourself off as a professional, you need to know how a professional behaves. "Do you know why he wanted to act like Aldo Conte?" I asked. "I mean, did he ever explain his plan to visit the Gardner Museum in Boston?"

"He say he have business, that's all. He needs to work so he can do his business. He spend all his time with Silvio and have no time for Theresa."

"But he made time for Angela," I said and watched a small flame of disbelief flash in her eyes. "You didn't know that they were together again in Boston, did you?"

For the longest time, she didn't answer. She pulled the cat to her, a woman scorned. A woman hurt. Finally, she said, "You know this is fact? He with her again?"

I reached in my jacket pocket and removed the security photographs Charles Raskin had given me of Angela Ricci and Francesco Vega. Theresa took them and studied them as if somehow the intensity of her stare would make the images go away.

When she handed the photos back, she said to the cat, "Come on, Niello, time for us to go." She stood, holding Niello firmly in her arms. "Lock up when you leave," she said moving toward the door.

"Wait a minute," I said catching up to her. "The men who jumped me had keys to this apartment. They didn't use the one under the mat. Who would Francesco have given keys to?"

"He has friends."

"Friends who go around beating up people?"

Theresa shrugged. "Maybe they thought you were stealing from him. Maybe they wanted to stop the robbery. Maybe they wanted to get your attention. You Americans don't understand violence like Italians do. First you get slapped around to get your attention. Later, when your attention wavers, you get hit harder. If that doesn't register, you get shot maybe to death, maybe not. You Americans run around shooting from the very beginning. There's no thinking behind it, just guns. Everybody has the guns. Here, we let the Mafia shoot the guns. You should pay attention to the Mafia or get yourself killed."

"Is that who you think beat me up?"

She shrugged. "Who else?"

"Why would the Mafia have an interest in protecting Francesco's apartment?"

Again, she shrugged. "I don't know his business. Now, I don't care about his business. Ask Angela, maybe she knows."

"Angela's dead."

Theresa Abutto froze, then nodded as if she approved of what I'd just told her. She opened the door and stepped out into the hall. I watched as the elevator gate opened and Theresa moved inside. She stared back blankly, petting her cat as the elevator doors closed, and the carriage groaned slowly down. So much for living the life, I thought, aware that complete vision was slowly returning to my damaged eye. I blinked a dozen times to speed matters along, locked the apartment door, and put the key back under the mat.

Walking a little gingerly on the cobblestones, I headed for Da Tonino on Via del Governo Vecchio, a narrow winding street dotted with boutique clothing shops, coffee bars, and restaurants. Da Tonino was one of my favorite places for lunch, and I was both sore and starving. The restaurant was small with tiny tables crammed closely together and always full of locals enjoying the day's specials. I sat at a table for two in the back corner and ordered eggplant strips rolled around a chunk of Asiago and baked in a smooth, rich tomato sauce. Veal meatballs came on the side along with a glass of house red.

As I ate and regained my strength, I thought about what Theresa had told me about Francesco's sudden turn toward the serious life. Apparently, that turn swooped Silvio along with him. What prompted it? What compelled a couple of "love the life" guys to shift gears and get serious about their futures? Did Francesco read the *Art World* article and suddenly think that impersonating Aldo Conte to gain entrance to Gardner was the first logical step ending with a robbery? That didn't make sense. Still, the fact remains that Francesco did impersonate Conte and did go to the Gardner under false pretenses. Just as the fact remains that two goons attacked me in Francesco's apartment. Were they looking for Francesco and attacked when they found me instead? Or was I the intended victim and the beating a warning to stay away? Who would want to do that? Regardless, they rummaged through my wallet and now know who I am and that I'm in Rome hunting for Francesco Vega.

I paid the bill and stepped out into the street with its growing crowds. I felt much better and wanted to walk and think about my next move when my phone rang. I answered it.

"Theo? It's Gina. You sound like you've just gotten up from a nap."

"A little groggy, yes."

"Are you all right? Shall I ring you later?"

"No, no, I'm fine. Might be jet lag you're hearing. I just got here."

"Got where?"

"Rome." I held the phone toward the street as three Vespas raced by. "The sounds of the city," I said, adding, "What's up?"

"Some information that may be useful to you. I did check into a few things as you asked. You may want to do more than scratch the surface of the Aldo and Silvio Conte family bond. Seems to be an interesting crack in it," Gina said. "Son is a disappointment; father's standards are unattainable. That sort of thing. Seems Silvio got in with a rough crowd to get back at his father. Apparently, the father-son battle is the main reason Aldo got divorced. His wife, Marianna, couldn't stand the family fracture that got worse and worse. Silvio didn't just want to embarrass his father, he wanted to hurt him."

"What did he do?"

"That information is not all that complete. Aldo Conte is revered in the classical music world as one of the finest violin makers alive. As you can imagine, not much dirt seeps out from the concert halls. From the instrument makers to the musicians and conductors, they keep things to themselves. Nothing should spoil the music, if you know what I mean."

"I do," I said. "Protect the institution at all costs."

"Yes, and its members. However, Marianna was not one to be silent when her marriage was threatened. She didn't want Aldo to keep silent. She wanted him to deal with Silvio, to stand up to him, expose him as the roughneck that he was. She wanted to make things in the family right, and she needed her husband's help to do it. When Aldo refused to help, they separated and eventually divorced. Details were not disclosed. Sorry."

"Don't be sorry, Gina. You've been your usual thorough researcher."

"You can't track down stolen artwork if you don't like digging through the files. Alicia says I might go blind any day, which reminds me of something else you should know now that you're in Rome. Alicia looked further into the Italian family who picked a fight with Niles Huygens over the value of a rare canvas. It looks like the family was run by the late *Don* Roberto Garcetti, recently deceased but during his lifetime, if you needed something done anywhere near Rome, you went to *Don* Roberto. He has one son . . ."

"Vincent," I offered.

"You know the family?" Gina asked.

"I know of the Boston side of the family. Vincent is in prison and his son, Peter, now runs things until Vincent gets out," I said. "What was *Don* Roberto trying to gain by fighting with Huygens?"

"Details on that are a little sketchy," Gina said. "Alicia's still investigating, but it may not have been *Don* Roberto who started the fight."

"Maybe Vincent started it," I said, thinking out loud. "Maybe the fight has something to do with robbing the Gardner."

"Sorry, Theo. Nothing points to that."

"Never hurts to ask," I quipped. "Speaking of asking, any idea how to get in touch with Marianna Conte?"

"Now Marianna Dossi."

"Remarried?" I asked.

"No. She's using her maiden name." Gina gave me Marianna's contact information. "I don't know how any of this will help, Theo. It seems a long way away from Rome to the Gardner Museum. You haven't asked, but do you want my professional opinion?"

"What are partners for if not for offering their professional opinions?"

"I hate to remind you, Theo, because it does resurface bad memories, but you know in my past life I was involved with the illegal removal of a painting from a small museum in Madrid."

"I remember you were forced into it," I said.

"That's right. Sala Ponte would have been ruined if I hadn't become involved. Anyway, I have gone over and over that dreaded event. I took one small painting from one small, out-of-the-way museum. Even that wasn't simple. Magnify it by however many pieces were stolen from the Gardner."

"Thirteen," I said.

"Magnify it by thirteen pieces, some not so small, and I come to one conclusion: Someone inside had to have helped, maybe even planned the entire operation. You'll find all your answers back in Boston."

"You sound just like Sanford J. Brothers," I said. "He's a board member who believes the inside job was carried out by his own security guards."

"It happens," Gina said. "Guards have access and opportunity."

"I hear you," I said. "I haven't ruled anything or anyone out. I'll poke around here for a few more days. The weather's fine, the food excellent, and the wine perfect. If I don't shake something from the tree soon, I'll go back home and make a nuisance of myself with Boston PD."

"They'll love that," Gina chimed in.

"Thanks, Gina. I'll be in touch," I said and ended the call.

I tapped in the number for Marianna Dossi and waited for someone to answer. A woman's soft Italian voice that sounded like it could make reading a legal document sexy came on the line. She introduced herself as Marianna Dossi. She would see me later that afternoon.

Chapter Eleven

I needed a car for two trips and decided to combine them with one rental. The agent handed me the keys and a road map. He pointed to the map when I gave him the address and asked the best way to Vega's Fine Leather. Rome traffic is like traffic in most cities with the addition of darting and slashing scooters and motorcycles tossed into the mix. Riders, some wearing helmets, most not, ride without fear as if each green light is the start of a new, important race.

I was heading out of Rome on highway 52 toward Vertibo where Marianna Dossi lived with a stop in a commercial district just past the Foro Italico, a huge sports center lined with sixty statues around a central stadium. My map indicated that Vega's Fine Leather would be found along this route. It took an hour but eventually the traffic thinned, and I found my turnoff.

The commercial district was a sprawling mix. At one end in front of large mounds of sand, rows and rows of terra cotta roofing tiles lay drying in the sun. Next to that was a garden center selling large ceramic pots, a commercial bakery came next with a truck parked in front being loaded for delivery. If my directions were correct, at the far end of the complex stood a large building where Vega's Fine Leather was housed. A box truck idled in front while a man maneuvered a load of furniture strapped on a wooden pallet out of the shop and into the back of the truck. When he was done, he waved to the driver who pulled away, revealing a sign for the upholstery shop.

I got out of my car, walked past the bakery with the air holding the aroma of baked bread, and went inside Vega's Fine Leather shop. To my left, at a desk topped with invoices and a computer, sat a man typing furiously on the keyboard while keeping a telephone balanced between shoulder and ear. He glanced my way, acknowledged me with a quick nod but kept to his task. I took the time to check out the space, which was a prime example of form follows function.

In the center of the expansive room were waist high tables where a young man painstakingly tightened red brocade fabric over the seat of what looked like a dining room chair. Beside that were ten or so chairs just like it in various stages of repair. Some were stripped down to their intricately carved wooden arms and legs, others had new webbing on their seats, and still others were covered in the red brocade. Even my untrained eye could see the high quality of the work.

Behind the tables were two women at sewing machines with folds of fabric stretched out before them, their attention on the clatter of their machines as the material inched along. Farther back in the building stood a man wielding industrial sized shears. He smoothed a paper pattern over fabric, pinned it securely to the table, and began cutting with confidence experience brings.

Along one wall were rows of wooden crates. These were set on end and had their tops removed. An employee stood over one, rummaging through the contents before finally pulling out a length of veneer. He checked the skirt of a small loveseat being recovered to see if the veneer matched the grain. Not satisfied, he moved to another crate to find the perfect match.

On the opposite wall bolts of fabric hung from racks. On the floor below the racks were additional crates, some filled with more pieces of wood, some with pieces of Styrofoam, others stuffed with what looked like white batting. I was about to look in other crates when I noticed that the man at the computer had gotten up and was standing behind me.

"Sorry about the delay, my good man, but now you have my undivided attention," he said with a perfect British accent, while he ignored me again. His focus on two employees rummaging through some newly opened shipping crates. "Anything?" he asked one of the men who disappointedly shook his head. "We've had a delivery issue that I've been trying to sort out. The tracking number indicates that the special-order French fabrics were shipped, but they haven't arrived and that's holding up several projects. That loveseat for one. But that's not your concern, is it? Now, how can I be of help?"

"I'd like to speak with Mr. Vega, if he's back at work."

The man cocked his head, surprised. "Back at work?"

"From his accident. A fall I believe Francesco said."

"Why would Francesco say any such thing? Giuseppe Vega hurt in a fall? Utterly preposterous is what that is." The man sped off toward the back of the shop.

I followed him into a large alcove, set up in miniature like the rest of the shop with tables for cutting patterns from leather, not fabric. In fact, the entire area appeared to be devoted to covering furniture in fine leather as several finished pieces lined one wall. Along the opposite wall stood shipping crates filled with leather hides of various colors.

"Very nice," I said, running my hand over an ornate chair covered in soft red leather.

"More than nice," the man said. "Beautiful. Fantastic. Our customers expect nothing but the best, and Giuseppe Vega makes certain they get it. Right, Giuseppe?"

At the sound of his name, an elderly man with a slightly stooped back looked up from the large sofa he was working on. He held a small tack hammer in one hand and copper brads in the other. Around his slim waist hung a tool belt worn with age. When he smiled, the dark lines in his weathered face seemed to deepen. He nodded and went back to fitting a piece of gray-green leather over one arm of the sofa. The sofa matched the drawing of the unusual couch I'd found in

Francesco's apartment. I looked again at the shipping crates and thought they closely resembled the crate drawn in pencil as well. Why would any of this be of interest to my attackers?

"Giuseppe Vega," the man said by way of introduction. "He doesn't speak much English, I'm afraid. His is, however, master craftsman, resident artist, and owner of this shop. I can assure you, his value is such that if he had a hangnail, we would all know it. So, no, he did not suffer a fall. Francesco must have been pulling your leg."

"Maybe I didn't hear him correctly," I said not wanting to argue the point and turned my attention on Giuseppe and his work. "What kind of sofa is that?" I asked. "It's very unusual."

"It's the kind that makes you pull your hair out," the man said. "More specifically, it's French Baroque with walnut stretchers and turned legs in the Os De Mouton style of the seventeen-hundreds. The owner made specific requests when he brought it in. The piece was to be taken apart. All framing was to be replaced with dried hardwood. The pine and fir used in the original frame as well as the screws, nails, and brads that attached the original leather to the old frame were to be kept so the owner could document the rebuild."

"I've had friends do the same thing when rebuilding an antique car," I said. "I never thought of it being done with furniture."

"*Special* furniture," the man said. "Os De Mouton of this period is very rare. As you can see, this example has the finely curved back and rolled arms that is typical of the period. But what makes this one exceptional is the straight stretcher connecting the legs. Most Os De Mouton sofas have turned stretchers, making them quite ornate. When Giuseppe finishes working his magic, the piece will reclaim its original beauty. That's why customers seek us out," the man said. "That's why I was hired, to make sure more customers know about the fine work done here. Even the dining room chairs you saw when you came in.

The pattern will match from chair to chair. Each one will be exactly alike. It takes more fabric to make that happen, and more cost, but it's a quality issue and the only way Mr. Vega wants it done. As you can see, Mr. Vega works on the most complicated projects. He's a master working with leather."

"What about Francesco?" I asked.

"Francesco saw how the business could grow if we could get the word out beyond our local setting. He hired me to make sure that happened." The man offered his hand. "Reese Ogilvy," he said as we shook. "My specialty is in bringing older, family run businesses into the modern era without damaging what made them successful in the first place. I've brought in the internet, modernized orders and shipments, the French fabric snafu an exception, while maintaining the highest quality. Mr. Giuseppe Vega insists on it. All of our employees do. It is a tradition begun by Mr. Vega's father. He started the business. Giuseppe took over several years ago. He's quite the perfectionist. And, as you can see, not suffering from any fall. Strong as an ox."

"Did Francesco ever work here?" I asked.

"No. And, sadly, he probably never will. Francesco has other interests, which is not to say that he has no interest in the shop. Like I said, he brought me on to increase efficiency. He stops by once in a while. He makes suggestions. Hands out a sketch or two when he feels like it."

"I think he sketched the sofa Giuseppe is working on," I said. "Any idea why he took an interest?"

Ogilvy thought a moment. "Special considerations for shipping the sofa when it's finished, I suppose. Part of the owner's unique request list was a shipping container comprised of wood. Double walls on all four sides. Special construction all the way. Francesco likely put some ideas together for that. When something captures his imagination, he works out the details in a sketch. He's very good at it. He drew a redesign of our shipping crates not long ago. He said we would cut costs if we made the crates a few inches wider, added a divider and packaged light items like leather hides or special fabrics on one side and veneers or fasteners or anything else heavier that would fit in the other. When a shipper sends us multiple items, that's how we do it now."

"How'd that work out?" I asked.

"Very well. Francesco was correct. Those double shipments do save us money. He's a clever man. I like him. But don't see him often. He stops by to make sure his father is doing well. Then, he's off again."

"He seems to be a hard man to pin down," I asked. "Any idea where he is now?"

"Haven't seen him in weeks."

"I wonder if his father knows."

Ogilvy spoke quickly to Giuseppe in Italian. The elderly man shook his head with a shrug and went back to work.

"No help there either, I'm afraid. They're close, but not all that close, if you know what I mean," Ogilvy said. "What's your interest in Francesco?"

"We share a mutual acquaintance," I said thinking of Clair Bowman. "If I was ever in Rome, she wanted me to look him up. That's all."

"Ah, woman troubles, what?" Ogilvy said with a knowing smile. "Sounds like Francesco. You can leave a message here if you like. When he comes by, I'll make sure he gets it. But if he's running from another female, I wouldn't hold my breath. A very unhappy lady with a cat was here looking for him not long ago."

"Theresa Abutto," I said. "I don't think she'll be bothering you anymore."

"No?'"

"No," I said as someone shouted for Ogilvy's attention.

"Duty calls," he said and headed off.

I followed his example and went back to my car. Marianna Dossi lived about an hour further north, and I didn't want to be late for my appointment. The address she gave had me zigzagging along narrow back roads boarded by rows of cypress. Eventually I passed through a stone archway that curved onto a lane no wider than a goat's path. At the end of the lane was my destination.

If grand palaces were statements of wealth, the Dossi family was rolling in lira. Set back at the end of a stone drive, the villa held a stunning architectural presence. Twice as wide as high and wrapped in a dozen Corinthian columns, the four floors beckoned. I parked in front and walked to the front door which opened as soon as I'd knocked.

A woman of old-fashioned elegance stood on the other side. She was dressed in what looked like a linen suit, light blue, with a pink flower pinned in front. A string of pearls hung from her neck. Her dark brown hair with a touch of gray in the front swept behind her ears from which dangled large pearl earrings. She held out her hand.

"I am Marianna Dossi," she said.

I took notice of her soft skin spotted with brown age marks and the slight tremble of her hand as I shook it. "Theo Perdoux. Thank you for taking the time."

"Not at all. I look forward to sharing information about the Contes. A mother's curiosity regarding her children that I don't see all that often. Please come in."

We crossed the hall to a specious sitting room with pistachio green velvet on the walls. I sat in the offered loveseat as Marianna settled in a nearby wing-backed chair. A servant entered with a tray on which sat a decanter and matching glasses.

"I hope you'll join me," Marianna said. "I always enjoy a glass of sherry at this hour."

"Gladly," I said as the man poured two glasses. He handed them over and left.

Marianna raised her glass in toast. "Salute."

"Salute," I repeated and sipped. "Delicious."

She nodded. "I understand you wish to discuss my time at Villa Conte."

"Yes."

"Beyond the misery, I loved it there," she said without emotion. "Aldo is married to his violins and his family's past. He never should have had a wife. He hasn't the time for one. Neither has he time for children, but they arrived, didn't they? Lia first, Silvio second. Silvio was always second. Children are very perceptive. Like dogs, they pick up the slightest shift in the emotional river. The strong ones swim to safety, the weak claw at the turbulence and go under. A parent tosses a line. A parent tries to help, but sometimes the line doesn't go far enough. When someone, anyone, offers to keep the child from drowning, the child grabs hold. That's what happened to Silvio. The consigliere reached out and Silvio grabbed hold."

"He became an associate with the Mafia?" I asked.

"You have to understand the complexity of that question, Mr. Perdoux. If I answer truthfully with yes, that makes Silvio a gangster. He was not that. He was on the outside looking in. But the door was never fully opened to him. So, yes, he became a Mafia soldier, a fringe player, but a soldier all the same. He felt he belonged somewhere. He found a home outside of Villa Conte. I don't think he was happy about it. I don't think he found any joy, but it was a place, and in that place he found a purpose. No one made him feel small like his father did. No one made him feel unwanted like his father did. That's the strength of the Mafia, Mr. Perdoux. They may be cruel, but they are also skilled at making the unwanted feel they belong. That's very powerful and why there will always be the gangs."

"Why was the door not fully opened to him?"

Marianna shrugged. "I can only surmise that they sensed what I sensed. Silvio was lashing out. Fighting with himself. He couldn't fully commit to anything while he was his own enemy. The Mafia, if nothing else, demands commitment."

"Did Aldo see what you did?" I asked. "Did he try to help his son?"

"He didn't know how. Aldo couldn't understand what was happening under our roof. Silvio? Our boy? A Conte not following the family tradition? A Conte not born with the skills to create magical violins? A Conte running wild in the streets of Rome?" The painful memory seemed to darken her expression. "Aldo was crushed."

"What did he do?" I asked.

"What could he do?" Marianna thought a moment. "I've asked myself that many times, what could Aldo have done to make life better for us? I don't know that he could have done anything more. Aldo knew people. In Rome, you know the types who line up on the other side of the legal. Not Mafiosi but rough people. People who demand attention. Aldo called in the people he knew and asked them to help. Put a fright into Silvio. Show him that his road leads to nowhere but prison. Anything." She sipped her sherry, collecting her thoughts. "There are few moments in life worse than the son attacking his father. But that's what happened. Silvio did not want to be pushed around by Aldo's people. Silvio fought back. With two or three of his accomplices, I don't now remember the exact number, Silvio broke into our bedroom late at night. I can still remember being yanked from my sleep as the door shattered from the pounding. Silvio burst in, his face red with rage. He jerked his father out of bed and slammed him to the floor where one of the others pulled Aldo arms out straight like a modern crucifixion. Silvio raised his boot over Aldo's right hand and threatened to crush it. Aldo shrieked. His fist opening and closing, his fingers curling. His life, his art, his soul lived in that hand that made the beautiful violins as his family had done for centuries. I watched the hatred grow in Silvio's eyes as he jammed down his foot. Aldo cried out in anticipation of the ruin and pain. But Silvio only meant to send a message. The boot struck the floor, missing his father's hand by inches. Without a word, Silvio and his men left us. Shattered. That's the only word to describe it. They left us both shattered."

I could picture the scene. I could sense the terror she and Aldo must have felt. "It must have been horrible," I said.

"And something you don't recover from. Some breaks never heal, Mr. Perdoux, and that was one. I knew I could no longer live in that house and find any peace, but I did nothing for the longest time. When I was convinced improvement was not possible, I decided to walk away from my children and divorce Aldo. Not an easy task in Italy, but something I had to do."

"How did Silvio react to that?"

Marianna thought a moment, then said, "His normal reserved chill. His encounters with life produced either a burst of anger or a reserved chill. Silvio knows no middle ground."

"And Lia?"

"Lia is like me, a realist. She sees life as it is, not as she would like it to be. And, like me, she realizes that some choices must be made selecting from options that are not appealing. I suppose that's a way of saying that had I been presented with better options, I would not have left Villa Conte."

"Are you sorry you did?"

"I regret I could not live my fantasy. I would continue my career, my children would grow strong, straight, and happy. My husband would love me. I suppose one consolation is that Aldo's attention went to a violin and not another woman. I'm the only one of our exploded family that has no current connection to the business of Conte violins. Aldo is the current master, Silvio teaches how to make inadequate copies, and Lia teaches one and all how to play."

"I heard pieces of one lesson," I said.

Marianna's pride broke through her smile. "Lia is not only my daughter, but also my student. One of many I tutored over the years. I am delighted Lia has continued offering instruction. People are better off with music in their hearts. That was what brought Aldo and me together: music. I held first chair in the violin section at Rome's Teatro dell'Opera when he and I met. I think we both lived the same fantasy for a while. Aldo would make beautiful instruments, I would make beautiful music on a famous Conte violin, and we would both live happily ever after. But children came and reality overtook fantasy. Aldo was not patient with children, and I had to learn to be. I gave up my career to raise them."

"That must have been very hard for you."

Marianne bobbed her head slightly. "Very hard," she said softly.

"Tell me about Aldo," I said. "Being born into such a well-known family must be both a blessing and a curse."

"For some of Aldo's ancestors, it was difficult. Think of the world's best in any profession. Their children are born into not only a family but also a legacy. The family and the world outside share expectations that the children will, in Aldo's family's case, make beautiful instruments producing exquisite sounds. Not so easy, Mr. Perdoux. Aldo's great-great-great uncle killed himself when he failed. He could craft the musical box, but the musical box did not make beautiful music.

He tried building and selling harps, relying on the Conte name to bring in business. When that failed, he hung himself. Aldo, on the other hand, thrived in his family's tradition. He possessed that wonderful blend of skilled craftsman and alchemist. His finished violins looked and sounded beautiful. A rare talent and in high demand in the classical music world."

"Apparently not in demand enough to easily support Villa Conte," I said, recalling my conversation with Aldo about upkeep and taxes.

"Not easily, no, especially when you are a poor businessman like Aldo. These old estates are not for the meek, Mr. Perdoux. No repairs come cheaply assuming you can find someone to undertake them. I speak of both my current accommodations and Villa Conte. Living here I, of course, could sell out. Aldo would find that impossible. How do you sell the family palace? His ego would never admit that he could not carry on the family home. He would do whatever it takes to keep it. The children must think the same, that's why you find Silvio and Lia living and working in the house." Marianna paused then added, "It must have been a bitter pill for Aldo to welcome Silvio into the fold after being attacked by the boy. But the need for money makes people do strange things."

"Do you think Aldo is afraid of his son?" I asked.

"Wouldn't you be?"

I pictured being yanked from a warm bed, spread out on the floor with a raised boot hovering over my hand, threatening my livelihood. It brought back the moment thirteen years ago in a dark cave in Northern Italy when my Nazi father pointed a gun to my head and threatened to shoot me.

It was the last time I saw him.

"Let's say I wouldn't turn my back on him," I said and asked if she had any contact with her children.

"Infrequent. I might get a note in the mail or a phone call when Lia thinks about it. I have no contact with either Silvio or Aldo, not that I expect any. When I moved back here, my parents were elderly and not well. My focus was on them, making sure they lived their last days well in this house. I heard nothing about or from my children until Lia wrote me that Silvio and his father had come to a resolution." Marianna sipped more of her sherry. "I was pleased to hear that. Villa Conte would once again be a house focused on the Conte tradition of making beautiful music possible."

"And passing on that tradition to Marcus," I said, adding, "You haven't mentioned your grandchild."

"I haven't, have I," Marianna said coolly. "Perhaps it's because I'm old fashioned. I believe children should come after one is married. Lia and I disagree on that to the extent that she has told me nothing of the father."

"You don't know who he is?"

"No. I don't. Lia has enjoyed her life with men. Even as a young woman, she preferred not to be tied down. Those were her feelings before my divorce, so I can believe that her behavior is not a reaction to that. I don't know where it comes from, but I don't approve and told her so."

"How did she react?"

"She didn't appreciate my opinion. But a parent's obligation is to challenge their children, don't you agree?"

"That sounds like a good approach," I said, "but I have no children to test the theory on."

"I don't know if you should be congratulated or pitied. Being an Italian Catholic, I will cast my vote with pity, since we believe children are the strength of both our country and religion."

I looked at Marianna over the rim of my glass as I sipped more sherry and tried to shift the conversation. "Does the name Francesco Vega ring a bell?" I asked.

"It is a name I wish to forget," Marianna said, a hint of bitterness in her voice. "Silvio looked up to him. I mentioned earlier that the Mafia filled voids in some lives, Francesco Vega did the same with Silvio. He was like Silvio's older brother. A brother he never had. He was also one of the men with Silvio the night he broke into our bedroom. Francesco held Aldo's hands to the floor."

"Nice guy," I said sarcastically. "He traveled to Boston recently impersonating your former husband."

Marianna offered no reaction. "Nothing surprises me when it concerns Francesco Vega. But why Aldo? Why would anyone want to pretend to be him?"

I explained about Francesco's trip to the Gardner, the eventual robbery and the murder of Angela Ricci. Marianna's expression remained composed.

"Angela's been murdered?" Her voice was soft, distant. "I'm sorry, of course, but not surprised. I suppose you know that Angela had a whirlwind romance with Francesco that ended in divorce. They were a wild pair chewing up life in big chunks. I wasn't so sure they'd survive their brief marriage."

"Why was that?" I asked.

"I don't know. Silvio and Lia used to dash around the city on their little Vespas. Francesco had a big, loud motorcycle. Angela used to sit on the back, her hands flinging about in the air, holding on to nothing as Francesco raced down the streets. It was like they were daring death to show its face. I guess it finally did, didn't it?"

"Had you been in contact with either Francesco or Angela recently?"

"No. Not in years. Do you think they were somehow involved in stealing those paintings?"

"It's very possible."

"And Angela's killing. Do you think Francesco murdered her?"

"It's a possibility."

"What are the other possibilities?" Marianna wanted to know.

"Angela got involved with one of Boston's rougher crowds. The Garcetti family," I said as Marianna's brows arched. "I take it you know them."

She reached for her sherry and took a long drink, collecting her thoughts. "*Don* Roberto Garcetti was a guest at Villa Conte on many occasions. His family is as old and well established in Roma as is Aldo's. His son, Vincent, and Vincent's son, Pietro, enjoyed many an evening swimming in our pool. So, yes, I know the Garcettis well. I know both their rough and smooth sides. I take it Angela did as well, if you think they might have been involved in her killing. Not Peter, I hope."

"No. A man named Nicolas Bianchi, one of the Garcetti's top men. If Vincent or Peter needed to threaten someone, Bianchi provided the threat."

"I don't know the name," Marianna said with a hint of relief.

"Why did you hope Peter wasn't a likely candidate?"

"I liked him," she said. "He seemed more reasonable than the others. Refined, almost. When Vincent went to prison, Peter came often to visit the ailing *Don* Roberto. His concerns for his grandfather's health seemed genuine, not like some who put up with the elderly to enhance their place in the will. Besides, he once showed an interest in Lia. I thought something might come of it."

"Did you know that Lia and Francesco once had a relationship?"

"A brief connection," she corrected. "Yes, I knew. Lia is strong-willed. If you tell her to do something, she's likely to do the opposite out of spite."

"So, you told her to stay away from Francesco?" I asked.

"You are perceptive, Mr. Perdoux. Yes, I spoke to Lia about my feelings toward Francesco. To begin with, he was much too old for her. I couldn't tell her that, of course. She needed to find out for herself that he was no good. And she did. Can I tell you anything else?" she asked, putting the lid on our visit.

I stood. "I don't think so," I said. "You've been very helpful. I appreciate it."

She walked me to the door. "My family has many faults, Mr. Perdoux. Perhaps their most egregious is their continued association with Francesco Vega. They should have been done with him a long time ago, but he continues to weave his way into their lives. If you learn why, you will likely find the answer to many of your questions." She opened the door. "If I can offer any other assistance, I am mostly here."

I thanked Marianna Dossi and drove back to Rome. I stopped at a petrol station in a cutout on the side of the road, filled up with gasoline, and returned my rental. Walking back to my hotel, I kept wondering how best to learn why the Contes kept associating with Francesco Vega. He didn't seem a likely candidate for an apprenticeship, a love affair, or a long-term friendship. Yet, every time I turned a page on the Conte book of life, Francesco Vega appeared in the margins. What was the connection?

Marianna Dossi was a thoughtful woman. I wondered if she knew the connection and was holding back to protect her family. Or one member of it. At the hotel bar I ordered a Negroni and took a seat away from the crowd. Halfway through my cocktail, I phoned Clair Bowman.

When she answered, I said, "Just checking in as you requested."

"Theo? Where are you?"

"At the bar in the Hotel Raphael in Rome tracking down the imposter Aldo Conte. I found the genuine article at his violin shop and believe him when he says his identity was stolen by a man named Francesco Vega." I sipped my drink. "What's been happening on your end? More television appearances?"

"Tomorrow," Clair said with an audible sigh. "The museum has been contacted with a demand. That may mean that Detective Flynn and some members of the board were right all along. Looking for this man Vega is probably a waste of time."

"Hold on a second," I said. "Back up. What is the demand? Who made it?"

"An attorney. Howard Moss. He would not say who he represented, but he did say that he had seen the stolen artwork and was authorized to negotiate its return."

"He saw all thirteen pieces?"

"So we are led to believe. It's exciting, isn't it, Theo? We're going to get them back."

"I hope that's true, Clair. Really, I do. But what are the terms? What does Moss want for his client?"

"A show of good faith is what he said. He wants cash and leniency, and he wants it announced publicly. Stanford J. Brothers and I are going on television tomorrow to announce that the museum has authorized a reward for the return of all the stolen items. In addition, the museum will not press charges once we have all the pieces back."

"How much are you offering?"

"Five million dollars."

"I thought the museum's coffers were empty," I said.

"Private investors are putting up the reward," Clair explained. "Civic support for our loss has been extraordinary. People realize how important the Gardner is to the city and want to help putting this disaster behind us." She let me have a moment, then asked what I thought of the tactic.

"More importantly, what does Brody Flynn think? I assume he's handling your negotiations?"

"He is, yes, along with the FBI. Flynn has cautioned us not to get our hopes up just yet. He said cash and leniency as a show of good faith likely means that Howard Moss is going to ask for more before the paintings are finally given back. He didn't say what else they might want. But it doesn't really matter, we don't have anything else to offer," Clair said.

"Crooks always think they can raise the ante. That's what negotiations mean to them. Get what you can, then get more. Brody knows the game," I said sounding as reassuring as possible. "Does he have any idea who Moss is representing?"

"If he does, he hasn't told me or members of the board. But what does it matter as long as we get those paintings back?"

"You're right, Clair," I said. "It doesn't matter if you get them back."

"So, you can pack up and come home, Theo. Forget about Aldo Conte."

"I don't think that's wise," I said. "Not just yet."

"Why?"

"You don't have the paintings back."

"But we will. I'm sure of it."

"And if you don't get them back, I'd have to restart my investigation. It's best if I play this out, at least until you know what the final demand is. Once you go on television and announce your good faith, how long will it be until Moss gets back to you?"

"Twenty-four hours."

"Let's hold off on me coming home until then. Fair?"

She paused a moment, then said, "Yes, Theo. I think that's fair."

"Good," I said. "I'd like you to give Brody a message. Tell him the name of the man who passed himself off as Aldo Conte is really Francesco Vega. Vega was once married to Angela Ricci. Second, ask him to keep tabs on the bank account of Charles Raskin after you announce your reward."

"I believe he's already had Chuck in for questioning on more than one occasion."

"How's Raskin holding up?" I asked.

"Fine, apparently. I mean fine for someone who believes he's being harassed. He's maintaining his normal guard schedule, which I greatly appreciate. I've seen no change in the man, and I still don't believe he's involved."

"He might not be, but then the possibility of banking five million might encourage him to talk."

"Speaking of talking, why don't you give Detective Flynn your own message?"

"I would, but I don't think he'd take my call. That's the last thing I want you to relay to Brody. Tell him I'm staying out of his way, but if he'd like to know what my digging has turned up, call me. He's got my number."

"Anything else you can tell me?" Clair asked.

"Yes. Don't be disappointed tomorrow. Rewards bring out the crazies."

"That will make me sleep better," Clair said. "Like I've had a peaceful night since this all started."

"Hang in there," I said. "Something's about to break. Whether it's here with me or in Boston with Brody, something is about to happen that will get your paintings back."

"I want to believe that, Theo. I've got to believe that."

"We've all got to believe in something," I said and hung up. It was too late to knock on the front door of Villa Conte and speak with Silvio, so I ordered a second drink and planned an early morning visit.

Chapter Twelve

Compo di Fiori exudes a hectic, carnival atmosphere in the early morning. Pushcarts filled with multiple kinds of salad greens beside counters stacked with onions and peppers are rolled in, small tents blocking the sun are erected as lemons, limes and oranges are off loaded from the 3-wheel Ape trucks. Bustle and noisy chatter fill the square with energy. A new day has begun in this place of orderly abundance.

A young man cut pomegranates in half and slid them into the jaws of a manual juicer. He pulled the lever and ruby-colored liquid poured into the paper cup. I bought one and drank it on my way toward the Tiber whose reddish-brown water ran swiftly within its banks. I wanted to kill enough time to avoid Aldo, a man I thought too protective of Lia when I spoke to her. I didn't want Aldo hogging the conversation when I met with Silvio. I had additional questions for Aldo, but this morning, I wanted Silvio to myself.

When I knocked on the front door, the housekeeper answered. She eased the door open wide enough for me to see Marcus gleefully dashing down the hallway, his nanny in measured pursuit. Typical behavior in a typical household, only this place was anything but typical. I told the housekeeper I wanted to speak with Silvio. She didn't welcome me inside.

"Is he here?" I asked as Lia stepped out from the music room and into the hall. She held a violin bow in one hand and the hand of Marcus in the other.

"What is it you want?" she asked stiffly.

"To talk to your brother—or to Marcus. He's the only one who seems interested in my visit," I said as the child looked up at me with wonder in his eyes.

Lia pulled her son closer, protectively. "You leave him alone." Her eyes narrowed to dots.

"Your brother, then."

"He can tell you nothing."

"Your mother seems to think otherwise."

A look of anger mixed with surprise flashed in her expression. "You spoke to Marianna?"

"Yes. Yesterday afternoon."

"I want you to leave our family alone."

"Nothing I'd like better. I'm on a short leash, Lia. One more day and then, I'm being called back to Boston, washing my hands of all things Conte. But, I can't leave without talking to Silvio. I don't like loose ends." When she didn't soften, I said, "I'm good at waiting. I have all day."

"I don't," Lia snapped, her eyes hard. "None of us do. You can have five minutes," she finally said, relenting.

Lia handed Marcus off to the approaching nanny, then nodded to the housekeeper who led me downstairs to Silvio's workshop. I watched as he selected various pieces of thinly planked wood and set a length on each of the six workbenches. Attached to each bench was a small vise and beside that a row of tiny hand planes and other tools laid out with precision.

Announcing myself, I said, "Looks complicated."

When he glanced up, I got a good look at his square face, framed with large, dark eyes and a thin nose. His mouth seemed in perpetual frown. He was about my size at six feet. He looked like he could handle himself if he needed to get rough. I could picture him about to stomp on his father's hand, his dark eyes blazing hatred. I could also imagine him having a heart attack as he seemed wound tight and nervous.

"My father said you'd likely come poking around." His voice edgy, uninviting, his accent harsh. "I don't know what I can tell you that hasn't been said. You're looking for Francesco Vega, and nobody in this house knows where he is. Nobody cares where he is."

"Isn't that a change of tune?" I asked remembering they were best friends. "You were once close."

"Were we?"

"What can you tell me about him?"

"I can tell you nothing."

"You don't know where he is. You don't know anything about him. Yet, he passed himself off as your father. You don't find that strange?"

Silvio shrugged.

"I understand he was a student in one of your workshops."

Silvio walked to the back of the room. When he finished rummaging through a stack of wood, he came back carrying a piece that resembled a club or shortened baseball bat, which he proceeded to pound threateningly in his open hand.

"I want to thank whoever worked over one side of your face. They left the other side for me."

When Silvio stepped toward me, I said, "I was a Boston cop, Silvio. I know most of the tricks and how to use them. Be a shame to make a mess of you and your workshop, which is what will happen if you take another step closer."

"I'm shaking in my boots."

"That's a good start," I said and wasted no more time. I yanked the club from his grip while landing a solid backhand to his jaw. My speed and power stung. Silvio slumped back to his desk, rubbing his jaw with one hand. "Now, let's get back to business. Francesco Vega was a student in your workshop, wasn't he?" I pointed the club at Silvio. "Wasn't he?"

"You don't give up, do you?"

"Not a good habit in my profession."

"Which is what?" Silvio asked.

"I'm a private investigator hired to find things. I'd never heard of the Conte family until a few days ago, when I was hired to learn why someone calling himself Aldo Conte wanted access to the Gardner Museum, which was robbed soon after. Turns out, that Aldo Conte is really Francesco Vega who was a student in your workshop, and from what your mother told me, a very good friend of yours."

Silvio sat on the edge of his desk finally getting the message that I was neither afraid nor leaving. "Francesco was a student here. He finished his work, did well, and moved on to help my father. He showed talent and was rewarded as an apprentice. That's all there is to it."

"Not quite," I pressed. "He left his apprenticeship carrying with him your father's identity. Before that, you ran through the streets with him and roughed up your father with his help. What did you hope to gain by that stupid stunt?"

"None of your business."

"That's the point, Silvio. It is my business. It's what I was hired to do, and I don't plan to go back to Boston empty handed. If you'd help me out, if you'd stop being a hard ass, and tell me what you know, I'll leave you, Lia and your father alone. How about it?" I ignored Silvio's hate-filled glare. "Francesco was in your workshop, he dated your sister, apprenticed with your father. I figure you likely had a pretty good take on Francesco. You certainly had enough exposure to the guy to figure him out."

"What was there to figure out?"

"Lots of things like why he flew to Boston to scope out the Gardner Museum. Like why he pretended to be Aldo Conte. Like what information was he after at the Pamphilj? Like why has he disappeared? Like where is he now?"

"I won't answer any of that," Silvio said.

"How about why he got serious all of a sudden? Starting around Christmas, he stopped 'living the life' and did nothing but work."

"You talked to Theresa," Silvio said. "She doesn't know what she's talking about. Francesco didn't spend a lot of time with her, that's all. She got put out. Angry. Theresa is high maintance, and Francesco didn't want to put in the effort."

"Because he was here working, according to Theresa Abbuto," I said and walked toward the back of the shop. "Was he working on something special back here?"

"There's nothing back there for you."

I kept walking.

"All right," Silvio said, his voice jacked up a notch. "Francesco used my workshop after I'd finished the day's classes. He needed a place to work, so I let him have some space."

I turned back to the front. "When was this?"

"He started in December and was in and out until sometime in February."

"Was he making something, building something? What was he doing?"

"He said he wanted to surprise his father with a new design. A shipping crate for large pieces of furniture or something like that. He used my shop to build a few models. He'd done the same with smaller crates that were successful. He wanted to try his luck with larger pieces."

"Crates for the sofa his father is working on?"

"I don't know."

"Come on, Silvio. You were doing just fine until then."

"I said I didn't know."

"But you helped him. Theresa Abbuto said you two stopped living the life at about the same time. Nothing but work, she said. Nothing but long faces."

"I helped him sometimes, all right? Only if he asked. Francesco liked to do most things on his own. He didn't like interference."

"But it was your workshop, and he was your best friend."

"You learned boundaries with Francesco. You didn't cross the boundaries."

"But he crossed them, didn't he?"

"How do you mean?"

"Stealing your father's identity. Francesco crashed through the Aldo Conte boundary and rode it right into the Gardner Museum. Did you know he was going to do that?"

"No."

"That's hard to believe, Silvio. First off, the timing is too perfect. Francesco goes all serious on Theresa about the same time he starts using your workshop. Then, in early January, he travels to Boston and meets up with Angela Ricci. He's at the Pamphilj when he gets back to Rome, making notes on the proper way to repair an Old Master. Do you begin to see a pattern here?"

"No."

"I do, and it points to you being involved. You and your best friend. How did Theresa put it? Always with a scowl, the two of you down here in the workshop planning a robbery, all serious about it. All se-cretive."

"You don't know what you're talking about," Silvio snapped, his eyes hot and narrow. "I'm not going to talk to a crazy man. You're like Theresa Abutto. She got everything turned around and went crazy in her head. There was no scowl, no secrets, no nothing. Francesco wanted her to go away, that's all."

"She did. She took her cat and left. You can pass that along to Francesco next time you see him." Silvio didn't take the bait, so I shifted tactics. "Who's Katzen?" I asked as Silvio's expression shifted in an instant. The subtle, nearly imperceptible change meant Katzen was a familiar name. "You know him, don't you?"

Silvio pulled back and regrouped. "Katzen? Was he a student of mine?" Silvio teased, trying to recover. "Or maybe he's a client of my father's. Let's go with that. Leo Katzen. The name has the ring of a violin player, don't you think? I do. Leo Katzen is an orchestra member who honestly believes a new instrument will improve his play. He's wrong, of course, but my father will encourage the fantasy. My father lives in a fantasy land. Conte violins. Conte history. Conte tradition. That's all he knows and all he cares about. You asked what I hoped to gain by roughing up my father. I wanted, for one brief moment, to focus his attention on me and not a violin. I believe I did that."

"And ruined your mother's life in the process," I told him.

Silvio stiffened. "My father ruins lives, not me. He's very good at it. What matters now is that my father and I have an understanding. He doesn't push anymore. He accepts me for who I am."

"And what is that, Silvio? I get snippets, but not a complete picture. You're a teacher, a craftsman, a member of a famous family, a . . ."

"What I am is out of tune," Silvio smirked. "That's what my father said when he examined my work. My craftsmanship as you call it." He picked up one of the wooden planks from the nearby workbench. "In a few hours the students will shape this piece of spruce into the top of a violin. They'll cut it from a pattern and do the same for the back. But that's only the beginning. The inside of each piece needs to be planed so that the outer edges are thinner than the center. How much? I give them guidelines, but it's not precise. Intuition comes into play here. Artistry. Once planed, the top and bottom are then glued to the side piece creating little more than an echo chamber that produces the sound once the neck is attached and a bow crosses the strings. I teach all that. I could even teach you to do that, but to get the sound of a Strad or an Amati or a Conte, that's where the artistry comes in. I teach how to build a beautiful box. Aldo Conte builds a beautiful box that sings. I don't teach that. I can't teach that. I don't know how it's done, and my father can't explain it. It just happens when he makes a violin. After a while, I recognized I could never compete with him, so I went in a different direction. I built a harpsicord. I was going to take the Conte name in new directions. When I showed my father what I had created, he played a few notes and said that it was out of tune. He also said he would display it in the music room as a reminder for us all that we should create what we know, not what we don't." Silvio inhaled a deep breath and released it. "My father pointed that harpsicord out to you, no doubt. It's one of his great pleasures. See the grand mistake my son made?" Silvio said bitterly. "Someday, I'll take an axe to it."

"Better it than your father," I said, suddenly aware of violin music drifting down from the upstairs music room.

"My workshop starts a few minutes after Lia's first student. I want you out of here."

I tossed the wooden club on Silvio's desk as he hurried past me to the side door. He jerked it open onto the garden and pool. I caught sight of the door's lock in case I wanted to come back. I was pretty sure I wouldn't be welcomed at the front door and the workshop's side entrance seemed a good alternative. I nodded a good-bye and left as students gathered in the garden.

I walked along the Tiber and headed in the direction of St. Peters, something nagging at me as I went along. I couldn't exactly put my finger on what was at the top of my being bothered list. It could have been the lack of confidence I had that anything any of the Contes told me was the truth. I wasn't sure why I had such a feeling, except that Francesco Vega, the man I was looking for, and the man I couldn't find, was entrenched in the lives of Lia, Silvio, and Aldo Conte. Like Marianna Dossi said, if I find out why he was so entrenched, many of my questions would be answered. And that was what was bothering me, my utter inability to gain any headway into finding Francesco.

I crossed over the bridge at Vittorio Emanuele II and decided to take out my frustrations on Charles Raskin. Gina Ponte's opinion matched Sanford J. Brothers. Both believed the Gardner heist was carried out by someone on the inside. I had Raskin's contact information and went about making his morning miserable.

I pulled the paper with his phone number on it from my pocket and dialed Charles Raskin's number. A woman answered, her voice thick with sleep.

"Chuck there?" I snapped.

"Who's calling?"

"Theo Perdoux. We spoke at the Gardner a few days ago. Put him on."

"Is this important?"

"Put him on," I barked.

Some murmuring in the background, then a friendly, "Mr. Perdoux? I didn't expect to hear from you again. The police, you know, they've been pretty much on my case."

"They sense you're involved," I said. "That's my feeling, too."

"Me? Wait a minute. I'm getting kinda tired of this, if you want the truth. I could lose my job if this keeps up."

"It's your job I'm calling about. The job you worked with Francesco Vega."

"That I worked with who?"

"When he came to the museum, Clair Bowman introduced him as Aldo Conte. I'm cutting you some slack here, Raskin. You thought the man was an expert, a renowned name in the world of classical instruments. Why worry about him? Why treat Aldo Conte like some bum off the streets? If he wanted a few minutes alone while you took a coffee break, what's the harm? The problem is, Raskin, the man you left alone was an imposter."

"What are you trying to do to me?" Raskin asked rattled. "My wife can't take any more of this. Neither of us can. I did nothing wrong."

"But you did leave Francesco Vega alone for a few minutes. Maybe you showed Angela Ricci how to get to the ladies room."

"No."

"For a few minutes."

"I said no."

"And for that time alone, what did he promise? Money?"

"No." There followed a long, tense pause. Finally, Raskin said in a low, soft voice, "He said he wanted a coffee. That's all. He said he wanted a coffee so I brought him one. Angela and I went downstairs and brought him back a coffee. That's it, I swear."

"How long was he alone?"

"Five minutes. Maybe ten. I had to heat the water."

"When you came back with the coffee, what was he doing?"

"Same as before, studying the Cavelli. It didn't look like he'd moved a step. I looked around, you know, to protect myself and didn't see one thing out of place or missing. I'm not stupid. I'm a security guard."

"Did Vega say anything about where he might go when he left the museum? Did he give any indication that he might be staying in Boston? Or visiting somebody? Anything at all?"

"Not that I remember. He thanked me for the coffee. He said it tasted American, watery and not very good. Listen, if I knew anything, I'd turn him in for the reward. Honest, I'd tell where the paintings were and turn that little prick in."

"Who told you about any reward?" I asked, surprised that he knew before the official announcement.

"Miss Bowman. She sent out an e-mail to the staff last night. She didn't want us to be surprised if we saw her today on television. You think I couldn't use five million? You think I wouldn't turn that pair in for five million? In a heartbeat."

"I'm sure," I said and ended the call that hadn't made me feel any better. Sometimes making someone as miserable as you works wonders. Other times, it doesn't. This was one of those other times.

Before I knew it, I was walking on Via Della Conciliazione. Ahead stood Piazza San Pietro and Bernini's colonnade, a marvelous spectacle of simplicity and order. Before getting there, I passed souvenir shops selling small tearful-eyed statues of Christ on the cross. I ducked around a cluster of Japanese tourists and kept walking toward St. Peters. I was about to climb the massive stairs, stairs that popes and thousands of others had climbed when my phone rang, and I veered off.

"Theo?"

"Brody?"

"Amateurs ruin the world, Theo. Artsy amateurs are the worst. Jesus God, I think I'm going to kill myself."

"What are you talking about?"

"I'm talking about Clair Bowman doing the nice and tipping off her staff about the reward that we were to announce later today. Only Clair

Bowman didn't figure that every reporter in the city would have his or her ear to the ground and pick up every tremor. So, I get up this morning and on the front page of the newspaper is a five-million-dollar headline. Makes me look like a dumb ass, Theo. I'd called a press conference to announce big news, and it's already in the papers. Makes me think I should be in Rome with you."

"She told you I was here?"

"After I yelled at her for five minutes."

"You still going ahead with the televised announcement?"

"Got to. Howard Moss laid out the demands. We're going to do as told to see if we can recover those paintings."

"Who's his client?"

"He's not saying."

"But you have suspicions."

"Dozens of them, but at this stage none of them matter. Moss is going to protect his client. If the deal falls apart, he doesn't want the police going after whoever committed the robbery. The guarantee of no prosecution is enforced only if we get the paintings back," Brody said. "Which reminds me, your tip about Angela Ricci and Francesco Vega being married. We'd already made that connection. You didn't have to go to Italy to find that out."

"If you remember, Brody, you encouraged me to leave you alone. Besides, I couldn't have met the authentic Aldo Conte without coming to Rome."

"What's your take on him?"

"He's old family evidently running low on cash. He's divorced, he's got a son who hates him and a daughter who had a child without bothering to get married."

"Sounds like the typical American family," Brody quipped. "The daughter's name wouldn't happen to be Lia, would it?"

141

"That's right. Why?"

"One of the names in Angela Ricci's address book. We're running a check on everyone including her and are hitting a roadblock with the Rome police. It's like everything else in that country. You stand in line at the bank for an hour to cash a traveler's check. When it's your turn, the teller puts up the closed sign. Off to lunch for three hours. How does a country function with a system like that? The whole damn country shuts down in the middle of the afternoon. My wife and I were there for a week and couldn't wait to get back to the States. It's a miserable country, Theo. You can have it."

"What about the Rome police giving you the cold shoulder on Lia Conte?" I asked.

"Cold as in the deep freeze. The *polizia* weren't helpful, and the *cababinieri* refused to cooperate saying they had no reason to investigate a private citizen. They suggested contacting the *polizia*. You can see where that was going," Brody said. "Round and round in circles."

"Maybe the personal touch would help," I said.

"I was hoping you'd say that, Theo. You could be helpful, since you're there and all."

"Have you got a name?" I asked.

"Roberto Filippo, Sergeant Roberto Filippo of the *Polizia di Stato*, something like our State Police. I'll contact him and tell him you're on special assignment working with Boston PD. That might grease the rails."

"And what exactly do you want me to find out?"

"Who stole the Gardner paintings? What else?"

"Very funny," I said.

"I'll send you the Sergeant Filippo's contact information. And, thanks, Theo. I owe you one."

Chapter Thirteen

Sergeant Roberto Filippo put down his newspaper and looked up from his desk when I entered his office, a small space without windows on the second floor of a military-looking building housing the *Polizia di Stato*. Filippo, a slightly overweight man of about sixty, stared fixedly at me as if he'd completely forgotten the appointment. Finally, his memory engaged, and he sprang from his chair and bolted around the desk.

"Ah, *dottore*," he said, shaking my hand with vigor. "Please, please, come in and sit." He motioned to the only other chair and retook his place behind his desk. "So, you are here about the Conte family." His index finger tapped a thick file in front of him. "I did some looking. A fine family. A family with history, not so hard to find in Roma, eh? No, not so hard to find. Is harder to find a family without history, that is my thinking. So, you are looking for what? You realize, of course, that I cannot open the entire vastness of my department to you and your investigation without proper authorization from my superiors, who at this moment know nothing of our meeting. How do you say it in your wonderful country? This is not the record."

"Off the record," I corrected.

Filippo beamed. "Off the record, *dottore*. Of course, off the record. You have some identification?"

I presented my detective's license. While the sergeant scrutinized it, I said, "You spoke with Brody Flynn of the Boston Police."

He handed back the license. "The picture doesn't exactly match your face. You have fallen and that causes the bruise, am I right?"

"I took a fall, yes," I said.

"Our streets." He shook his head as if personally responsible for the condition of the streets. "A stone gives way. The rains create a river. Two days ago, a sinkhole swallowed a dog. No one is safe, *dottore*. You are living proof. I hope you notified the proper authorities where this fall took place so that the street can be repaired and no one else will suffer."

"Brody Flynn," I said as a reminder.

"Oh, yes. A voice full of tension, full of stress. I asked him how he'd been sleeping." Filippo shook his head as if worried for an old friend. "I hope he lives a long life, but my doubts are that he won't. You need to send him some good news, no? Good news would make his life easier, maybe let him live a few more years. Who knows?"

"Nobody knows," I admitted. "Brody Flynn must have told you of my interest in Lia Conte," I said, trying to wrangle the conversation to my purpose.

"Ah, yes, yes. The older of the two children. Her ancestors are from the north, not far from Milan. They go back hundreds of years, *dottore*. A fine family with history." The sergeant seemed to look at something floating in the air, then said, "Imagine making a living building violins. I don't know how it can be done. Of course, it wasn't always done well even for the Contes. They had troubles from time to time."

"When was this?" I asked.

"Two-hundred years back. A little longer, maybe." He opened the file and studied the page before him. "Yes, *dottore*, two-hundred years back. Some troubles with bankers. A suicide in the family. The plague. The Conte family seems to live with money troubles. Like the rest of us, no?"

"Anything more recent than two-hundred years?" I asked.

144

"Of course. But to that matter of making a living building violins. Remarkable, don't you think? I could never do it. As sure as we sit here, *dottore*, I tell you I would starve." He cut me a sharp look. "Do you play? The violin? Do you play such a lovely instrument?"

"No," I said, my frustration growing.

"Then, you would likely starve, too. I can't make the instrument, and you can't play it. What good are we?"

"About Lia Conte," I said again. "Her name was found in the apartment of a woman murdered in Boston."

"I see." Filippo thought a moment, then said, "Guns? Killed with guns?"

"Shot. Yes."

"You Americans shoot to solve your problems. We Italians yell at one another, then have a glass of wine. If we are lucky, the wine leads to passion. Who was this woman shot?"

"Angela Ricci."

"Ricci, Ricci," the sergeant said, glancing again at the file. "She was in Roma. Ten years back or so. Magistrate Antonio Levy handled the case of the shoplifters."

"Shoplifters?" I repeated. "Plural? Ricci and who else?"

"Francesco Vega."

"Were they prosecuted?"

"Jailed overnight. Fined. Released." The sergeant leaned forward on his desk and spoke as if revealing a top secret. "Had they some smoking materials with them, some marijuana cigarettes or the hashish, they would still be in prison. We Italians are unforgiving when it comes to Americans invading our country and smoking the marijuana cigarettes. We lock them up for a long time, *dottore,* a very long time."

"What did they steal?"

"Roman coins said to have been found under mosaics at Hadrian's Villa and a few small pottery vessels. The antique dealer was himself a crook known to sell fakes to tourists. However, he did not appreciate being taken advantage of and threatened prosecution when the pair walked off with what he called his rare antiquities. Common fakes is what they were. Italy has a terrible problem, *dottore*, with unsavory types stealing our national treasures and selling them overseas. The chain of thief to shipper to buyer is difficult to break. Maybe impossible, since Italy's treasures are the most sought after in the world. Had it been me, I would have put the man Vega in jail for twenty-five years and let the woman, who is it? Ricci? Yes, I would tell the judge to put her behind bars for ten years. I have no reason for the difference in sentences, but that is how our judicial system works. It doesn't always make sense. Take, for example, how we deal with the Mafia. We have a dedicated police division in this city for all things Mafiosi. Special investigators, special prosecutors, special courts, special judges. We make arrests and have trials that last years. The appeals last years more, *dottore*. It hurts me to say that the Mafia still thrive in our country, in this very city." He tapped the file again. "In here are reports that Silvio Conte for a time had such leanings that, I am happy to say, appear to be over. The family continues to work in music and nothing else. In fact, the same can be said for Francesco Vega. How do you say it in your country? Francesco arranged his life around."

"Turned his life around?"

"Yes, *dottore*, that is it. He turned his life around when he started classes with Silvio and began a romance with Lia. Is it Lia you want to talk about, no?"

"Yes. Very much," I said relieved that he remembered. "What can you tell me about her?"

"A lovely woman. Smart. Talented."

146

"Any trouble with the authorities?" I asked.

"With the police? No. With her priest? Yes. The child, you understand. The priest did not approve. With her father? Also a yes for trouble with him. We have in our file a record that Aldo Conte called the department on two occasions reporting his daughter having run off. Not for long periods, you understand. A few days, a week." Filippo shrugged. "Divorce is difficult for some and that appears to be the case with Lia. She was very fond of her mother and hated that her marriage ended and that she left Villa Conte. Lia is high spirited. A rebel, *dottore*, the kind of woman requiring much attention. You look like a married man, you should know these things. How many children? A man like you, handsome but with an injury to the face. If you don't mind my asking, what became of your eye?"

I told him about the thrown rock landing on the side of my head.

Filippo's frown sagged. "People should not attack authority. No. Never. I bet your children helped you get well, no? How many? Five is my guess. You are the father of five healthy children. All boys, I hope. How old is your oldest?" he asked.

"No kids. My wife and I divorced," I said, not interested in pursuing my family history.

"Ah, you married a rebel no doubt. You did not pay enough attention to her. Me? My wife is the glue of the house. She keeps me and the children together. If we step out of line, she boxes our faces. Especially our girls, girls can be trouble when they are lovely, and ours are. Would you care to see pictures?" the sergeant asked eagerly.

"Some other time," I said. "Do you have anything in your records connecting Lia to Angela Ricci?"

"Not that I saw. Of course, they could have met on one of Lia's trips to your fair city."

"Lia was in Boston?"

"Yes, *dottore*, according to one of the reports Aldo Conte filed, she was certainly a visitor once when she ran off with a man from there. He was in Roma visiting family, you understand. Something he did quite often as his grandparents were elderly. We take care of the elderly in this country. It is a matter of national pride. Somehow Lia and the man became acquainted, and when he went back to Boston, she went along."

"Who was the man?" I asked.

Sergeant Filippo checked his notes, then looked up at me. "Pietro Garcetti, son of Vincent, grandson of Roberto who died recently." The sergeant made the sign of the cross. "Lived to be nearly one hundred. What is the name of your Boston police detective?"

"Brody Flynn," I said.

"Brody Flynn will not make one hundred. Too much stress with all the guns and shooting in your country. Not good, *dottore*, not good."

"What can you tell me about Peter Garcetti and Lia Conte?"

"Very little about how involved they were with each other if that is what you mean. Of course, I can guess. Both were young and eager like we all used to be. The families were acquainted with each other. They visited. They drank wine." Filippo tapped the cover of his file. "This is not a complete dossier, *dottore*, just a few notes I have made and kept since Villa Conte was broken into two years ago. I would have no reason to file a report on the Conte family had it not been for the unfortunate crime. Insurance companies, you understand, want everything in duplicate, and my superior wants it all in triplicate. It's surprising I am as efficient as I am, given all the forms I fill out."

"What was stolen during the break in?"

"Yes, of course. I do not need to look at my notes, *dottore*, as I was in charge of the investigation. If you have not visited Villa Conte, you should do so. It's a beautiful palazzo, one of many grand structures in our city. Unfortunately, they are often targets for a criminal element. Statues, paintings, rare tapestries are often the prizes the thieves go after. Never have I been called to a property to investigate the theft of a violin. A Stradivarius. An instrument worth over two million dollars American taken from the music room in the middle of the night. Fortunately, the beautiful instrument was insured."

"Was it ever recovered?"

"No. No trace of the violin was ever uncovered. It was as if the instrument vanished into thin air. I had my suspicions, of course. That is how we survive, no? We in positions of authority are paid to have suspicions."

"What do you think happened to the violin?" I asked.

"I think Francesco Vega took it with the help of his friend, Silvio. I could never prove it, of course, but that is what I think happened to the violin. Both men denied any knowledge, as you can imagine they would. Aldo gave Silvio an alibi. He said the boy was sleeping when the robbery occurred. And Lia swore she was out for the evening with Francesco. As you can see, *dottore*, the hands of my suspects are clean. Aldo Conte was heartbroken over the theft. That violin, he told me, was very dear to him. Other than the instruments made by his ancestors, the Stradivarius was the prize of his collection. I was of the mind that his pain was so great, so sincere, that he might eventually tell me the truth and turn in Francesco and his son. Of course, that never happened."

"Why do you think they wanted the violin?" I asked.

"That is the question I asked. What would two young men want with a musical instrument, even one of great value? The motive was what? Money? I rejected money as a motive, *dottore*, as there are far more items of value in Villa Conte that would be far easier to sell. If not money, then what?"

"A poke in the eye," I offered.

Filippo smiled knowingly. "You heard that Silvio with the help of his friend dragged Aldo from a deep sleep and threatened him. Marianna filed a police report on that unfortunate attack that Aldo denied ever happened. Our hands were tied when he wanted the family name kept out of such a sordid business. The opposite was true when his violin was stolen. Aldo's grief caused by his loss turned to frustration and later anger when the insurance company refused to pay."

"I thought you said the piece was insured."

"It was. Or, I should say, a Stradivarius was photographed and documented following insurance company regulations along with all the other musical instruments in the Conte collection. The insurance company, Sardi and Fenzoni International, had difficulty confirming that the violin stolen was the Stradivarius. At least, that is what they claimed. It was no more than a typical insurance company delaying tactic. There was no dispute that the Stradivarius was missing. Eventually, Aldo Conte and his insurer went to court after failing to reach a settlement. In the end, Conte was awarded the money."

"Then, money was the motive," I said.

"Only if Aldo was himself involved in the theft," Filippo answered. "I do not believe him capable of stealing what he spends his life building. No, *dottore*, the truth lies in another place, a place I have not found."

"And you're convinced Lia had nothing to do with it?"

Sergeant Filippo nodded approvingly. "You think like an officer of the law, *dottore*. Lia happened to travel to Boston immediately after the robbery. Upon her return, I brought her in for questioning. She claimed no knowledge. And before you ask, yes, I spoke with Pietro Garcetti when he next visited his grandfather. I was very thorough with my interrogation of him, but he offered nothing. That is the family way. Even if you know something, it is best to remain silent. Roberto, Pietro's grandfather and a fine man, made the rules that all followed. You did not disobey *Don* Roberto. May he rest in peace." He made another cross with the flip of one hand. "*Don* Roberto held tightly those under him. No one made the journey across the line and lived happily."

"You mean no one crossed him and lived."

Sergeant Filippo bobbed his head. "That is the truth, *dottore*. I believe Vincent Garcetti lives the same way in your country. He's surrounded by a protective family who say nothing to the authorities. Too bad Vincent did not attend his father's funeral."

"Vincent is in prison," I said.

"Yes, yes, I am aware. I saw Pietro at Roberto's wake. He said his father hurts about not being at the funeral. I went to pay my respects. I always enjoyed my conversations with *Don* Roberto even though I never learned anything."

"Your criminal investigations often led you to the Garcettis?" I asked.

"Of course. Many times. Roberto owned many businesses and ruffled the skin of many competitors. There were fights, fires, break-ins . . ."

"Murders?"

"On occasion someone died before he should have, yes. Often they disappeared never to be seen again. *Don* Roberto had no idea where any of them went. At least, that is what he told to me."

"Did he ever speak of a man in Nice who specialized in the theft and resale of stolen art?"

"What is this man's name?"

"Niles Huygens."

Filippo didn't hesitate. "Huygens, yes. Everyone acquainted with the loss of expensive items knows the name of Niles Huygens. But, *dottore*, *Don* Roberto did not introduce me to this man. Pietro did."

"Peter Garcetti?"

"Yes. Pietro used his grandfather's wake and funeral as an opportunity to introduce himself to those who might be useful to him as the head of the family here in Roma."

"What about Vincent?" I asked. "Power is usually handed down to the eldest son."

"A man in prison is limited," Filippo said. "In my country contact with the face, the shake of the hands, a kiss on the cheek, wine, all of it is important. Pietro Garcetti engaged in all of that while his father did not. Pietro now runs the family here. He made it clear he wanted to meet certain people and Niles Huygens was one who came to the funeral."

"What was the nature of their business?" I asked.

Filippo shrugged. "I was not privileged to hear such details. I attended the wake and went to the funeral. I met many men who came to honor the life of *Don* Roberto and to bestow good wishes on his grandson who clearly wants to wake a sleeping giant."

"How do you mean?"

"I mean *Don* Roberto lost interest in family affairs. He let business drift. Others took advantage. Pietro made it clear that would not happen in the future," the sergeant said as someone knocked on his door. "*Pronto!*"

A fellow officer burst in, barking something in Italian to his sergeant. Filippo pushed himself up from his chair and stretched to his full height.

"Another meeting, *dottore*, you understand," he said, ushering me out. "Have a walk, get some sun. You look like you could use some color on your face. The sun would help that terrible bruise. I would love to join you but meetings. They will be the end of us, don't you think?"

I shook the sergeant's hand. "You've been very helpful," I said.

He wagged his finger at me. "I have *not* been, *dottore*. This is not the record. My superiors . . ."

"I understand," I said and left Sergeant Filippo striding off toward another meeting.

For the first time since I'd arrived in Rome, I felt luck turning my way. Sardi and Fenzoni International Assurance insured the majority of high-risk fine art in the world. I knew of it because Gina Ponte insured the contents of her art gallery with them, and on one of my Barcelona trips, I met her insurance agent.

Over coffee at an outdoor bar not far from Sergeant Filippo's office, I searched the local directory and found a Rome number for Sardi and Fenzoni. I didn't know what I might learn from a chat but thought it worth a try. I called the number and introduced myself as the business partner of Gina Ponte looking for information about a contested claim.

The voice on the other end put me on hold. My coffee grew cold while I waited. Finally, a woman's voice came on. I explained again that I was looking for information about a claim filed about two years ago regarding a stolen Stradivarius.

"Two years," the woman mused. "A very long time to now be bringing up the Conte business."

"Then, you know what I am referring to."

"I do, yes. I came to work with Sardi a few months after Mr. Conte and the company went to court. Human Resources started using the claim as a case study, training new employees on how not to treat our customers. I was one of the first agents to get the training."

"What can you tell me about the case?" I asked.

"Very little, really. We respect the privacy of our clients."

"Of course."

"Our training after the Conte case stressed the importance of client relations. We are in the trust business. Clients buy policies from us, because they trust that, when the time comes if ever, we will be there for them, supporting them, providing the insured funds within a reasonable amount of time."

"Your reputation is impeccable," I said, hoping for more about the missing violin and less about the mission of Sardi and Fenzoni. "Why did your company not pay the policy immediately?" I asked.

"A reasonable amount of time is not a fixed point, you understand. People might disagree as to when it arrives."

"So, you let the courts decide," I said.

"In the end, yes. But not just when an amount should be paid, but *if* it should be paid."

"You thought you were dealing with insurance fraud?"

"We never made such a claim and never would. The one undisputed fact is that a rare violin was stolen from the Villa Conte music room."

"Who stole it?" I asked.

"The Italian authorities never arrested anyone. Our own investigators created a list of possibilities, but no charges were ever filed."

"Care to offer any names?"

"I'm afraid not."

"Silvio Conte?"

"I can't say."

"Pietro Garcetti?"

"Sorry. No comment."

"Francesco Vega?"

"Same answer."

"If I recover the violin, it would be a feather in your cap," I coaxed. "Answer me this, Sergeant Filippo who investigated the robbery told me that Francesco Vega had been arrested for shoplifting. It wouldn't be much of a stretch to think he could up his game to include stealing a priceless violin, would it? I mean, theoretically speaking."

"Theoretically speaking, no, it wouldn't be a stretch. However, my non-theoretical answer is our company's position which is that it could not definitely be proven by our investigating authorities who took the Stradivarius. Mr. Conte owned several pieces in his rather extensive instrument collection. Sardi and Fenzoni wanted to make sure that all involved were abiding by the terms of the written policy."

"But, in the end, you paid."

"The full amount, two million dollars. Mr. Conte is a well-re-spected maker of fine instruments. We did not want to maintain a lengthy court presence in an apparent adversarial position against him."

"David vs. Goliath and all the bad publicity that comes with it."

"Well put."

"You never said you thought Conte was guilty of fraud."

"Customer relations training would never permit us to do so."

"I get it," I said, thanked her and hung up.

Chapter Fourteen

Sometimes information takes a while to show its true value. The fact that Peter Garcetti had cut out his father and taken the reins from *Don* Roberto was just such a piece of information. Add to that a visit to Rome by Niles Huygens so the two men could talk. Huygens wasn't the type to make the trip unless he could profit by it. Was Garcetti selling something? Gardner paintings? Likely not, I thought. Howard Moss is making a deal to give the pieces back. It wouldn't make sense for Peter to broker a deal with Niles Huygens using the same pieces. So, what was going on?

Time was running out to answer that question if I was going to keep my word to Clair Bowman and fly back to Boston. I decided to spend some of that time with another visit to Vega's Fine Leathers. This time I'd wait in the parking lot until Giuseppe Vega left work. I didn't speak Italian enough to question him, so I would follow him in hopes that he would lead me to his son. A basic rule in any investigation is that the husband is a prime suspect in his wife's murder and that a parent is most likely the person shielding their child.

Giuseppe, here I come.

The rental agent dampened my enthusiasm when he gave the news that all the cars were spoken for. He offered me the rental of a scooter. I declined. Sitting on a Vespa waiting for something to break at Vega's Fine Leathers was not going to happen. The attendant then gave me the address of a second rental car location a few blocks from the Piazza di Spagna. I hopped in a cab and gave the driver the address.

The piazza with its fountain in the shape of a leaking boat and the steep steps leading up to the public gardens of the Pincio are a magnet for tourists. This sunny, early June day was no exception. My taxi crawled through the traffic, eventually worming through the crowded piazza and deposited me in front of a rental car shop one block from the fountain. I paid and got out.

I was on my way inside the rental office, when I stopped and wheeled back toward the men seated across the street at the outdoor café. One of the men sitting alone, fingers drumming on the round glass tabletop, appeared anxious, out of place. When he pulled off his dark glasses and wiped the sweat from his brow, I recognized Pietro Garcetti. He was nearing fifty with wavy black hair, light olive skin, and dark, narrow eyes. He wore a blue checkered shirt open at the collar revealing a large gold chain hanging around his neck. Peter's reputation was that of a very smart yet ruthless man capable of out-thinking most and out muscling all. He was Vincent Garcetti with brains.

I waited across the street hidden behind a magazine kiosk. Garcetti kept his eyes on the street. In a few minutes, a taxi slowed, then stopped in front of the café. The blocked traffic instantly erupted in a cascade of honking car, bus, and Vespa horns. Peter shot to his feet, waved his arms, and shouted something to the driver in the car directly behind the taxi. The driver shouted back, creating a greater spectacle out of the chaos. Peter charged the car. His menacing stare enough to shut up the driver. Nerves calmed, Peter moved quickly to the taxi, then yanked open a rear door. An energized Marcus Conte spilled out with Lia right behind.

Peter bent down as the boy jumped joyfully into his waiting arms. When Peter stopped spinning the boy around, he kissed Lia who beamed with delight. Then, like any other family out for a stroll, they were off with Peter in the middle, holding hands with Lia and Marcus. I stayed back, hiding in the jostling foot traffic. In a few blocks, we turned off onto Via Margutta, a short street halfway between Piazza del Popolo and Piazza di Spagna.

The three-story manse Peter approached had none of the grandeur of Villa Conte. Instead, like the other buildings on the block, it radiated a simple, sturdy dignity while calling out for attention. Chips in the stone façade and porch needed repair as did a few of the large wooden shutters that framed all of the many windows. Still, it was a grand house that Peter approached with familiarity. At the massive wooden door, he took out his key and inserted it into the lock. The threesome entered the front hall as I walked past and took up residence in a corner trattoria across the street. As I waited for my espresso, I thought back to what I knew of Peter Garcetti's Boston life: married, four children, MBA from Dartmouth's Tuck School of Business, and head of the Garcetti family while his father served his prison sentence.

Based on police reports I'd read over the years, Peter had put his college degree to work modernizing the Garcetti family businesses ranging from offering personal loans to weekly garbage collection to a string of car dealerships specializing in used vehicles sold to those who needed wheels but had neither money nor credit. The cars were low end, the interest rates, like those for personal loans, highest of the high end. Like his father, Peter kept his hands clean and oversaw his businesses from his Boston office. Unlike his father, Peter craved the next deal, the next opportunity to generate more power and wealth. He was always on the hunt, pushing aside the competition when anyone dared challenge him.

According to Sergeant Filippo, Peter and Lia traveled to Boston together soon after the robbery of the Stradivarius. Before that, Vincent and Peter had been guests at Villa Conte, enjoying a swim in the pool. Plenty of opportunity, I thought, for Peter and Lia to explore their romantic interest, interest that evidently led to a son.

Beside the bar I found a pay phone with a telephone book attached by a chain. I looked up the name Roberto Garcetti and found that he had lived at Via Margutta, 10. I paid my bill and walked across the street. I pressed the door buzzer and waited. I pressed it again and heard the lock click open. A man holding a roll of clear packing tape opened the door. Like the men buzzing here and there behind him, he wore white coveralls.

"You the man moving, no?" he asked.

"I'm not moving, no," I said.

"With the truck. Moving, no?"

"Ah," I said catching on. "No, I'm not the man with the moving truck. I'm here to see . . ." Before I could finish, Peter Garcetti climbed down the last step and spoke to the man with the tape who hustled off to seal another box.

Peter's expression was a heated stare of antagonism. "As you can see," he said motioning to the boxes stacked along one wall of the hallway, "I'm rather busy. Who are you and what do you want?"

"Theo Perdoux," I answered. "I'm a private investigator. What I want is a little conversation."

Garcetti's eyes flashed recognition. "Nick Bianchi told me about you," he said, not bothering to hide his disgust. "So has Lia. You're making quite a pest of yourself with the Contes. You're not going to do that with me."

"Just doing my job," I said. "But if this is a bad time, we can talk back in Boston. Your wife may want to be a part of it when we talk there."

Garcetti hesitated, then pulled back the door. I stepped in to the normal chaos of packing for a move. Behind us, two men carefully lifted a massive mirror from its wall hangars and lowered it to the marble floor where the man with the tape wrapped it in a quilted blanket.

Another man appeared carrying a wooden packing crate that the mirror slid into. When he bent over to load the mirror, I spotted the revolver clipped to his belt. A second look at the other men revealed more guns.

"Expecting trouble, are you?"

Garcetti cocked his head. "Why do you ask?"

"Your moving men are packing crates and guns."

"I've had threats," Garcetti said evenly. "Nothing to be concerned about. Besides, these men work for me in various capacities. Packing up my grandfather's house is one."

"Moving out, are you?"

"Moving in," Garcetti said. "My grandfather was not capable of keeping up the house during the last years of his illness. Everything of his goes in storage. Once the place is empty, I will make the necessary repairs."

"Quite an undertaking," I said.

"My grandfather left his house to me. I accept the responsibility."

"Your grandfather did well for himself," I said.

"He had a good long life," Peter said as a child's joyful shriek drifted down from upstairs.

Without a word, I followed Peter up the wide, winding stairs and toward the playful sounds coming from a third-floor room designed for a child's fantasy. What looked like a small circus tent sat in one corner. Opposite were a tricycle and a rocking horse. Along one wall stood a child's soccer net. Marcus occupied himself peddling a replica of a red Ferrari around the center of the room, head back, laughing with joy as Lia chased him around. When she stopped, her eyes bored in on me.

"I don't mean to spoil the party," I said.

"Then, leave," she quipped.

"Let him have his say," Peter chimed in. "I don't want to see him in Boston. Is that understood?"

"Understood," I said, dodging the race car as it sped by. "Your son, I take it."

"Yes," Peter said. "A very happy boy as you can see. We plan on keeping him that way."

"I want everyone to be happy," I said. "Including me."

"And you think you will find happiness here?" Peter asked. "I'm afraid you'll be disappointed. Our focus is on cleaning out this house and making it livable. Nothing else. Certainly nothing to do with Francesco Vega. He's who you've been pestering the Contes about, isn't it?"

"I've talked to them. Yes."

"Francesco Vega has evolved into an unfortunate situation. The Contes gave him every opportunity to make something of himself, and he found ways to close the door on those opportunities. It's unfortunate, but nothing more than that."

"I take it you know Francesco," I said.

"We've met."

"In Rome or in Boston?" I asked and caught the slightest flicker of resentment cross Garcetti's expression.

"You're trying to draw me into something, Mr. Perdoux. I don't like that. My contact with Francesco Vega was here in Rome, when he was suspected of stealing a rather significant item."

"Significant like a Stradivarius?" I asked.

Garcetti nodded. "I've been told you were good at your job when you were a Boston cop. I can see that you're still good. How did you learn that Vega stole the violin?"

"I have a contact here in Rome. He told me about the robbery and that you and Lia left for Boston shortly thereafter. Did you take the violin with you to sell it on the black market?"

Lia's quick burst of nervous laughter caught me off guard. "You need to get a new contact," she said. "We had nothing to do with stealing the Strad or trying to resell it."

Garcetti raised one hand for silence. "Let Perdoux make the accusations, Lia. We shouldn't offer anything until we know what he's giving for what we know. It's like a poker game, Mr. Perdoux. Lia and I are holding all the cards. What are you adding to the pot to see our hands?"

"How about five million dollars?"

"A nice round figure," Garcetti said evenly. "How does one win the hand?"

"Give back the stolen art."

"You seem to have made quite a jump. First, you are asking about a violin, now you are talking about missing paintings. What connects the two?"

"Francesco Vega for certain. Silvio Conte likely. Maybe even you."

"Go on."

"Let's start with the Stradivarius," I said. "I had a conversation with the insurance company who paid the two million. They haven't accused anyone of fraud, but that could change if I were to provide them with new information."

"Which would be?" Garcetti asked.

"That Francesco Vega and Silvo Conte were involved in both the theft of the Strad and the Gardner paintings. The depth of that involvement is unclear, but the circumstantial evidence is enough for them to reopen their investigation. Insurance companies hate to be taken advantage of," I said as Lia cut Garcetti an anxious look. "All it takes is one call from me to get the ball rolling. If it rolls from the stolen violin to the stolen paintings, lots of people could get hurt. Maybe even spend the rest of their lives in jail. I don't think Aldo Conte would survive that."

Like any professional poker player, Garcetti studied me, looking for any sign that I was not telling the truth. Finally, he said, "What would it take for you not to make that call?"

"The truth. Not only about the Stradivarius, but also about the Gardner heist."

"By the truth, you mean you want my confession. All right, I confess that I had nothing to do with stealing either the violin or any paintings. However, I will gladly tell you the real truth, not the one you believe to be true."

"Verified, how?" I asked.

"By practicing your trade, of course. By making a pest of yourself. Eventually, someone will tell you what I say is the truth."

Lia shifted from one foot to the other. "What will you do once you learn the truth?"

"Depends," I said.

"No," Peter said with authority. "That's not the way the game is played. We're not handing out information that lets you decide our fate."

"Or the fate of others," Lia said. "My father could not live through another prolonged investigation that questions his reputation. All he has is the Conte name. Tainting it with even the hint of fraud would crush him."

Garcetti took charge. "We will tell you about the violin and you will not hold the truth against the Contes. Agreed?"

"You didn't mention Francesco," I said.

"No, I didn't," Peter said. "Nor did I mention your father."

I felt a quick stab in my chest. "What has he got to do with any of this?"

"You didn't answer about the Contes, Mr. Perdoux. You will not hound them with what I am about to tell you, agreed?"

"Agreed," I finally said, fully aware that I was being played like a Stradivarius. "Now, about Wilhelm Barr."

"In due time." Peter pulled in a deep breath and released it. "First, let me tell you something about my grandfather. His father and mother worked tirelessly up in the hills on a stony piece of land where they raised their family. My grandfather learned the value of hard work from his parents. He also learned that being poor produced a life of doubt and worry. Would the late spring frost kill all or just some of the crops? Would the rains ever come? Would the rains ever stop? My grandfather vowed to make for himself a different life. A life he and others could respect. He began his journey in the world of work in a bakery. He would leave for work every morning at four to bake the day's bread. An infrequently told story about Italians, Mr. Perdoux, is that few of us any longer bake our own breads. Like the French, we go to the nearest bakery. Within a few years, my grandfather not only owned his own bakery, but also delivery trucks. He saw the value of claiming routes for his trucks only, so that no other bakers could service the village stores. With the routes all his own, my grandfather began delivering to the bottlers grapes and olives from the fields. When the wine and olive oil was bottled, he delivered cases to restaurants and markets. Within a few years, he was both powerful and wealthy enough to buy this house. Because he was respected, people from the small villages came to him to settle local disputes. Law enforcement and the judicial system in this country is slow and inefficient. My grandfather's justice was swift. Often, he enlisted the help of men of strength to make certain his solution of the dispute was abided by. That is how the humble Roberto Garcetti became *Don* Roberto."

"Quite a legacy," I said. "Are some of those men of strength down-stairs packing?"

Peter nodded. "Some of *Don* Roberto's men have decided to stay with me. They are very proud of his legacy and want to continue to be a part of it. I want that as well, which is one of the reasons I want to bring this house back to its original glory. My grandfather would have appreciated that."

"What about your father? Would Vincent approve of what you are doing here?"

"My father is an angry and hurt man. Prison does that. He peti-tioned prison officials for permission to come to Rome to see his father before he died. That permission was denied. All my father can think of is getting out, getting his freedom back. Redoing an old house is the farthest thing from his mind."

"What about his grandson?" I asked as Marcus peddled by. "Does your father approve of your life here in Rome?"

"I don't seek his approval," Peter said stiffly. "That's one of the lessons I learned from Francesco and Silvio. Both of them sought ap-proval from *Don* Roberto. He had no interest in them, which only made their need for acceptance all the greater. What could they do that would make my grandfather welcome them into his extended family? Their answer was to present my grandfather with a prize of great value. It proved a foolish move that backfired, because rule number one is that you never steal from your own family. Never."

"They stole the Stradivarius to impress *Don* Roberto?"

"They did. Silvio left the back door of the music room unlocked," Lia said. "Francesco walked in after we'd all gone to bed. The Strad-ivarius was in a special case. The lock was easily broken. He removed the violin and left. During the morning's cleaning, our housekeeper discovered the loss and alerted the family. Father called the police immediately."

"And you and Peter dashed off to Boston to get rid of the evidence," I said.

"I told you before, we left for Boston, yes. Peter wanted to show me around his city, that's all," Lia said. "But the violin didn't go with us."

"It's upstairs," Peter said calmly. "It's been in this house all along."

"*Don* Roberto was saddened, disappointed with the gift. He would not accept anything Silvio stole from his own father," Lia said. "Instead, *Don* Roberto informed our father that he could have the violin back. But to take it back was to point the thieving finger at his own son. That a Conte could be a thief was one thing, but the thief of a rare Stradivarius from father's prized collection was a level of betrayal that my father could not accept. He decided to do something else, something to protect the family's reputation. He decided to report the robbery and to file an insurance claim."

"Even though he could have had the Stradivarius back at any time," I said.

"Even though he could have, yes."

"As my grandfather got older and less agile, Lia visited and played for him. It was one of his few remaining pleasures. Beautiful music on a Stradivarius while he watched his great-grandchild play. I appreciated the gesture very much," Peter said as Marcus traded his red convertible for a soccer ball. "*Don* Roberto did as well."

"How did Silvio and Francesco take *Don* Roberto's rejection?"

"They tried not to show their hurt, but a sister knows. Silvio was crushed. Francesco was simply bitter. My brother turned to making his workshops better, more efficient. Francesco sulked then went away for a few weeks. When he came back, he enrolled in one of Silvio's classes learning how to make musical instruments. Francesco is not without talents. He paints well. He studied the Old Masters in school. Once he learned the techniques of making classical instruments, he would be a valuable addition to any museum."

"Like the Palazzo Pamphilj," I suggested.

"Precisely. Silvio recommended him for that position. I don't know why it didn't work out."

"Maybe it did," I said. "He stayed long enough to get the information he wanted. Same with your father. When he knew how to impersonate Aldo Conte, he went to Boston to play the part. The question is, who did he report to once he left the museum?"

"Which brings us full circle, Mr. Perdoux," Garcetti said. "You have your contacts in Rome and I have mine. Would you like to know what they say is the answer to what your father had to do with the Gardner robbery? He set it in motion with a man known as Hans Katzen guiding the entire enterprise."

"You're sure about that?"

"I trust my contacts, yes."

"How did Francesco Vega fit in?" I asked.

Garcetti turned to Lia and said, "I think Marcus could use a nap." Lia took the hint and collected her son. When they left the room, he said, "There are some things best kept secret. Silvio's involvement in all of this would break Lia's heart. She thought he'd straightened himself out once Aldo kept his involvement in stealing the violin a secret."

"Family blackmail, you mean," I offered.

Garcetti shrugged. "Something like that. Silvio was to toe the line. If he didn't, Aldo would turn him in."

"So, why did Silvio risk everything and get involved?"

"He followed Francesco. He always did. Katzen barked orders, and they obeyed."

That explains Francesco's phone conversation that James Alberts told me about. Katzen called, and Francesco snapped to attention.

"What did Katzen promise?"

"Money. A payday they could never have imagined. Your father is a very generous employer."

"So I've heard," I said.

"He's also an expert at staying in the shadows."

"Which makes me wonder how you learned so much," I said. "Very few know as much about my father as you seem to."

"Jealous?"

"Curious."

"I told you, I have contacts here in Rome, in Boston, wherever I need information, I get what I need."

"Does that include inviting Niles Huygens to Rome? What sort of information were you looking for from him?"

"The kind he's expert in. Niles Huygens Appraisals is the best in the business. My grandfather's collection is extensive. Before taking the artwork from the walls and putting it in storage, I wanted an accurate appraisal of what *Don* Roberto had collected over the years. I hired Huygens to do the job. You look disappointed, Mr. Perdoux. Were you expecting me to admit to something else?"

"Fencing stolen paintings," I said. "Niles Huygens is best in that business, too."

"Back to that, are we? I told you who was involved in the Gardner robbery. Your father devised the plan, Hans Katzen made sure it was carried out with the help of Francesco Vega and Silvio Conte. Since you can only lay your hands on one of those men, I suggest you press Silvio for answers," Garcetti said and moved out into the hallway.

I followed. "You must know what role Silvio played in all this."

"Specifics, I don't know. All I know is that Silvio was involved. I wanted to know how deeply so that I could protect Lia's feelings if need be. She worries about her brother. She doesn't want to see him in trouble."

"How involved was he?" I asked.

"He didn't travel to Boston like Francesco, if that's what you mean. His efforts were all done here in Rome in his workshop. He did some work, but he kept his distance."

"I've been in his shop," I said thinking back to the student work-stations. "I didn't see anything that ties into robbing a museum. Any ideas?"

"I gave you my idea. Talk to Silvio," Garcetti said as we climbed down the stairs.

"What can you tell me about Angela Ricci's involvement?" I asked.

"Involvement with Nick?"

I shook my head. "Involvement with the robbery."

"Very little."

"Who killed her?"

Garcetti shrugged. "Nick Bianchi would like to know that," he said. "He had a certain fondness for the lady."

"Nick had a good time telling her about my father."

"I heard something about that," Garcetti said as we reached the bottom of the stairs.

"I find it curious that you both know quite a bit about Wilhelm."

"Information is king, or haven't you heard?" Garcetti opened the front door and waited for me to leave. "Let's call this hand a draw, shall we? I'm sure there will be others to play. Maybe next time Nick will join us. He loves a good game."

"Nick's coming to Rome?"

"Landed at the airport a few hours ago."

"You've got a house full of holdovers from *Don* Roberto's rein, why call in your top man?"

"I have a special task for him. Now, if you'll . . ."

"One more thing," I said before he could finish. "Packing up your grandfather's house and putting it all in storage. Could be a great place to hide what was stolen from the Gardner, don't you think?"

"Goodbye, Mr. Perdoux," Garcetti said and closed the door behind me.

I went out to the street into the bright warm sun. As I jostled my way through the crowd, I couldn't help wondering why Garcetti was offering Silvio to me on a serving platter. If he really wanted to protect Lia's feelings about her brother, why tell me he was part of the robbery? Why not lie to protect him? Why point me to his workshop which was where I was headed.

Chapter Fifteen

Piazza del Popolo is a large chaotic roundabout from which one broad street enters and three major streets fan out into the heart of Rome. It's a good place to hail a taxi, which I was about to do when an e-mail message labeled 'Urgent' pinged on my phone. I wouldn't have stopped to read it if it hadn't been sent from Art Recovery International. ARI is an organization dedicated to locating missing artwork and serves as an informational clearing house connecting dealers, collectors, museums, and agencies like mine. Gina Ponte and I joined years ago and have found their assistance tracking down stolen canvases invaluable. I stepped out of the traffic beside the church of Santa Maria del Miracoli and read the text.

> TO: All Member Agencies
>
> FROM: Anna Kroll, Recovery Manager
>
> RE: CHRIST IN THE STORM OF GALILEE
>
> On March 18 of this year, thirteen artworks were stolen from Boston's Isabella Stewart Gardner Museum. Information circulating about Rembrandt's *Christ in the Storm of Galilee* indicates that the canvas was separated from the thirteen and has been offered for sale.
>
> If you have been contacted about the illegal sale of this item or if you know of anyone offering *Christ in the Storm of Galilee* for sale, contact this office immediately.

Something was not right here, I thought when I'd finished reading. What happened to the five million dollars offered for the return of all thirteen? I flipped through my contacts and phoned Clair Bowman.

"Clair," I said when she came on the line, "I just read the ARI bulletin about the Rembrandt. What's going on?"

"Nothing's going on. It's all chaos," Clair said, the strain clear in her voice. "Everything's upside down, Theo. I was ready for the press conference announcing the reward and guarantee of no prosecution when Howard Moss called it off."

"Why? It was his game."

"He said there had been a change. His client was pulling back, rethinking. I feel like a fool," Clair said exasperated. "I told the staff about the reward last night and it leaked to the papers. Once again, the board is disappointed with me. I feel badly, but not as badly as the thought that that wonderful painting could end up in some ruthless collector's gallery. *Christ in the Storm of Galilee* is special. Any collector without scruples would love to own the only seascape Rembrandt painted."

"That's not good, Clair. If the paintings are getting singled out and sold to collectors, you'll never get them back."

"Anna Kroll said the same thing."

"Did Anna have any leads on who offered the painting for sale? Any names associated with Niles Huygens come up?" I asked, knowing that Huygens didn't advertise. If word circulated that the Rembrandt was offered for sale, it didn't come from Huygens.

"No names, but she thinks the rumor may have started in Europe. The painting might be there now. I'm just sick about all this, Theo."

"Which may be why Howard Moss pulled back. His client wants you to squirm. He wants you think all is lost, so you'll agree to anything to get the pieces back."

"That's a cruel negotiating tactic," Clair spit out.

"But one that works," I said and asked if she had told Brody Flynn to keep an eye on Charles Rankin's bank account?

"Yes. Nothing's changed as far as I know. Of course, Flynn is not likely to tell me anything. I think he'd appreciate it if I left town. Which might be what Chuck Raskin did. He didn't show up for his shift yesterday. There was a message on my office machine saying he might be a bit late. But late turned in to a no show. Even his wife doesn't know where he is."

"Or she isn't telling," I said. "Keep me informed when Raskin makes an appearance. He's cracking and might be willing to talk."

I ended the call and hailed the first available taxi that dropped me off at the rear entrance to Villa Conte. Since Lia wasn't giving violin lessons today, I hoped that Silvio was taking Saturday off as well. I opened the garden's iron gate, walked past the swimming pool and tried the door to Silvio's workshop. It was locked but easily opened with the aid of a credit card slid past the strike plate. I pushed the door open and listened.

I stepped into the empty room. There was just enough light from the windows to let me move without running into anything. I inched my way past the student's benches and made my way to the back of the room where Silvio stored wood. If Francesco spent time here working like Theresa Abbuto claimed, he needed space of his own. He needed privacy.

Behind a stack of lumber I found a door to another room that looked promising. I turned the knob and went inside, greeted by the strong smell of turpentine. The room was small with good light coming through the windows along the outside wall. A painter's easel occupied the center of the space. On it was an amateurish attempt at capturing Rembrandt's artistry in the painting *Christ in the Storm of Galilee.* The paint was dry, the colors neither rich nor bright, the brush strokes uneven and made without confidence. It was so easily identifiable as a fake that I imagined the artist painted for a purpose other than fooling anyone.

Along the wall opposite the windows was a bench topped with brushes of various sizes stuck in old coffee cans, paint tubes, small jars of dried pigment, cans of linseed oil, a roll of heavy linen, cleaning rags and other painter's supplies. Off to one side, on a rectangle of plain white paper sat a small mound of what looked like soot or crushed charcoal. Beside it was a mixing cup with no more than a few tablespoons of liquid. I sniffed the liquid. Linseed oil. I tipped the cup until a drop of the black mixture slid out onto one of the rags. I placed the rag next to a swatch of black paint on the forged Rembrandt. It was then I noticed that someone had repainted a section of black at the bottom edge of the painting. I looked at the fake more closely and saw the purpose of the painting as yellows, reds, blues were also repainted in small sections along the bottom of the canvas. Someone was experimenting with color, trying to match those on Rembrandt's original. Not an easy process, and one that takes time and trial and error unless they had a background in painting. Or, I thought, watched the art restoration professionals at the Pamphilj conservatory while they restored an old painting.

According to James Alberts, Francesco took copious notes. The notebook, I thought, must be here containing the color formulas. I started looking in a back corner. Leaning against the wall were tall lengths of aged lumber complete with worm and old nail holes. A glass jar filled with aged tacks sat on the floor beside the wood. In addition to the jar of tacks, a coffee tin held several screws and hand-forged nails. I unscrewed a glass jar that smelled of solvent and wood stain. I put the lid back the way I'd found it and examined the pile of wooden stretchers leaning against the base of the easel.

They were small, about twelve inches by twenty. There were five in all. All were precisely made and to my eye, built sturdier than necessary if they were built to hold a simple canvas. Two of the five held no canvas. Three did. One remained in its original condition of stretched linen tacked tightly over the frame. The second looked as if it had been primed with a commercially bought gesso over the linen. The third was primed with an off-white mixture that seemed to be a combination of thin hide glue and crushed chalk both of which sat beside the can of commercial gesso. Old Masters used a mixture of glue and chalk as a primer to smooth the surface of rough canvas before applying paint. I was made aware of this technique when helping to verify the authenticity of a disputed portrait. Chemical analysis of the paint and gesso helped my client prove she'd been sold a forgery.

Someone singing one of Rodolfo's arias from *La Boheme* startled me. The voice sounded like the happy voice of Silvio, but I couldn't swear to it, since I hadn't any experiences with a happy Silvio. As the voice strained through the high notes, he came closer to the studio. I knelt down around the corner of the bench, my insides tightening in small knots. Outside, the singing grew louder and more off key, then it began to fade. I waited in silence for a few minutes and that is when I spotted the notebook sitting on top of the wooden stool slid under the bench.

I stood near the windows where the light was strongest and opened it. The first few pages were notes jotted in English. "You are Aldo Conte, an expert. Act like it." "Show respect for the staff and the Cavelli." "Don't rush. A professional is expected to be thorough."

After the prompts, were photographs of Rembrandt's *Storm in the Sea of Galilee*. There were six photographs in all, only one of the front of the painting. The remaining pictures, along with precise measurements, were details of the stretcher's corner construction, spacing of the canvas tacks, condition of the stretcher's wood and finally the overlap and paint coverage of the canvas on the stretcher. Francesco obviously wanted access to the Gardner to take these pictures.

Did Charles Raskin help him take the original from the wall, shoot the photographs of the back of the canvas and then rehang it? Or did he make sure no one bothered Francesco while he took the measurements and shot the photographs? But why?

I picked up one of the small stretchers and compared its construction to the photographs. It looked identical, which explained why the small stretcher was overly built. It was a model, and, like the others, was a practice piece. Was Francesco planning to reattach the *Storm in the Sea of Galilee* on a stretcher identical to the original except for size? Francesco had books on Rembrandt in his apartment. He was likely aware that Rembrandt's *Portrait of Catrina Hooghsaet* had been cut and reduced in size to fit a smaller, more modern frame. Many Old Masters suffered the same fate when the paintings changed hands.

A few pages after the photographs, a page marked 'Pamphilj' at the top listed the names of dry pigments followed by weight in grams followed by the number of drops of Linseed oil added to create the desired paint consistency. These recorded formulas must have been part of the copious notes James Alberts said Francesco made during his aborted trial period. Was Francesco going to touch up the Rembrandt after attaching it to its new stretcher? Had it suffered serious damage when cut from its frame?

After the Pamphilj pages was a detailed sketch, along with measurements of each part of the frame for the sofa Katzen had delivered to Vega's Fine Leathers. Folded next to the back cover were the pages of sketches I'd found in Francesco Vega's apartment and had taken from me when I was knocked out. A handwritten note scrawled in English at the bottom of the page containing the sofa sketch read, "You were to leave nothing behind. No more fuck ups. B."

B? Barr? Was this the piece of the puzzle finally tying Wilhelm Barr to Francesco? Francesco must have met up with the two thugs after they knocked me out, which meant he was still around. How else would he have gotten the threatening note? Where did he go once he read it? I decided to pressure Giuseppe Vega to find out.

My trip to Vega's Fine Leather was off the back burner.

I rented a car and sped north through the city. At the industrial park, I circled the area, staying clear of the delivery trucks and forklifts loading roofing tiles on flatbeds. I was about to pull into a space when I spotted the two men who attacked me in Francesco's apartment. The large, stout thug who wielded the gun onto the side of my head was seated behind the wheel of a white box truck. The other man who looked more like someone dressed for a day at the office, got out of the passenger's side and was walking briskly toward the upholstery shop.

Caution and patience are acquired skills in my profession. Ignoring either can lead to major problems, even death. The two men in the truck were capable of serious violence. They'd proven that in Francesco's apartment. Absently, I rubbed the side of my face. It was a sore reminder of their attack.

I found a space between two commercial trucks near the back of the lot and backed in. I switched off the engine and got out, inching my way crablike toward the man behind the wheel. He was about twenty yards ahead with his window down smoking a cigarette. I dropped to one knee, watching. The man's focus stayed locked on the leather shop's front door as his partner in crime opened it and went inside.

I crept along, keeping one of the big trucks between the box truck and me. The forklifts made enough noise so that I wasn't worried he'd hear me approaching. That he might see me was a different matter as his attention shifted to what went on around him once his friend went inside. Bolted to the truck's doors were large side mirrors providing the driver with a clear look of what was behind.

When my target was twenty feet away, I waited until he puffed the last of his cigarette. As his eyes shifted toward the dash, I guessed to find the ashtray, I sprang toward the open window, grabbed the driver's head and slammed him face first into the steering wheel. He sagged in the seat and let out a beefy groan. When he reached for the door handle to come at me, I stopped him with a hard fist between his ear and jaw. The thug's head wobbled, then he slumped across the front seat.

I yanked open the truck's door and searched him. He had a Ruger on the seat beside him. I slipped it in my coat pocket and felt through his clothes for his wallet. The picture on his Italian driver's license said his name was Leonardo Severino. He was thirty-five years of age. I put his wallet back, checked my surroundings to make sure no one had seen me before walking back to my car. While I waited for the man in the leather shop to find his friend, I checked the gun. It was a .45 caliber Ruger with a fully loaded magazine and one shell in the chamber for a total of 8 shots.

In ten minutes, the second man stepped out of the leather shop and walked steadily toward his friend. When he spotted his injured partner, he stretched himself to his full height and scanned the area, looking for the culprit. I bent low, the dashboard blocking anyone from seeing me. When I looked up, the man shoved his wounded partner to one side and jumped behind the wheel.

I started my engine, anticipating his exit. It came in an instant with dust and gravel chattering against his wheel wells as he spun out of the lot. I jammed the shifter into drive only to swerve out of the way of an approaching flatbed blocking my progress. I slammed my open hand against the car's horn sending out a blast. By the time the driver paid attention and inched forward giving me room to pass, Severino and his pal were gone.

I shoved the gun in my waistband and raced into the leather shop. As before, the office manager sat behind his desk, a phone scrunched between his shoulder and ear, talking while tapping hurriedly on his keyboard. Work in the shop seemed as busy as the man on the phone, but I was in a hurry and didn't want to waste time.

"The man who was just here," I blurted. "Who is he, and where is he going?"

The office manager looked up, irritated. When he held up one hand to quiet me, I reached over and took his cell phone from the other. I pushed the cancel button and handed it back to him.

"The man," I said.

A stunned look grew in Reese Ogilvy's expression. "You can't . . ." he stammered, glaring at me. "One man comes in yelling. You come in taking my phone. What is this?"

"What was that man yelling about?"

"What he always yells about: His sofa. Getting it out of here will never be soon enough. Now you," he said as if a memory had caught up with him. "You came the other day asking if Giuseppe was back at work after his imaginary accident."

"That's right," I said. "Now I'm here asking about the customer who just left."

"Hans Katzen," Ogilvy said. "We're preparing his project for shipping now. A leaky truck, a leaky container ship letting water drip on that beautiful leather and its ruined, so we wrap it in plastic. Once we finish the plastic wrapping, then we crate it as Mr. Katzen requested. He wants to pick it up later today after we finish with the wooden crate."

"What time will he be back?"

Ogilvy shrugged. "We close at six. Before then. Do you have an interest in the rehab of an original seventeen-hundred Flemish Baroque leather sofa like Mr. Katzen?" he asked, standing. "Not many people do."

"I have an interest in Hans Katzen," I said. "But I would like to see the finished product."

The office manager grabbed a folder and led the way. "There's really little to see at this point," he said. "You might be able to make out some details through the plastic."

Had I not previously seen Giuseppe's work on the sofa, I would have had no idea as to its beauty. The plastic wrapping hid most of the detail. One detail I could see was that the sofa's legs did not reach the top of the wooden pallet on which the sofa sat. The sofa's frame rested on a wooden box. I bent down for a closer look and asked Ogilvy about it.

"A preventative measure during shipping," Ogilvy said. "All of our furniture prepared for shipping rests on a pallet. On top of the pallet is a wooden structure that the furniture's frame sits on. It's little more than a box really, but it keeps the legs from damage during shipping. Chair and sofa legs are the weak link in construction. They're quite sturdy holding vertical weight, but horizontal movement, such as you would find on a container ship sloshing through the waves, loosens the joints. Owners get quite unhappy when they uncrate their prized possession and find that it wobbles. Francesco came up with the solution preventing that, and it's proved quite successful."

While Ogilvy spoke, I stepped behind the sofa and found an area where the layers of plastic permitted a peek of Giuseppe Vega's fine craftsmanship in the delicately rolled arms and the tufted gray-green leather back. The smooth seat was outlined with what looked like bronze brads. The overall effect was spectacular.

"There you see before you a wonderful example of the work produced here," Ogilvy said. "Mr. Katzen demanded specific details in this remarkable sofa, and he got those specific details in the finished product." He flipped open the folder he carried and removed a photograph of a sofa that had all but fallen apart. "This is what Mr. Katzen brought to us. A wreck, wouldn't you say?"

A careful look showed one leg broken, aged dry leather ripped in several places exposing the white padding, and a twist in the frame as if the sofa fell from a great height. "I'm surprised it could be saved," I said.

"That was exactly the issue I raised with the client. It couldn't be saved. We used the broken pieces to make an exact pattern of the original. Katzen was pleased with that, but wanted all wood from the original frame, plus the original brads, put aside, so that he could document the project. We complied, of course. In the end, everyone seemed pleased with the result." Ogilvy put the picture away. "One of the pleasures of working here is to be around such quality. Giuseppe is a genius."

"You said Katzen came in yelling. Doesn't sound like he was happy."

"Katzen is a nervous man. Jittery. When he takes time to relax on his new sofa, I hope he calms down," the office manager said proudly, as two men arrived carrying parts of the shipping crate. "The ends of the shipping crate. Double walled as you can see," Ogilvy announced as the men began screwing one of the end pieces to the base of the pallet. "When they attach the front and back pieces and put on the top, the sofa will be protected from all possible damage in transit. The only thing we can't protect against is the ship going down."

"What's the final destination?"

"That I don't know. Mr. Katzen wasn't divulging that information. Very unusual, I admit, since our price estimates include delivery, but when I presented him with a shipping manifest, he said he would take the piece from here as soon as crating was finished. He wants one last look before we screw on the top."

"And you have no idea where he's taking it?"

"None. He did say he was moving out of his apartment today. That's why he was antsy when he came. He'd packed his old place and wanted to make certain the sofa was ready, so he could leave town. Understandable, don't you think? Lots of moving parts that can drive a man crazy."

I looked inside the double walled end piece attached to the pallet as the men worked attaching the other end. My hand easily fit inside the space between the two walls.

"What's the point?" I asked.

"Strength," Ogilvy said. "It's not uncommon for the outside wall to get cracked or splintered during transit. A shattered piece of sharp wood could easily pierce the leather and ruin the finished product. It's *very* uncommon for the inner wall to suffer damage."

"Francesco's idea?" I asked.

"That's right," Ogilvy said, adding, "You look like something is bothering you."

"Just thinking," I said, wondering if Katzen and Francesco were building the perfect smuggling container. "The double walls, the box on the bottom, all places someone might add things for transit. Things they didn't want discovered."

"You're talking about contraband," Ogilvy said.

"I'm talking stolen paintings," I said. "Remove a painting from its ornate frame and it would easily fit between the double walls. Ones cut from their frames could be rolled and slipped inside the box on the bottom. A clever thief might ship everything stolen from the Gardner in this one shipment. The person taking delivery would be a millionaire several times over."

"Impossible," Ogilvy defended. "This is a respectable shop. Giuseppe Vega would never allow such a thing.

"I'm not talking about Giuseppe. I'm talking about Francesco and Katzen. Did Francesco send a shipment here from Boston sometime after March eighteenth?"

"Shipments come and go every day. I really don't think . . ."

"Would you check your records?" I asked. "That would solve the matter."

Ogilvy tucked the folder under one arm and headed back to his desk where he sat and pulled up the recent shipping manifests on his computer monitor. I stood behind him, scanning the screen as he scrolled through the pages. Recorded shipments from March, April, May and part of June slid across the screen. On March 19 a shipment left from Newark Liberty International Airport in New Jersey. That was the only shipment from the US.

"What was delivered?" I asked pointing to the March 19 date.

Ogilvy's finger slid across the screen. "Twenty-five yards of Schumacher's Feather Cream in pale blue. I remember the order distinctly. A customer wanted an American southwestern look for some pieces in her sunroom."

I sank as if someone had doubled gravity. "That's it?"

"That's all there is. You can see the deliveries for yourself."

I studied the screen. "What about the column over here?"

"Those are shipments from here, not deliveries." Ogilvy studied the entries. "This one deals with that troublesome French fabric I've been trying to get here in the shop for weeks. I try not to deal with boutique fabric designers, but they had what the customer wanted. They sent the wrong color. The shipment recorded here on March twelve indicates I sent it back with instructions to correct the order. To date, it hasn't arrived."

"There's a second shipment out of here on the twelfth. It doesn't say what was shipped or to where. You didn't note any details. Why?" I asked.

"Because I didn't have any details," Ogilvy said. "That shipment was handled by Francesco. I just assumed he was testing out another improvement on his crate designs. I told you he had an interest in making that part of the business more efficient."

"He tried out his designs often with similar shipments lacking similar details?"

"When he thought he'd devised an improvement. Yes. Anything that provided better service to our clients and saved with operating expenses was always welcome. But you're talking about the possibility of shipping contraband. I will vouch for Giuseppe and Francesco as having nothing to do with such a thing, I will not vouch for Hans Katzen." Ogilvy looked around to see if anyone was listening. "Sizing people up is part of my job, you understand. The way they talk about furniture and fabrics and costs gives me some idea if the project they wish to undertake is really something they can comfortably afford. Bad reputations for a shop such as ours begin when the client is pleased with the end result but struggles to pay for it. It's much better for all concerned to order a less expensive fabric or, in the case of Mr. Katzen, opt for something other than a complete rebuild. That's a long way of saying that when he came in with the project, he did not exude confidence that he had the means to pay for such an expensive effort. In fact, I don't think he understood what he was getting into in terms of cost. I simply wasn't sure he could afford it. The amount of fine quality leather, the special order fasteners and lumber and linen alone cost in the thousands. I confess that Mr. Katzen did not immediately strike me as a man of means, so when he placed the order for the sofa and left the required deposit, I followed him to see where he might go. You can understand my apprehension. A significant amount of time and money would be tied up in a project such as this. I wanted assurances that Mr. Katzen lived in a suitable domicile to accommodate such a fine piece of furniture. I was greatly disappointed."

"His villa was too small?" I quipped.

The office manager frowned. "His villa was an apartment in the modern city of Latina about an hour south of here. Not only an apartment, but in a relatively new high-rise no less. Imagine, a modern apartment for a classic piece of furniture such as this. Mussolini ordered several of those modern towns built throughout the country. It was his vision to make Italy up to date with the rest of world. Too bad he didn't have any taste. Frankly, I thought that very thing about Mr. Katzen. Why would he order a very expensive period piece of furniture when he lived in an apartment building made of tacky steel and glass? It made no sense then, and it doesn't make sense now. I'm not entirely sure that the sofa will even fit in the elevator. Of course, I didn't tell him that, as I didn't want him to know I'd followed him."

I asked for Katzen's address and wrote it down. "Having those thoughts makes me wonder why you agreed to the project."

"Francesco said I'd been hired to manage such special projects and that I should accept this one as a professional challenge. Put that way, I couldn't really say no."

"Did Francesco have anything else to do with the project?"

The office manager shook his head. "Not to my knowledge. Katzen came in a time or two with drawings. I couldn't swear, but they looked like Francesco's work. He has a certain style, a certain flair when he sketches anything. Even the shipping crates he drew to show off his new idea of putting a divider down the middle was distinctively Francesco. Katzen's drawings had that flair."

"Did you ever see Francesco and Katzen together?"

"No."

"How about Leonardo Severino and Francesco?"

"Never heard of Severino," Ogilvy said.

I jotted my phone number on a piece of paper. "I want to know when Katzen shows up to take delivery," I said.

"I think I can manage that," Ogilvy said. "Sometime today, I'm sure of that."

I thanked him and headed for my car. The drive south to Latina took me through patches of farmland and small vineyards interspersed with drab apartment buildings constructed close to the highway. Laundry hung from many of the balconies creating a fluttering patchwork that waved as I sped by.

I drove for an hour before seeing the first sign for Latina. I turned off the highway onto a two-lane road that funneled into a medium-sized city, which, at first glance, had little to recommend it. Its modern and drab shopping center looked right out of the 1950s. It would have been right at home beside the miles of strip malls built in Florida. Past the shopping mall, a row of mid-rise apartment buildings framed the street, many with small yards sprinkled with children's toys. Mussolini apparently had a vision but very little taste.

I turned right at the first sign for Torre Pontina, a once gleaming glass and metal skyscraper that looked like it belonged on the bad side of downtown Akron. I followed the arrows past the underground parking garage thinking that the box truck couldn't pass under the low ceiling. I spotted it parked in the semicircle that curved along the front of the apartment complex. I pulled into an empty space across the street and shut off the engine.

It took nearly half an hour for the front door to open. Severino set a suitcase in the opening so the door couldn't close, then he and Katzen stepped out, both carrying cardboard boxes that looked heavy. They were all business, no chatter between them. Severino opened the back of the truck and slid in their loads next to other packed boxes pushed all the way to the front. There weren't many, maybe a dozen boxes in all. I saw no stacked furniture or hanging clothes. A truck this size could easily carry the contents of a good-sized apartment or the leather sofa back at Giuseppe's.

These guys had something else in mind, and it began to show itself when Severino rushed back inside. Katzen followed. In seconds, they hauled out a large flat object wrapped in moving quilts supplied by companies like U-Haul. *Christ in the Sea of Galilee* was a large canvas so they could have been carrying that. They could also be carrying a mirror or a marble tabletop. My guess went with the painting.

I checked the urge to rush the truck and held back to see what they would do next. Carefully, they loaded the object into the truck on edge and secured it to the side with straps. While Katzen convinced himself that it wouldn't move, Severino retrieved the suitcase and set it in the truck. He closed the back doors, got behind the wheel beside his partner and drove off.

Moving day had begun.

I eased into a line of cars behind Severino and followed him as he maneuvered through the traffic with the confidence of a driver who'd made the trip many times. In just over an hour, we were off of the highway and hostage to Rome's narrow streets. Via Merulana provided some space, still the traffic snailed along to the intersection of Via

Cavouri, which deposited us at the base of Santa Maria Maggiore where local police officials waved their arms making terrible traffic worse.

Severino snaked through the congestion, then turned right toward Statzione Roma Termini. I tried to follow, but the stiff arm of the police held back traffic for long enough that when I did make the turn, the box truck was nowhere to be seen.

I drove to the train station parking lot and circled past the waiting buses, looking for the truck. A harsh horn blasted from an angry bus driver, sent me wheeling around the corner. I felt pushed along in the churning flow of traffic. There was nowhere to stop, nothing to do but inch forward, which was the speed of my investigation. However, something Peter Garcetti said about my father swirled in my brain. *He is to be admired for setting things in motion then stepping back into the shadows.* I wondered if Wilhelm really had set all of this in motion. Was he the B of the note threatening Francesco? Or was someone else behind it? Peter Garcetti, maybe? How could either one of them arrange access to the Gardner so Francesco could remove a large Rembrandt from the wall, measure and photograph it? Was the answer in the *Art World* article? I decided to find out and drove to my hotel to work the phone. After two calls, I had the person I wanted.

Chapter Sixteen

Molly Brennan's biographical sketch at the end of her article stated that she lived in Boston and was a widely published freelance writer who specialized in the arts. I dialed the number the receptionist at *Art World* had given me. When a woman answered, I introduced myself and asked if she was the author of the Cavelli guitar article.

"I am," she answered warily. "I take it there's no problem."

"No, not at all. Why should there be?"

"Because nothing about that piece was normal. At least, for me. Other writers work that way, but I don't usually get involved with that sort of thing. It leaves a bad taste; you know what I mean?"

"I don't really," I admitted.

"Besides, that piece came out months ago. Why the interest now?" she asked.

"I'm tracking down leads to anyone who may be involved in the Gardner Museum robbery."

"The robbery?" she repeated, startled. "How could that article . . .?" She stopped. "You don't think that I had anything to do with it."

"No, I don't."

"Good, because I didn't. I told the police that when they asked me questions, and they seem satisfied that I am what I say I am, which is a freelance writer specializing in the visual arts. Painting, mostly. Eighteenth century mostly. I've done a few pieces over the years focusing on the Gardner, but never anything connected to music. It really is out of my area of expertise."

"Then, how did you get the idea for the Cavelli article?" I asked.

"It wasn't my idea," Miss Brennan said. "I'm a little embarrassed to say that it wasn't really entirely my article. That's what I mean about this process not being normal. The research for the piece was already done as was the slant someone wanted. How might this rare old instrument be salvaged? That sort of thing. All I had to do was make a pitch to *Art World* and then crank out a draft. I did, the publisher liked the idea, and we were off and running."

"Who made the pitch to you?" I asked.

"I'd have to dig in my files to tell you that."

"Does the name Wilhelm Barr ring a bell?"

"Of course. Anyone with an art background knows his exploits," she said. "Nasty business from a nasty man, if what I know is true."

"Then, he wasn't the man who suggested the Cavelli article to you?"

"Barr?" Her voice shot up. "No. Not in a million years."

"He could have used a different name," I said. "He likely did. Could you describe the person who made the pitch?"

"Impossible," Miss Brennan said. "I never saw him. The pitch came in the mail. Once I agreed to write the piece, the research packet came in the mail a week or so later. When I had a contract from *Art World*, a cashier's check for five thousand arrived special delivery. *Art World* paid twenty-five hundred upon publication. It was the most I'd ever made on one article and the shortest amount of time spent working it into shape."

"Who signed the check for five thousand?" I asked.

"That I do know," Miss Brennan said. "As a freelancer, you have to keep track of your finances. Plus, I was a little suspicious of a check drawn on a foreign bank. The money was good, so I went along. Hans Katzen signed the check. Now that I think about it, he was also the man who pitched the article idea. Guess I don't need to call you back, huh?"

"No need," I said as the connection ended.

It was foolish to think that my father would have in any way identified himself as the one who pitched the Cavelli article idea to Molly Brennan. And the fact that Katzen's name was associated with the pitch and the signed check didn't bring me any closer to proving that Wilhelm or Peter Garcetti was involved in the Gardner robbery. But it reinforced the notion that the Gardner robbery was very well planned and begun with the Cavelli article.

I was thinking that Wilhelm would be drawn to such an opening gambit when my cell phone rang. Brody Flynn was on the other end.

"Things are heating up," Brody said when the poor connection stopped crackling. "Not boiling over, but definitely getting hot."

"The Howard Moss pull back," I surmised.

"Who told you? Clair Bowman? I don't know what I'm looking forward to more, getting her out of my hair or having a root canal? I'm leaning toward the root canal, no Novocain. Just start drilling."

"She's in a tough spot, Brody."

"She's paying your freight; you've got to defend her."

"Her hunch about the phony Aldo Conte might turn out to be right."

"You've got something?"

"I do. Francesco Vega is working for a man named Hans Katzen. He was the name behind getting the *Art World* article about the Cavelli guitar published. I say 'name' because he's a front. He's working for someone else."

"Who put him up to it?"

"Could be my father," I said calmly. "I'm not one hundred percent sure, but I'm beginning to warm to the possibility. Katzen is the man everyone sees. Francesco Vega and Silvio Conte do the dirty work, and Wilhelm Barr stays behind the scenes raking in the profits once he sells the artwork. It's the way he works."

"Got any proof?" Brody asked.

"Not yet. But see how this fits with what you have. The *Art World* article gets Francesco special treatment into the Gardner where he takes detailed photographs and measurements of one of the Rembrandts. Charles Raskin either helped him or looked the other way while Francesco and Angela did their work. Once they have the details, Francesco heads back to his studio in Rome and paints a copy. Art Recovery International gets wind that the Rembrandt is for sale on the black market."

"You mean a forgery is for sale."

"That's right."

"Wilhelm has no history of selling forgeries," Brody said.

"I realize that's a problem," I said. "That's one reason I'm not completely convinced he's involved in any of this. Pointing the finger at him could be something told to me to put me off track."

"Who did the telling?"

"Peter Garcetti. Have you ruled him out?"

"No one is out," Brody said. "That is, if they're alive. JoJo Weems was found stuffed in the trunk of a stolen car and parked in front of Angela Ricci's house. One shot to the head just like Angela."

"Who'd want to take out one of Nick Bianchi's bodyguards?" I asked. "I saw him at Sully's a few days ago acting big, strong and tough."

"Well, he ain't tough no more," Brody quipped. "Seems JoJo and Angela were chummy. One of the neighbors identified photographs of Nick, JoJo, and Francesco as recent visitors coming and going with great frequency."

"Nick wouldn't take too kindly to one of his guards screwing his lady. D'you think he found out and took JoJo down?"

"I think he found out that JoJo and Francesco both were screwing his lady. Nick is like a bowling ball in a bag of glass when he's been wronged. He likes breaking things. Which is why I'm calling, Theo. Nick is on his way to Rome. Francesco Vega is on his radar screen. Nick tore this city upside down looking for him, now he's headed your way. That puts you and Nick on a collision course looking for Francesco Vega. Nick's got friends in Rome, Theo. Be careful. Peter Garcetti is already there setting things up for Nick."

Setting things up sounded an awfully lot like setting me up, I thought and wondered if Peter had done just that with his show of family tenderness with his son. Was his display of affection toward Lia meant to distract me? Soften me up? Catch me off guard?

"You still there?" Brody asked.

"Yeah, thinking that's all."

"Well, think about this. When we had Nick in for questioning about JoJo and Raskin . . ."

"Raskin?" I asked, cutting him off. "What's up with him?"

"He's missing. As expected, Nick denied any knowledge of who killed JoJo or where Raskin might be hiding. The only thing he kept saying was that he was sorry that Angela never got to her meeting at the Five Horses with Purdy. That name mean anything to you?"

"It means we now know who killed Angela," I said.

"I thought the same. Angela, JoJo, and maybe you next. Keep alert, Theo. I'm a little far away to be of any help."

"Thanks for the tip, Brody," I said and rung off.

Nick Bianchi entering the mix left a bad taste. In the foul mood I was in, I wanted to chew him up and spit him out. Since he wasn't near, I decided instead to roust Silvio Conte. If need be, to punish him until he told me the truth. At this point, I wasn't particular about which truth. Did he know who Katzen worked for? Did he know where Francesco was? Did he know if my father was pulling the strings?

Take your pick, Silvio, but stop the lies.

Chapter Seventeen

I left my hotel and in half an hour, fell in behind a group of nuns walking swiftly, bowed heads covered in white veils and collars, hands clasped in front entering the convent church of Santa Brigida, a solemn picture of order. Church bells faded as I rounded the corner and ran to silence when I climbed the steps to the front door of Villa Conte. I knocked, surprised that Aldo Conte was the one who answered.

"I need to speak with Silvio," I said, making it clear this was not a social call.

"He's not here. The housekeeper and nanny have the day off. I'm here by myself. What is it you want?" Aldo asked with cold distaste.

"Where is he?" I snapped. When I didn't get an answer, I said, "I know about the Stradivarius and the insurance fraud. With one phone call, I can have that investigation reopened."

Aldo's expression twisted in stunned disbelief. "I don't think there's really anything to talk about," he said, pushing the door.

I stuck my hand out and kept him from closing it. "Francesco and your son tried to be tough guys to gain entry into the Garcetti family. When that failed, Francesco ran a little wild and ended up pretending to be you. If he stole the Gardner paintings, I don't know, but he stole a Stradivarius, so why not think big and hit the Gardner? That's what's to talk about, Mr. Conte. That and your involvement in all this," I said and bulled my way inside.

Conte stood frozen, then slowly like a beaten man, led the way upstairs into a second-floor art gallery whose walls were lined with what I took to be family portraits interspersed with paintings of the Apostles and triptychs of the Madonna and child whose innocence seemed out of place among the stern-looking portraits. An impressive display of marble busts completed the room's holdings. Looking over the gallery tested the limits of excess. In the center of the room on either side of a low ornate coffee table two brocade loveseats faced each other. Aldo sat in one, I the other. He removed a pipe from his jacket pocket, filled it with tobacco, and lit it. The smoke rose and disappeared above his head.

"I spend a lot of time in this room. It's comforting, relaxing. I feel as if my ancestors are looking down at me, judging my life without saying a word." He motioned to the far end of the gallery where a full-figured portrait of a stately gentleman looked out in our direction. "Marcus Conte," Aldo said. "The skilled genius who started it all. I seek out approval in the expressions found in each portrait and in their comforting, never blinking eyes. Eyes that I honestly believe would produce tears if somehow I failed to maintain the Conte tradition. That is a fear I live with, you understand. Through my incompetence or mis-management or stupidity, I would cause the end of the Conte legacy. Never mind that at my age, I cannot produce the number or quality of instruments that I did in my youth. What is to be done? Neither my son nor my daughter can make a Conte violin. Lia can play them, Silvio can make what looks like one, but it doesn't sound like a Conte. Our family hope lies with Marcus, my dear grandson. He needs to be given the chance to succeed. He needs the chance to experience growing up in this house with these ancestors looking approvingly at his develop-ment." He relit his pipe. "A few years ago, it looked like that might not be possible. Villa Conte was in grave economic trouble. Taxes, re-pairs." Conte shrugged. "The amounts were staggering."

"So, you decide to file a false insurance claim," I offered.

"Not at first," Conte said. "I didn't really know what I had in mind, only that I had to do something. Selling some of our collections seemed the best solution, but those activities take time for appraisals and then auctions. I didn't have that much time, and I certainly didn't want it known that we were in financial trouble. So, any items up for sale had to be kept in the strictest confidence. I've seen what happens to families fallen on hard times. First, they move to the top floor and open their villas to paying guests. If that doesn't produce enough income, they sell their prized possessions. It's a downward spiral since tourists only want to pay to see the treasures, which are now in the hands of the auction house. Eventually, the estate goes on the block, and the once proud family spends the rest of their lives blaming each other for their ruin."

"You paint a grim picture," I said.

"It's grim, and it's accurate." Conte rose from his seat and walked to the loggia, looking out the arched windows at the city before him. "The irony of all this, you understand, is that in Italy in general and in Rome in particular, everyday life is not grim at all. It is a magnificent gift, an always changing wonder that absorbs all who live here. You cannot escape the delights, one after the other, each one more impressive than the last. Right here between Villa Conte and my violin shop are buildings Michelangelo designed, sculptures by Bernini and frescos painted by Caravaggio. Beautiful, not grim at all." Conte turned back to me. "Who wouldn't fight to keep such a life?"

"Tell me what happened," I coaxed.

"What happened is that for once in his life, Silvio took the lead. He and Francesco worked it all out. Silvio left a door ajar so Francesco could come in after we were all asleep. The Stradivarius was insured for the greatest amount, so it was the obvious choice. I want you to understand that I had nothing to do with the initial planning. I was as shocked as anyone when I woke up that morning to find that the Strad was gone."

"But it didn't go far," I said.

"No. I didn't realize that the real reason Silvio and Francesco wanted the violin was to buy their way into *Don* Roberto's good graces. He rejected their gift, you understand, and offered to give the piece back to me. I'd already begun the process of claiming the insurance money and didn't think it wise to bring the instrument home. Besides, I didn't want it discovered that Silvio, my own son, was involved. So, I turned down *Don* Roberto's generous offer and kept silent."

"Did all involved keep quiet?" I asked.

"I'm not sure what you mean," Conte said, returning to his seat.

"I mean honor among thieves is a myth. Given your son's history with you and Francesco's record, it doesn't take much to imagine that one or both of them threatened to expose you unless you bent to their wishes." When Conte blanched, I knew I'd hit a nerve. "What did they want?"

"It wasn't Silvio, really. We were getting along. Lia, Silvio, and me we were making our life together work. Besides, we had the insurance money. Our debts were paid, but then, things began to change. Someone got to Francesco. That's the only thing that makes sense. One day he was his carefree self, the next day he was this very serious, very driven man I couldn't recognize. I didn't want to be around him."

"But you took him in as an apprentice," I reminded him.

"His apprenticeship was their demand. I never would have taken him otherwise. I took Francesco into my shop after he threatened to expose my involvement in the insurance claim. However, I made sure he stayed out of the way. Which was fine for him, since he wasn't there to learn about violin making. He wanted to observe me dealing with customers so that when the time came, he could behave like a professional. Why he wanted to learn how a professional behaved, I did not know until I heard about the museum's robbery and that my name was associated with it. Aldo Conte suspected of being a thief? I was shocked, you understand. Shocked and deeply saddened."

"It's one thing to gain access to the museum, quite another to rob it. Do you think either Silvio or Francesco actually stole those paintings?"

"Of course not," he said without hesitation. "For one thing, Silvio never left Rome."

"Maybe he did his part downstairs in the painter's studio."

"Silvio is not an artist."

"Francesco, then. I saw the detail of the stretchers they made. I found the formulas for mixing pigments. There's even a crude attempt to copy *Christ in the Storm of Galilee*. Who hired him to paint that?"

"I don't know. I know only that Silvio would not be part of selling forgeries."

"He's not a choir boy, Mr. Conte. Maybe it's time you zeroed in on that fact. He attacked you and stole a rare violin. Who's to say what he might do next?"

"It's Francesco. He's behind it all," Conte said bitterly. "I warned Silvio to stay away from him, but he wouldn't listen."

"Francesco is not the brains for this, Mr. Conte. Someone is giving the orders, and Francesco and your son are following them. I need to know who that person is."

"I don't know."

"Let's start with the Garcettis. *Don* Roberto, Vincent, and Pietro."

"*Don* Roberto is dead; Vincent is in prison and Pietro is the father of Lia's child. None of them could be involved."

"Why not?"

"I told you, *Don* Roberto is dead, Vincent is in prison, and Pietro is part of my family."

"Vincent still runs his operation from prison. He puts out orders, and they get carried out. Prison walls are not high or thick enough to prevent that."

Conte puffed on his pipe as if dredging up a memory. "I know he was hurt and angry that he never got to visit his dying father. The prison officials would not allow it. Even *Don* Roberto's funeral, Vincent was not allowed to attend. Pietro said his father was like a crazy animal when he heard that he could not come to the funeral. No one was safe to be around him, but does that mean he would then plan to rob a museum of some paintings? Why?"

"To trade them for his freedom," I offered. "It's been done before. The museum gets back its stolen artwork and the thief gets out of prison. Everybody wins. Especially when there's a safe distance between the man planning the robbery and those carrying it out. I know Francesco and Silvio were involved. The artist's studio downstairs proves that. I also know their contact was Hans Katzen."

Conte seemed puzzled. "Katzen?"

"Do you know the name?"

"No. I was just thinking that he might have been part of a small group Pietro organized for a short trip to Nice last summer. But that was not the name."

"Any ideas?" I asked.

"Woods, Weeds . . ."

"Weems? JoJo Weems?"

"That's right. Weems. He and Nicolas Bianchi went to Nice on business with Pietro."

"A show of force to Niles Huygens," I said.

"I don't know what it was," Conte said. "They weren't gone long. I had the impression the meeting went the way Pietro wanted. He's a very determined man. I'm sure you still want to claim that either

Vincent or Pietro Garcetti are the masterminds of the Gardner robbery. I tell you again, it's not so. Vincent and I are about the same age. Over the years, we talked about our lives, our families. It surprised me how much we were a like."

Conte could be doing time just like Garcetti, I thought but didn't say it. Instead, I asked, "In what way?"

"In the way we worried about our sons. Pietro was not happy growing up. He wanted to be a man. The things of boys, teasing girls, sports, school, all bored him. He did not run the Boston streets like Silvio did here in Roma, but Vincent worried that he might, so Pietro was enrolled in boarding school. Strict discipline. Strict hours. Everything strict. Once he stopped fighting the rules, once he figured out how to work the rules to his advantage, Pietro began to like his surroundings and stopped hating his father for putting him in such a place. When he graduated, he went on to college and eventually to graduate school. He wanted to learn the bones of business. What companies fail? Why? What could have been done to prevent the failure? Vincent was proud. Not only had his son gone to college, he'd gotten his MBA from an Ivy League school. He married a girl he'd met at Dartmouth. They started a family, and Pietro began work helping his father run the Boston businesses. I can imagine how Vincent felt. My heart soared when Silvio said he wanted to continue the Conte name, making fine instruments. Both Vincent and I ended up disappointed."

I knew about Silvio and asked how Peter Garcetti had disappointed his father.

"Changes," Conte said. "That's what Pietro wanted to make. Make the businesses modern. Vincent didn't want changes. He didn't want modern. He wanted to run things like he'd run things for many years, the way *Don* Roberto had taught him. That was the battle. That was their war." Conte relit his pipe and watched the smoke curl. "During the worst times, Pietro took refuge here with *Don* Roberto. That is when he began taking an interest in Lia. I cautioned her about his marriage and commitments in Boston. He would never give up what he had there. None of what I said mattered. Pietro and Lia were going to build a life here. That is what they've done. Pietro would not risk all of that to gain his father's release."

"What makes you so sure?"

"Because Pietro does not want Vincent out of prison. Lia has not told me that and Pietro would never admit it, but that is the feeling I have based on my own son. If Silvio were the head of this house, he would not want me coming back to take over. He would want to stay in charge, and that is the situation Pietro finds himself in here in Roma. He is now the boss. He wants to stay the boss. You will have to find someone else behind the Gardner robbery if the motive is to get Vincent Garcetti released from prison. Now, if you'll excuse me, I need to get ready for Silvio's students. I'm helping him out today."

"Where is he?"

"At my shop. A customer is picking up his violin. We are trading responsibilities this afternoon. I am conducting a workshop on the finer points of making a violin, while Silvio tends to a customer picking up the instrument I repaired." Conte looked at his watch. "Silvio will be closing the shop soon. There's a café around the corner from my shop. If you miss Silvio at the shop, you may find him at the café."

Chapter Eighteen

Twenty minutes later, I turned on to via di Moretta and stopped across the street from Conte's violin shop. A light blue *Polizia di Stato* car was parked in front. One officer was taking a statement from a neatly dressed man wearing a sport coat and tie. The man nervously gestured into the shop with uncontrollable hands. A few curious on-lookers slowed but moved steadily on as if the police in front of a violin shop were an everyday occurrence. When I saw Sergeant Filippo through the shop window, I crossed the street and knocked on the glass to draw his attention. He seemed puzzled at first, then his expression brightened when he recognized me.

"*Dottore!*" He stood in the doorway looking very official in his uniform. "I think I would not see you again. How is it that I do? As I recall, you don't play the violin, and I cannot make one. Isn't that right? Yet, here you are at the violin shop."

"You have an excellent memory, sergeant," I said, extending my hand. "What's going on here?"

Filippo's grip was swift and professional. He pointed to the nerv-ous man making the statement. "A sad ending for that musician," the officer said. "He came to pick up his violin that *signor* Conte had re-paired only to find it in worse shape than when he dropped it off. I am no expert when it comes to musical instruments, *dottore*, but I would say with confidence that it is a total loss." Filippo seemed to study me for the first time. "You are simply passing by? Or do you have further business with the Conte family? More questions about Lia, yes?"

I shook my head. "No," I admitted. "I came to see Silvio. He was supposed to be here."

"He is," Filippo said, pointing. "He's in the back."

Filippo stepped aside and let me pass. Slouched on a wooden stool, his shoulders drooped, his back curved leaning against the wall sat Silvio. He didn't look up as Filippo and I moved around the workbench on which sat a violin with broken strings and a hole through the front large enough for a fist.

Filippo waved a hand toward the broken instrument. "The violin in question," he said grimly.

"What happened?" I asked.

"Nothing according to Silvio," the sergeant said. "He wouldn't have called the police to report anything. The man picking up his violin phoned us. He found Silvio near the back of the shop on the floor. His violin is where you see it, a broken mess, no? What do you think, *dottore*? I will tell you what I think. I think Silvio is not telling the truth. The Contes have a way about them when it comes to telling the truth. It is most difficult for them to get the words out. I think back to Aldo Conte and the theft of the Stradivarius. Did he report what really occurred the night it was stolen? I'm never sure that he did. And now, Silvio is suffering from a beating, but he says nothing happened. Even that man's lovely violin is fine. Strings broken? No. Hole in the front? Not that Silvio can see, because nothing happened here. I might as well go and make out my report," Sergeant Filippo said, leaning down toward Silvio until their faces were inches apart. "Silvio Conte, I give you one last chance. I have my pencil ready. Your statement, if you please. Who beat you and why?"

Silvio's eyes slowly focused on the sergeant. "I fell," he said without conviction. "I tripped and fell damaging our customer's violin. It was my fault. I'm sorry you had to come out for no reason."

Filippo sucked in a frustrating breath and stood to his full height. "Even though little meaning will be included in my report, it will be made out in triplicate as required." The sergeant scribbled something on a pad and handed me the paper. "My phone number, *dottore*. Should you learn anything from this young man, be good enough to call, yes?"

"Yes."

Outside, the two officers said something to the musician who trampled off, arms still waving. The officers got back in their police car and drove off leaving Silvio and me inside. Silvio shifted his position and winced like a man suffering.

"Broken rib?" I asked. "Laughing and breathing, they hurt like hell. But there's not much to laugh about at the moment. Who did this to you? And if you answer tripped and fell, I'll yank you off that stool and finish the job they started. Who did it?"

"Why don't you leave me alone?"

I reached over and jabbed Silvio under one arm. He cried out.

"No doubt about it," I said. "Broken ribs. Let me try poking you here."

Silvio swatted my hand and yelped like a child at the pain caused by his quick movement.

"Looks like a professional worked you over. Lots of heavy hits to the body. How did you like it?"

"I didn't."

"See? You're not so dumb after all. How many were there?"

Silvio studied the floor near his feet.

"What did they want, Silvio?" I waited and heard nothing. "All right, Silvio. Have it your way. I'm going around the corner to the café. I'm going to order a glass of wine. If you don't join me and answer some questions by the time I pay my bill, you can fight the big boys by yourself. From the looks of you, it won't be much of a fight."

I turned and walked out.

Café Lucifer was a narrow establishment with tables on both sides with a space for waiters to squeeze by in between. Halfway in was a small bar with stools and standing room. Outside under an awning flapping in the breeze were more tables. I sat at the corner table in full sun, soaking up the warmth. I ordered a glass of house white and enjoyed the sharp, cold, citrus taste as it slid down. Across the street, a boy kicked a soccer ball against the side wall of an apartment building. The rhythm of his kicks and the wine seemed to relax me. I had half a mind to gulp the rest of my drink, pay up, and dash off before Silvio had a chance to show up and complicate my life.

I didn't and he did, walking stiffly like a man in great pain. Gingerly, he sat down across from me. He leaned across the table, his eyes tiny black bullets shooting hatred my way.

"One thing I hate about Americans is that they always think they know everything. You. Angela Ricci. Pete Garcetti. You know it all, and you know nothing."

"Are you finished?"

Silvio ignored me as his anger flared. "You come to Roma looking for Francesco, and what have you found? Nothing. What have you learned? Nothing."

I pushed back from the table and stood. "All right. I'm finished."

"That's right. Go back to America. I'll take care of business on my own."

"By the looks of it, you've done a fine job so far. In a week, you ought to be able to take a deep breath without pain." I leaned across the table. "Grow up, Silvio. You're out of your league."

I turned to leave then stopped when Silvio called out. "He wanted to know where Lia took Marcus. He already knew the rest of it."

"The rest of what?" I demanded and turned back.

"Francesco's real business. The smuggling. He already knew when the stuff came in, when it went out. He knew Francesco shipped a painting to Rome. That's what he wanted. What he demanded."

Silvio's breathing was shallow and painful. "He wants *Christ in the Storm of Galilee* by nine o'clock tonight or he'll kill Marcus."

"He'll have to get him first," I said thinking back to the guns I saw on all Garcetti's movers. "Peter knows of the threat," I said and sat back down.

"How could he?"

"I don't know that," I admitted as the waiter took our order for a glass of wine for Silvio and a refill for me. "But he obviously wanted Lia and Marcus with him. He's got a small army downstairs pretending to be movers. Tell me about who beat you up? How many were there?"

"Just one."

"Did you recognize him?"

"No."

"Describe him."

"Short. Stocky. Strong and quick like a wrestler. Little finger on his right hand was missing."

"Tell me about the smuggling," I said.

"What are you going to do about Marcus?" Silvio demanded.

"I don't know yet," I said. "As long as the boy is safe, nothing. Tell me about the smuggling."

"It's nothing big. Something to do. Francesco started dabbling in moving counterfeit goods years ago, right after he started building shipping crates for his father. It was an opportunity to make some extra money. From time to time, I'd help out. Little stuff. Knockoff stuff. Cheap watches with Patek Philippe labels. Worthless handbags from Gucci. Every now and then some pills. No hard drugs. Just a little something to perk up your day."

"What was the setup?" I asked.

"Vega's shop was the setup," Silvio said. "It was perfect. Shipments came and went every day. All legit. Francesco decided to tinker with the shipping containers. With a divider, he could have a legal delivery on one side and an illegal one on the other. No one was the wiser."

"Did Giuseppe ever get suspicious?"

Silvio winced as he shook his head. "Never. Giuseppe never had a clue. Still doesn't. That was the beauty of it. The leather shop operated as normal with a bogus shipment here and there."

"What was your part?"

"Late at night, when the shop was closed, I'd help Francesco unload or load a shipment. Whatever he needed. Sometimes I build a special crate."

"Did you help Francesco unload the Gardner paintings?" I asked.

"No. That business was different," Silvio said. "Everything about that job was different. Once we signed on, we couldn't come and go as we wanted. We couldn't mess around. Everything was serious. Precise. Nothing could be left to chance. We had a guy giving orders."

"Hans Katzen?" I tossed out.

"Yes."

"Why did he pick you two?"

"I asked that very question," Silvio said. "Katzen said we were a good fit. We had the necessary skills. We'd stolen the Stradivarius. We knew how to ship contraband. We could do the job without much training. All we needed was to commit. That's the way he put it. We had to commit for the duration. From day one, it was serious focus all the way to the end, about five months."

"Why so long?"

"Setting things in motion took time. First came the article about the Cavelli, then Francesco had to get into the Gardner, I had to build an exact replica of the stretcher before Francesco could begin to paint the copy. The months went by fast."

The waiter set the wine down and hurried on.

"How'd Katzen know about the Stradivarius?"

"I asked that, too. He said he knew everything there was to know about me and Francesco. What he didn't know, he would find out. I shouldn't spend my energy asking any more questions."

"He wasn't going to tell you anything," I offered.

"That's right. He put a task in front of us, and we got to it. It was just like the military."

Wilhelm's military? I wondered. "Tell me about the moving parts," I coaxed.

Silvio drank half of his glass and let out a deep breath. "The easiest way to look at this," Silvio began, "is to think of the Gardener robbery as two thefts taking place at the same time. The one Francesco, Angela and I were part of was precise and focused. The other was carried out by amateurs acting like animals. We used the amateurs to our advantage so that Francesco could carry out of the building Rembrandt's *Christ in the Storm of Galilee*. The original was never cut from its stretcher like the Vermeer and some of the others. Getting the Rembrandt out was key. All along, getting that painting was our goal."

"Two robberies?" I mused.

"At the same time. Yes. 'A precise action' Katzen called it."

"Why focus on that one painting?" I asked.

"Money. It's a one-of-a-kind seascape. Never be another one. It had to arrive here in perfect condition, or the deal was off. That's why Katzen trained us like we were military. No screwing around. Millions of dollars were riding on us doing everything right."

I thought back to the empty frames hanging on the Dutch Room walls when I interviewed Charles Raskin. I mentioned them to Silvio and said, "Somebody's not playing with a full deck. I've been to the Gardner since the robbery and seen the empty frames."

A flash of pride darting across Silvio's expression. "Genius, don't you think? The entire operation was genius."

"Walk me through it," I said.

"You need to start with the article about the Cavelli guitar. I needed specifics before I could make an exact copy of the stretcher. Its construction and fit had to be precise or it would be spotted as a fake. Francesco pretending to be Aldo Conte got me those specifics."

"That explains the photographs Francesco had in his notebook of the back of the canvas," I said.

"That's right. How else could we get measurements and photographs of the Rembrandt without drawing attention to our purpose? You can't simply walk into the museum with a camera and a laser measuring tape. But if you were Aldo Conte invited to examine the Cavelli guitar for possible repair, then questions wouldn't be asked. You'd be expected to come with a camera and tape. In addition to size, I needed to see the kind of wood used in the original, the heft of the linen and how it was attached to the stretcher. What kind of corner joints did Rembrandt use? How much overlap did he allow when he tacked the fabric to the wood? What was the spacing of the tacks? Francesco's job was to get me measurements and photographs so that I could answer all those questions. Once I got them, I could easily build an exact copy of the stretcher that looked identical to the one Rembrandt used in the sixteen hundreds."

"An expert could easily see that the wood you used wasn't from that period."

"Of course, they could," Silvio admitted with a wry smile. "That's where the Flemish Baroque sofa in need of reconstruction came in. Artists often used reclaimed wood for stretchers and frames. Not because they were trying to fool anyone, but because they were poor starving artists. They built stretchers from what they could salvage.

Old furniture was a very good source, and Katzen found the perfect piece. After Francesco's father took the sofa apart, I claimed all the wood I needed for the stretcher. I also reused some of the original tacks to secure the linen. When I was done, an expert could not tell the difference from the original. In fact, the museum people never questioned the authenticity of the stretcher. They were just sick nothing was in it."

"Building a stretcher that fools an expert is one thing, copying a Rembrandt that fools experts is an entirely different matter," I said. "I doubt Francesco has that kind of talent. Few do."

"We weren't trying to fool experts with a completely forged painting," Silvio said. "For weeks, Francesco focused on the edges of the canvas, that part left behind *if* it had been cut from the stretcher. The Gardner experts would be examining those edges attached to a perfect stretcher, not a completed forgery. Keep in mind, beside our Rembrandt was a Vermeer that had been cut from its stretcher. Katzen knew when they saw both, the museum folks would think both had been treated in the same fashion."

I thought back to Francesco's studio where I'd seen the rough copy of *Christ in the Storm of Galilee* with its amateurish center giving way to more skill along the edges. Francesco was clearly experimenting with technique, honing his skills.

"What happened when he finished the forgery?" I asked.

"When dry, we shipped it to Boston."

"Walk me through the robbery," I said.

Silvio sipped his wine. "Francesco and Angela drove a van to the museum and waited for the others. Katzen never told us who the two men dressed as members of the Boston police were, not that it mattered. All we needed to know was the time they planned to hit the museum. When Francesco saw them go inside, he and Angela carried the forgery up to the second floor. While the guards were being tied up in the basement, Francesco and Angela switched paintings and rehung the fake Rembrandt. By the time they got the original into their van and started driving to New Jersey, the other robbers left the basement and were upstairs sacking the place."

"The success of your scheme depends on the other robbers cutting the forgery from its stretcher and making off with it," I said. "How did you know they would do that?"

"Katzen said they would."

"Do you mean he was giving them orders, too?"

"I don't know, maybe. Maybe he had an informant. All I know is that everything Katzen said would happen, happened exactly the way he said it would. He said the other robbers had a list and that the Rembrandt and Vermeer were at the top of the list. The robber's instructions were to cut the large canvases out of their frames, roll them up and carry out the smaller pieces."

"Where did they take them?"

"I don't know. Francesco and Angela drove to a New Jersey airport where a shipment of fabric was being held in storage. Francesco brought the fabric back to Rome with him and shipped the Rembrandt in the crate. Right after that, Francesco disappeared for good."

"You mean he'd gone missing before?"

"Yes. Right after he came back from measuring the Cavelli. He was nervous when he came home. Antsy. I told him to snap out of it, that we had work to do if we were to keep on schedule. It didn't matter. Before I knew it, Francesco disappeared for a week or so."

That would explain why Clair Bowman could make contact, I thought. "Where did he go?" I asked.

"I don't know. But I'm almost certain he was upset that Angela was our Boston contact. Katzen promised someone would be there to help out. He never said who."

"How did Katzen explain Angela's involvement?"

"Katzen gave orders, not explanations. When Francesco cleared his head and came back, we got to work."

"Did you know that Katzen and Severino have been watching Francesco's apartment?" I touched the bruise around my eye. "They gave me this when they found me inside."

"What were you doing there?"

"Looking for a notebook. I found it in the paint studio at the back of your workshop. B left a note warning Francesco not to screw up again. Any idea who B is?"

Silvio shook his head.

"Does the name Barr mean anything to you?"

"Should it?"

"Someone was giving Katzen orders."

"I don't know who that was. I know Katzen was afraid of him. He never mentioned a name. He just said that none of us would be happy if we disappointed the man calling the shots."

"Did you know that Katzen was picking up the leather sofa later today?"

"No."

"Do you know where he plans to ship it?"

"No. He paid me and that was the last I had any contact. I know nothing else," Silvio said.

"I understand your use of the wood to make an exact copy of the stretcher, but once that was achieved, why go ahead and finish the sofa?"

"Customs. Francesco said that less than five percent of the Vega leather shipments were ever inspected. But if customs did open the crate, they would only find a beautiful piece of furniture and nothing else. The Rembrandt would be hidden in a side panel specially designed by Francesco."

"Is that where the painting is now?" I asked.

"I don't know. When Francesco disappeared, I lost all contact."

"The man who beat you, what else did he want other than the painting?"

"He wanted Katzen's address. He was on his way there next."

"He's already gone from Latina," I said. "I was just there."

"Katzen has another place in the city down by the train station." Silvio gave me the address. "It's on the first floor of an apartment building."

"Let's go," I said, standing.

"Me? Why?"

"Because I don't trust you, Silvio and I wouldn't want to walk into a trap."

"But I'm telling you the truth."

I tossed some bills on the table. "You coming? Or do I have to drag you?"

Chapter Nineteen

Silvio's car was behind the violin shop. He winced each time he shifted gears or cranked the steering wheel. The area surrounding the train station pulsed with rushing crowds pulling luggage or wilting under the weight of backpacks.

"What does Lia have to do with any of this?" I asked as Silvio drove one block past the station and painfully muscled the wheel to the right.

"Nothing."

"Hard to believe," I said. "You live in the same house. You work in the same house. She must have had some idea something was up, something was different."

"Marcus requires a lot of energy," Silvio said. "Her focus, her attention is always on Marcus first, Peter second. My comings and goings came in a distant third."

"Her focus is on Peter even though he has a wife and four kids in Boston? He's not going to give up what he has there."

"Lia understands that. Whose life is perfect?"

The street in front of the apartment building was clogged with parked cars. Silvio stopped at the end of the street, then pulled two wheels onto the sidewalk. He shut off the ignition. I got out of the car, walked around to the driver's side, and opened the door.

"You lead the way," I said as Silvio strained to get to his feet.

As we made our way under the awning that led to the front door, I wondered why Katzen needed a second address. If Wilhelm was giving the orders, was this where he'd been hiding? This was a modest apartment building, not the style Wilhelm usually demanded. Or was it where Francesco hid?

Through the security glass, I could see an elevator and a long narrow hallway past it. An elderly woman stepped out when the elevator doors creaked open and walked toward me.

"Act like a rental agent," I said to Silvio. "Talk up the virtues of living here. Quickly."

Silvio fell in line, chattering like a salesman. I nodded. I smiled, acting like I understood every word. I examined the quality he spoke of and beamed at the woman when she stepped past us. I kept the door from closing and went inside, Silvio leading the way down the hall. At the end, a door stood partially open, the jamb splintered at the lock.

I pulled the Ruger from my jacket pocket and eased the door open into the living room that had seen better days. Cushions from the small sofa were tossed on the floor beside a broken table lamp. A short hallway led to the bedroom where I found the man's body. He was fully dressed on the floor at the foot of the bed.

"Do you know him?" I asked Silvio as I rolled Leonardo Severino onto his side. He'd been shot once in his forehead.

"He was one of *Don* Roberto's trusted men. He works for Peter Garcetti now."

"You mean he did," I corrected and checked for rigor mortis. "He's been dead for hours," I said. "The man who beat you didn't do this. He may have come here looking for the painting, but by then Severino was already dead."

"Why kill him?" Silvio said. "Who would want to?"

"I don't know," I said, thinking back to following the box truck from Latina to the train station where I lost sight of it. Did Hans Katzen kill Severino? Why would he? "We'd better get out of here," I said, stepping around Silvio. Before I reached the front door, my ringing phone startled me.

"Hello?"

"You asked me to tell you when Mr. Katzen was arriving to pick up the sofa. His friend Severino just phoned with wonderful news. Francesco is coming with them this evening. They might be a bit late but not to worry because Francesco has keys. He will lock up. Isn't that wonderful?" Ogilvy said. "The sofa leaves and Francesco returns. Ying and yang, don't you think? The rhythm of the universe."

"Who did you say phoned?" I asked.

"Mr. Severino. I took the call a few minutes ago."

"And he was in good spirits?"

"He seemed so. Why?"

"Nothing," I said. "When do you expect them to come after the sofa?" I asked collecting my thoughts. I had a dozen questions that I was sure Ogilvy couldn't answer, like where Francesco had been for the past few weeks.

"Near closing. But like I said, Francesco has keys. It's not unusual for him to pop in and out. Shall I tell him you're coming to see him?"

"No," I said. "Don't say anything. I want it to be a surprise."

"That's what Severino said. He didn't want me to tell Giuseppe that his son was coming to the shop. He didn't want me to tell anyone. He wanted it to be a surprise."

"Let's keep it that way," I said and looked for the number Sergeant Filippo had given me. I found it and made the call after hanging up on Ogilvy.

"*Pronto.*"

"Perdoux here, sergeant. You asked me to call you if I learned anything new from Silvio Conte."

"Ah, *dottore*, I thought I recognized the voice. I am about to drink a coffee with my superior who wishes a discussion about an unfortunate incident with some American tourists adding liquid to some of our fountains that now make the bubbles. My superior believes this to show the utmost disrespect to our city. My opinion doesn't matter as I prefer bubbles to you Americans wading in the fountains, although neither is to my liking. What have you learned new about Silvio Conte, *dottore*?"

"I learned that his partner, Francesco Vega, is going to make an appearance this afternoon. I thought it might be a good idea if the police were along so that they could make a legal arrest. You interested?"

"Arrest for what?" Filippo asked skeptically.

"Stealing a Rembrandt and shipping it into this country." When Filippo didn't jump at the opportunity, I said, "I thought it might be an easy way to impress your superiors. To show them how a dedicated professional officer of the law operates."

"Yes, *dottore*, I can see that."

"Then, you are interested?"

"I would be honored. I will put in a call and have police cars and armed officers at the ready. Where will this appearance of Francesco Vega take place?"

"I think it's better if we leave the police cars and the other officers out of it. We don't want to scare Francesco away with a show of force," I said and told him where I was staying. "I'll be back at my hotel in about half an hour. Meet me in the lobby, and we'll go in my car."

"A sneak attack," Filippo said gleefully.

"Exactly."

"Under the covers."

"Right. Under the covers." I ended the call and turned to Silvio. "I need your car."

"Where are we going?"

"Me. Not you."

"You can't just leave me here with a dead body."

"Try and prevent another, Silvio. Go to your sister. Make yourself useful protecting Marcus."

"What are you going to do?"

"I'm going to intercept Francesco and get the Rembrandt. Tell Peter when I get my hands on it, I'll bring it to him. Hopefully, before nine o'clock. Now, get going."

When I got back to the Raphael Hotel, Sergeant Filippo was at the front desk chatting with the attractive woman who registered guests. He broke away when he saw me.

"I went back through my Aldo Conte file, *dottore*. Francesco Vega was someone I spoke with as part of my Stradivarius investigation. As I believe I told you, he took classes from Silvio Conte and turned around the direction of his life. Now, you believe he is back to the life of a thief?"

I got behind the wheel and started the engine. "He and Angela Ricci were arrested for stealing some coins," I reminded him. "From what I now know, he's graduated to stealing artwork worth millions."

The sergeant nodded as if reaching his own conclusion. "Turning around a life is not an easy thing," he said. "Like the giving up pasta for the good health. But, *dottore*, pasta is good for the health. Pasta and vino. My father lives to this day at one hundred years because of a diet of vino and pasta and my mother's love."

A bus dropping and picking up riders slowed our progress and gave Sergeant Filippo more time to ruminate.

"To admit this, *dottore*, might sound a wrong note, but in my life upholding the laws of my fair city, I have wondered how it is that Roma has lasted all these centuries. You Americans don't have the history for such reflection, but we Italians have years and years and more years of wars and sackings and emperors with boyfriends and popes with wives who have ruled us. Many were cruel. Others simple minded.

Through it all, the country survived. At times, it thrived. God must look out for this country. If all the politicians and Mafiosi and officers like myself disappeared, Italy would remain because of God's good favor."

"I can't argue against you," I said, not wanting our focus to be on God or country. I wanted it on the task at hand, which was getting that Rembrandt to Peter Garcetti before time ran out. Nothing else.

"No one can argue against these facts," the sergeant rambled on. "It is like Francesco Vega who is now a criminal. No one can argue against the facts. Do you expect trouble, *dottore*, or do you think when he sees me in the uniform of the *Polizia di Stato* that he will see the error of his life and surrender?"

"I'm not sure," I admitted, turning on to the access road. Our destination was minutes away. "He's supposed to be inside an upholstery shop crating a shipment."

I pulled into the parking lot and drove past the box truck backed up against the shop's loading area. I parked out of the way and shut off the motor. I looked over at Sergeant Filippo and wondered if it was such a good idea to bring him along. Would he get in the way? I wondered and got out of the car.

"Ready?"

Filippo nodded and kept pace. I stopped at the front of the box truck and looked inside the cab, the Ruger in my right hand. The cab was empty. I motioned for Filippo to swing along the driver's side while I inched along the passenger's side. The back door of the truck was closed as was the door to the loading area of the shop. Not surprising since at this hour the shop had closed for the day.

Behind me, cars kicked up gravel and dust as they left the lot. I waited at the customer's entrance, listening for sounds inside. Men, no matter what they're doing, made noise. Capping the lid on a large shipping crate makes lots of noise.

"Trouble?" Filippo asked in a whisper.

"We're about to find out," I said.

I slowly pushed open the door. The workspace was fully lit and quiet. At any moment, I expected someone to jump out from the shadows as I made my way deeper inside. Sergeant Filippo was behind me and to my right.

I signaled Filippo to ease ahead while I made my way toward Ogilvy's desk on the opposite side of the room. The light indicating messages blinked red on his telephone. I checked the desk for a sign that Francesco had changed his mind about showing up, but the desktop was clear except for the blinking phone and the computer.

The last I'd seen of the partially crated sofa was deep within the shop at Giuseppe's secluded work area. I was on my way there when Filippo's voice broke the silence. He stood ten feet from the forklift, his service revolver pointed at the driver.

"The trouble is finish for this man, *dottore*. This man is dead."

I raced to the sergeant who was examining the body of Hans Katzen who sat at the controls of the forklift, his head tilted skyward. He'd been shot once in the head. Filippo lifted Katzen's right arm.

"No dead long," the sergeant said.

The forks of the lift were under the wooden crate containing the sofa as if Katzen were about to lift it and haul it out to the box truck. I looked quickly around hoping to spot Francesco. When I saw nothing, I stepped toward the crate. The lid had been put on top and nailed down. I looked around and found a hammer and crowbar.

I handed the hammer to Filippo and started working with the bar. In no time we had the lid free and lifted off. Francesco Vega was laid out on top of the leather sofa. Like Severino and Katzen, he'd been shot once in the forehead. Unlike Katzen, he'd been wrapped in clear plastic. Dark blood pooled in the low spots near his neck.

Sergeant Filippo made the sign of the cross. "This not what I was expecting, *dottore*," he said, shaking his head. "Francesco Vega will not be arrested. Who is the other man?"

"Hans Katzen," I said and told Filippo where to find the body of Leonardo Severino. "Like these two, he'd been shot."

"For what purpose?" Filippo asked. "What's to be gained with their deaths?"

"I'm not sure yet," I admitted. "Silvio told me this crate was built to hide the Rembrandt Francesco stole from the Gardner Museum in Boston. Help me get the caps off," I said, noticing that one of the side panels and an end piece did not have the caps attached. "They must have been shot before they could secure the caps," I said looking inside each. "They're empty."

We started removing the cap of one of the long side panels that was about chest high and seven or so feet long. The two end panels were the same height and a little over five feet long. All of the panels were secured to the base of the crate with a combination of nails and screws. With the top on the crate secured, a tank couldn't damage the leather sofa inside.

As Filippo pulled nails, I jammed the end of the crowbar into my side of the cap and yanked. The wood creaked and moaned but finally gave way. I lifted the top off of the panel and exposed what amounted to a narrow envelope about four inches wide. The Rembrandt on its stretcher would easily have fit inside, but I didn't see a painting. Instead, I pulled out a narrow cardboard box suitable for holding a flat television screen. Beside it was an identical box that Filippo retrieved.

The sergeant took a knife from his belt and opened the blade. He cut along the top of the first box. Inside were row upon row of small leather boxes embossed with the gold insignia of Patek Philippe. I opened one of the boxes and took out a gold watch worth thousands on the retail market, if genuine. I handed the watch to the sergeant as I opened the second box. It, too, was filled with watch boxes.

"There must be close to a thousand watches in these two cartons," I said and wondered aloud why they hadn't been taken. "Why kill two men and leave the bounty?"

Filippo nodded and took out his telephone. "We've stumbled on a major smuggling ring, *dottore*. I need to call for assistance so this crime scene can be properly documented."

While he made his call, I went outside. I jerked open the back of the box truck, hoping to find the Rembrandt. The crate once secured to the side and large enough to protect the painting was gone. The cardboard boxes I'd seen earlier had been turned over, their contents strewn across the floor as if a madman had gone berserk. In a box tossed on its side, the contents leaking out, I spotted the signed six-month lease for the Latina apartment. There was no name on who leased it. Attached to it was a paid in full receipt. The payment was made in cash.

I shoved the box aside and picked up an envelope marked 'Possibles.' Inside was a single sheet containing simple evaluations beside initials. The notations were brief, direct, in English and in the same handwritten script as the note left at the bottom of one of Francesco's sofa sketches.

FV: Talented. Lacks direction. Will play for price.
SC: Works hard. Has own shop. Driven to cash.
HK: Loyal. Follows directions.
LS: Loyal. Tough. Will do as told.
WB: Craves a challenge. Shuns limelight. None better for task.
CR: Unreliable. Relapse. Don't bother.

"Find something?"

I turned to see the sergeant behind me. "Yeah. A mess," I said and slipped the paper in my pocket.

"My team will be here any minute," Filippo said. "I don't know how to put this, *dottore*, but for me to claim the top position in this important criminal investigation, I need to appear in charge. Smuggling is one thing, but three murders . . ."

"You want me to get out of your way," I said knowingly.

"If you would be so kind."

"I understand," I said.

"Then, I don't have to explain to my superiors how you have a weapon, which, in my country, you should not have. You must have the paperwork, *dottore*. Can you produce the paperwork for carrying such a weapon?"

"Not on me," I said.

"Of course. If you should leave, you might find it."

"Exactly what I was thinking," I said and jumped down from the truck.

"We will speak again, *dottore*. Not to worry." Filippo puffed his chest. "Once I have this investigation under control and the criminals who did this under arrest. I think that will be soon as I am known as the dog that bites."

"Good luck, sergeant," I said and hurried toward my car.

Chapter Twenty

I heard the sirens before I saw the flashing lights as a line of police cars sped toward the dead bodies. I was glad to be out of there and on my own. I had a lot to think about, and a lot to sort through, starting with who would want to get rid of Francesco, Severino and Katzen? Did the killer steal the Rembrandt? Or had it ever been delivered to the shop?

I parked Silvio's car at my hotel and ducked into the nearest café. I ordered a glass of red wine and took out the list. The answer to who put the list together might be hidden in the mess of box truck papers, but that was now in the hands of Sergeant Filippo and his men. It wasn't difficult to see that the initials identified possible team members. FV, the talented one lacking direction had to be Francesco Vega. The hard worker with his own shop was clearly Silvio Conte. HK was the loyal and now dead Hans Katzen. The same for the loyal and tough Leonardo Severino identified as LS. WB craves a challenge, shuns the limelight and is none better for the task points to my father, Wilhelm Barr. The unreliable CR, I spent no time trying to identify as he was rejected from the team.

Who put this list together? I wondered. It had to be someone other than Wilhelm since he would not refer to himself as a possibility. He was in charge, or he wasn't. He hired men to rob the Gardner, or he didn't. It had to be someone else. Someone who wrote the list in English. Reese Ogilvy was a prime candidate. He knew Francesco, he ran the upholstery shop and likely knew of the smuggling operation. He also knew Francesco and Katzen were heading to the shop. Did he lie about the call from Severino announcing their arrival? Did Ogilvy kill Severino and the other two so he could steal the Rembrandt? If he did, why initial the threatening note to Francesco with a B? Maybe because Ogilvy didn't write it, Nick Bianchi did. I mulled that possibility over as a shadow crossed my table.

I sipped my wine as a man pulled out the chair opposite mine at my table. He was about my height, just over six feet and beefier than me, maybe two-hundred and fifty pounds. He had a round face, tanned skin and black wavy hair. I guessed him to be in his mid-forties. He leaned across the table, his hands folded in a show of extreme confidence. I saw immediately that one finger was missing.

"Someone wants to talk," he said with an accent I couldn't quite place.

"Are you the delivery boy?"

"Among other things."

"As in the guy who pounded Silvio Conte senseless?" I asked. "You did a good job."

His blank stare gave nothing away. He stood, dropping a few lira on the table for my drink. I followed him outside and around the corner where his car waited. He got behind the wheel with me beside him in the passenger's seat.

"Where are we going?" I asked and got no answer. "Who wants to see me?"

We rode in silence around Piazza Barberini and onto the Via Veneto through the ancient stone gates of Porta Pinciana into the beautiful sprawl of the Borghese Gardens. The driver slowed his pace as the street became clogged with bicyclers and walkers enjoying the early evening air. When the car stopped, the driver pointed to a park bench a few feet back from the street under a plain tree.

"Wait there," he said.

I got out of the car. He drove off toward the gallery as I took my seat on the bench. I sensed the movement behind me and looked at my father stepping out from behind the massive tree. Even under his wide-brimmed straw hat pulled low over his forehead, he was recognizable. His summer suit was finely cut, his light blue shirt pressed. Although not wearing a tie, he appeared formal, yet very comfortable. It had been over ten years since I last saw him. What blond hair I could see below the hat was mostly gray and thinner. Still, he looked fit walking toward me with the aid of a cane, the limp the result of a war injury.

"You don't look surprised to see me," he said evenly, his German accent coloring each word.

"I thought I might," I said, trying not to stare at the man beside me. He'd been an officer in the German army, a man who looted and killed, and a man who thirteen years ago saved my life at great risk to his own. That he was my father should have softened my feelings toward him, but it didn't. "Things were pointing in your direction."

"Too many things. Let's walk, shall we? My leg still gets stiff if I don't move."

We joined the crowd of families strolling in the park through a maze of paved streets. At the first intersection, I spotted Wilhelm's driver in his car pulled to one side. He was keeping a close watch on us.

"About seven or eight months ago," Wilhelm began, "I got word that an American mob boss wanted to have a conversation. If I wanted to participate, I was to place a phone call. I did not want to participate. A few weeks later, word reached me again that an intermediary, a man by the name of Howard Moss, had important information for me. This time I made the call. Moss told me that Vincent Garcetti had devised a plan to rob an American museum, so that he could barter his way out of prison. He wanted me to make sure all the elements fell into place and wanted to hire me to make sure that happened. I told Moss I didn't deal with convicted criminals. Their conviction proves they are not very good at their chosen profession. My life in South America was good. I needed nothing. I went about my business and let Howard Moss and Vincent Garcetti do the same. Without me."

"Did they ever mention the name of the museum?"

"No, not that it would have mattered," Wilhelm said.

"Then, all the hints that you were involved in robbing the Gardner were to set you up?"

"That's what I'm saying." Wilhelm led the way around a pushcart vendor selling soft drinks. "My supposed involvement keeps the heat off them. Why look elsewhere if I pulled the job?"

"So, you didn't hire Hans Katzen?"

"No."

"Francesco Vega?"

"No."

"Severino?"

"None of them," Wilhelm said.

"Why send your man to rough up Silvio Conte?" I asked.

"He went to speak with Aldo Conte. He's the one in the family most protective of Marcus. We didn't know Aldo wouldn't be there, but it didn't matter. We learned what we needed. A bonus would have been the whereabouts of *Christ in the Storm of Galilee*. I thought he might tell us."

"Why would he know?"

"Families talk. Peter Garcetti is part of his family. Peter picked up where Howard Moss and Vincent Garcetti left off. Not that he ever contacted me. He didn't see the need. What he saw was the groundwork for the perfect crime. Pull a job then make sure the guilty fingers point to someone who's known to never show his face. He'd never come out of hiding to defend himself for fear of being arrested for past crimes. Makes perverted sense, don't you think? Only Garcetti underestimated me. Just as the fools who pulled off the Stedelijk Museum robbery underestimated me."

"The Swedish authorities were sure you did that job," I said. "If you didn't, who did?"

"Someone who wanted it to look like I was involved, but it doesn't matter," Wilhelm said. "They won't bother anyone again."

"What are you planning to do here?"

"Protect my reputation and myself."

"You can't expect me to help you," I said, sounding more jarring than I'd intended.

"I neither ask nor expect anything from you," Wilhelm said as a flash of anger quickly vanished from his expression.

"Then, why do you want to talk?"

"Vincent Garcetti is a vengeful man. He has nothing to do with his time in prison but think of ways to get back at those who have slighted him. I'm at the top of his list since I rejected his offer. Peter obeys his father when it suits him. He may believe that you and I have a closer bond than we do and will come after you to get to me. With both of us out of the way, they're home free."

"You're warning me?"

"Providing information, that's all. I don't want the Garcettis to think they'll get to me through you. Your being vulnerable might lead him to believe that they are."

"I'll watch my step," I said coolly. "What are you going to do?"

"I've already begun. I'm on the offensive. I'm here to clean up the mess Garcetti's people have created. A mess has a way of spreading. I will avoid the mess."

"Your man made a mess of Silvio Conte. Why beat him up?"

Wilhelm shrugged. "I thought he might know where *Christ in the Storm of Galilee* was hidden. When I decided I had to come to Rome, I made plans to sell the painting. The buyer gets the painting tonight."

"Assuming you get your hands on it," I cautioned.

"Peter Garcetti loves his boy. I will get the painting."

"Why not leave Marcus out of this?" I asked.

Wilhelm cut me a steady look. "It is ironic, don't you think, that a child may play a role in how this comes out? When your mother told me you had been killed in an allied bombing raid, I didn't believe her, even though she showed me your tiny grave."

"I was with the Zacharys on my way to England."

"So I later learned," Wilhelm said. "She never should have told such a lie. Worse, she never should have kept you from me. That one event changed all of our lives. Now, here we are all these years later speaking about the fate of another child."

"Don't do it," I warned. "Leave the boy alone."

Wilhelm stopped and raised his cane above his head signaling his driver to bring the car. When it pulled alongside, Wilhelm said, "Nick Bianchi is a man to be wary of. He's been lurking about."

"I'll keep my eyes open."

Wilhelm opened the car door and got in the back seat. "I'm sure we'll see each other soon," he said and closed the door. He stared straight ahead as the car pulled away.

Chapter Twenty-One

If Wilhelm Barr was telling the truth, and he was set up, the person who could shed some light on that was Howard Moss. I grabbed a seat on a park bench and looked up the number for Moss, Knopp, and Tierney Attorneys at Law   I called the number and listened as a pleasant receptionist rattled off the firm's names. When I asked to speak with Mr. Moss, she put me off. When I said I had information about the Gardner robbery, she stalled. When I said I knew where the stolen art was, she put me on hold.

Like any lawyer who bills by the hour, Howard Moss made me wait until my blood pressure spiked. Finally, he came on the line, his voice a low monotone and direct.

"I know all about you, Mr. Perdoux," he began. "I know your reputation, your successes and failures and your interest in solving the robbery of the Isabella Stewart Gardner Museum, to date one of your failures. However, contrary to what you might believe, I am no longer involved in that negotiation."

"I know you backed away from your initial offer," I reminded him.

"That's a neutral way of putting it. I prefer to say I was dismissed."

"By whom?" I asked.

"Private investigators are like attorncys when they ask questions. You know the answer before you ask. Or you should. Wilhelm Barr hired me. But you already know that."

"Why were you dismissed?"

"Another question you already know the answer to. Come, come, Mr. Perdoux. Your father decided not to give the Gardner bounty back to the museum. More profit could be made selling Vermeer's *The Concert* and Rembrandt's *Christ in the Storm of Galilee* than the Gardner people could ever scrape together. He went with the money. Only someone jammed a wrench in his plans when they stole the Rembrandt out from under him."

"Francesco Vega?" I asked.

"That's the name I heard. When Wilhelm learned the painting was missing, he told me to get lost. He would handle things on his own from here on."

"Francesco Vega was found dead earlier today."

"That's how your father handles things, isn't it? No surprise there."

"Hans Katzen and Leonardo Severino were also shot, execution style."

"I don't know the names," Howard Moss said. "What was their connection to Wilhelm?"

"I don't know that there is one," I said. "I spoke to him not half an hour ago. He said Vincent Garcetti had you put out feelers to Wilhelm about pulling the Gardner job and he turned you down. Twice."

"And you believed him?" Moss snapped.

"I do."

"Then you're a greater fool than I thought," Moss said and ended the call.

A taxi dropped off a passenger, and I jumped in the empty seat. I told the driver the name of my hotel and sat back as the cab wound its way out of the park and toward Piazza Navona. It was a thirty-minute ride, and one I spent thinking about the sudden appearance of Wilhelm Barr in this case.

In my mother's diary, she wrote about her torrid affair with the dashing German officer. Simone was nineteen when I was born and aware that her involvement with Wilhelm was a dreadful mistake that broke her parent's hearts. They didn't understand Simone's thirst for life in the midst of war, a thirst that left her emotionally parched.

Wilhelm had lied to her about the possibility of a future together. He had used her like he had used others, and my mother swore to get her revenge.

Wilhelm was not in Paris when I was born. When my mother learned of his eventual return and his plan to take me back to Germany, she arranged for her cousin, Helen Zachary and her war correspondent reporter husband, to whisk me from Paris and raise me as their own. When Wilhelm learned of Simone's treachery, he stuck her and shot her parents when they refused to reveal where I had been taken. His last atrocious act against the Perdoux family was to steal their art collection and pack it off to Germany with hundreds of other collections.

Those acts were the beginnings of my parent's hatred for one another. A hatred that lasted until Simone died thirteen years ago. Her last wish was that I continue her work hunting down the location of her father's art collection. That work has expanded into searching for other looted artworks with my partner, Gina Ponte. My mother would be proud of what Gina and I have accomplished. Just as she would be horrified to learn that Wilhelm was poised to steal another small boy.

Simone stopped him once. I wondered if I could do so again.

I paid the driver and hurried into the Hotel Raphael. Sergeant Filippo, a sullen look of doom on his face, pushed himself up from one of the plush lounge chairs and walked over.

"Ah, *dottore*, so glad you have come. My feelings are not good the way I wished you to go away from the upholstery shop so that my authority could be on display. I am sorry," he said, draping an arm around my shoulder. "We can have wine and talk, no?"

"No," I said. "Something's come up, sergeant. Something that can't wait."

"Always in a rush, you Americans. A suspicious man might think you had something to hide. But there is no option. We must have a conversation."

I heard the threat in Filippo's voice. "What are you getting at?" I asked.

"Me? I get at nothing. It's my superior, *dottore*. When I mentioned to him as I was filling out my report that you had in your possession a weapon without proper paperwork, he thought it wise to investigate the possibility that it had been used in a recent killing. You have the gun, is that not so?"

I felt the handle in through my jacket pocket. "I do."

Filippo patted my back. "Excellent. Then, we have no worries. We will drink the wine and talk," he said, leading the way up to the rooftop bar. A light breeze cooled the evening air. Filippo ordered from the attentive waiter. When he brought the carafe of red and two glasses, Filippo seemed to grow more serious. "These murders, *dottore*," he said with the shake of his head. "These murders mixed in with the smuggling, how is one to proceed? In the truck we found a box of labels. Inside the shop in packing crates, we found hundreds of counterfeit leather belts, shoes, jackets, wallets and all manner of so-called fine Italian leather products. It's easy to sell the fake goods with an authentic looking label."

"Did you find any artwork?" I asked. "Any paintings?"

Filippo shook his head. "None." He sipped his wine. "Severino, Katzen, and Francesco Vega were all executed, *dottore*. In each instance, one shot to the head. The style of a professional. The question is, why?"

"To keep them quiet."

"Killing them would accomplish that, yes. But to keep them quiet about what? Smuggling a few watches? Some leather goods?"

"Silvio said Francesco was shipping a valuable painting in the side panel of the crate built to protect the leather sofa. The painting wasn't found so someone must have stolen it and killed the men to cover his tracks."

"Possible," Filippo mused, turning his wine glass as he thought. "I asked Giuseppe Vega and Ogilvy to come to the shop to explain the contraband. Neither man knew anything about it. They were shocked. Francesco a thief? Francesco dead? Giuseppe is having a difficult time. However, I believe him when he says he knows nothing about any smuggling. He is an artist, a craftsman. I feel sorry for the poor soul, looking down into that wooden crate at the body of his son. Dead and laid out on such a beautiful piece of furniture. Cruel, don't you think, *dottore*? A killing, yes, but a cruel killing. Not like the other two. Why put him on the sofa his father worked so hard on? It was like putting him in an enormous coffin."

"I wondered about that."

"And?"

"Francesco had been warned about leaving documents around that could be traced back to the man calling the shots. On top of that, he and Angela started up again."

"How do you know these things?"

"For the documents, I read a warning for Francesco not to screw up. For his involvement with Angela Ricci, Detective Flynn told me."

Filippo thought a moment, then said, "Who issued this warning?"

"Nick Bianchi," I said. "My guess is, he killed those three men."

"Bianchi," Filippo repeated. "The business manager, Ogilvy, mentioned that name. Bianchi came to the shop earlier in the day looking for Francesco."

"Probably casing the place. A careful hitman likes to know what he's getting into before he strikes. And," I said, "Nick Bianchi is good and careful. Do you think Ogilvy was telling the truth? Do you believe he knew nothing about the smuggling?"

"About that I am not certain. Some of the crates were constructed cleverly with a divider down the center. The front half contained fabrics and hides, the back half jewelry, more watches, even a few with laptops. Inferior goods, all of it. No duty paid. No taxes. It's a sophisticated counterfeiting operation, *dottore*. Is it possible that the office manager did not know what was in those containers?"

I drank some of my wine. "Francesco Vega designed those crates with the dividers," I offered. "He knew."

"So, Ogilvy said. He also said they were designed for legitimate business purposes. There is another element, *dottore*, a disappointing element I am afraid. The fancy leather couch. We had to order Giuseppe Vega to remove it from the crate and take it apart down to the wooden frame. I hated to make such a demand, but after we found evidence of smuggling in some of the other crates, I had no choice."

"What did you find?"

"A hidden compartment built in the seat containing white powder and thousands of pills, all sealed in hundreds of small plastic bags. My government goes after smugglers of all kinds, but especially those peddling narcotics. We will have specifics when the analysis is complete, but right now we can say that the leather goods and watches are of minor concern."

What was it Silvio had said about Francesco's smuggling operation? Little stuff? Every now and then some pills. No hard drugs. Just a little something to perk up your day. Was Silvio lying? Or did he not know the full extent of Francesco's operation?

"I think we should talk with Silvio," I said. "He must . . ."

"No, *dottore*. My supervisor thinks the Contes should be left alone. Pietro Garcetti spoke to my supervisor about how you have threatened the family."

"Threatened how?"

"The stolen Stradivarius. Reopening the case. The details, I don't remember, but my supervisor said to me that for all concerned that case was closed long ago. The violin is gone, the insurance paid. We have moved on."

"The Stradivarius isn't gone," I said. "Peter Garcetti has it."

"He said you would make such a claim."

"Garcetti has it in his house. It's been there all along."

"And therefore, a fraud has been committed, and the case must be reopened so that Aldo Conte, a respected member of our community and his very good friend, Pietro Garcetti, can see their reputations ruined in the morning papers." Filippo shook his head slowly as if he'd given up all faith in my opinion. "You need to understand, *dottore*, *Don* Roberto had many friends in my department."

"Including your supervisor?" I said knowingly.

"Of course."

"Look sergeant, the Garcettis are behind this entire mess. Peter's pointing an accusing finger at me because he knows I won't go away on my own. He wants you to push me out."

"Push? No, *dottore*, no pushing. It's my supervisor, you understand, not Pietro Garcetti. My supervisor wants me to bring him your gun. You, of course, will come along to answer a few questions."

"So you can arrest me? You know I have no permits to carry that gun."

"Which may have been used in three murders."

"Sure it has been, if you believe Garcetti," I said as I reached in my pocket and held the Ruger under the table. "I don't want to do this, sergeant, but you're not listening to me. The gun you think killed Severino, Katzen and Francesco Vega is pointed at your belly. If you think I killed those three men, you know I won't hesitate to shoot you."

Sergeant Filippo slid his eyes across the room, then settled back on me. "What are you going to do?"

"I'm going to walk out of here and you're going with me."

"No, *dottore*."

"Move." I pushed the barrel of the Ruger into Filippo's fat belly. "Walk to the stairs."

The sergeant stood and inched past me. I made sure he could feel the barrel of the gun in his back.

"One of my officers is meeting me here, *dottore*. A warning to you is something in my favor, no?" Filippo asked as the elevator doors slid open and a young officer wearing the same uniform as the sergeant jumped out, spewing in Italian.

"What is it?" I asked. "What's he saying?"

"There is trouble at Peter Garcetti's," Filippo said. "Lia Conte and her son have been taken hostage."

Wilhelm had made his move.

Before the young officer could say more, I yanked him aside and sent him sprawling into Filippo. I pushed the button for the lobby and rode the carriage to the ground floor as Sergeant Filippo's loud voice commanding me to stop echoed around me.

Chapter Twenty-Two

Silvio's car was where I'd left it.

I fired the engine and dashed into traffic. Like Italians before me, I kept one foot on the accelerator and one hand on the horn. Weaving through streets, I soon pulled to a stop near Peter Garcetti's house. A handful of police milled around out front. In a few minutes, Sergeant Filippo with the young officer driving, skidded to a stop, blocking much of the street. I stayed put when they got out of their car and raced into the house.

I watched as a line of police came and went through the front door. Much of my business is taken up with waiting and you have to learn to live with it. I would rather be doing something else, but there wasn't anything else to do but sit and look and wait.

In half an hour the police presence had thinned. I kept waiting for Filippo to make his exit when my passenger door flew open, and Nick Bianchi slid into the seat beside me. His presence was like a dark cloud.

"I thought I recognized you, Purdy," he sneered. "I was checking the perimeter of the house and there you were. What do you think you're doing here, Purdy?"

I reached quickly across the seat and grabbed Nick by his lapels. I yanked his face down hard on the dash. "Angela's not here to impress, Nick. And you're not impressing me. We're done with Purdy, you understand?" When he didn't answer soon enough to suit me, I gave a quick jerk and bounced his head off the window. "Understand?"

He was angry, his eyes hard and wide. "You ain't getting away with this," he gruffed.

"Understand?" I asked as his head again bounced off the glass.

"Yeah."

I let him go as some dots connected. "The night you were telling Angela about my past, it was all fresh to you because you'd been doing your research for Vincent, right? He wanted details about my father. He wanted to know everything about him. Isn't that right?"

"Keep guessing. You might figure it out some day," Bianchi said and rearranged the shape of his jacket. When he'd finished, he held a Beretta in one hand and searched my pockets with the other until he found the Ruger. "If it was me, Purdy, I'd shoot your ass right now. But I've got orders."

"Orders that included taking out Angela Ricci?"

"Can't remember."

"How about Francesco, Severino, and Hans Katzen? They're more recent. You ought to be able to remember a few hours ago."

"Get out of the car," Nick said.

I got out with Nick sliding out behind me.

"Who's got the painting?"

"Move it."

"How about Marcus?" I asked. "How'd you manage to let the boy get away?"

"Not me. The doorbell rang, and the man said he had the truck outside from the moving company. He was there to pick up the last few pieces. One of Peter's men let him in, and that was it."

"What'd this guy look like?" I asked.

Nick described Wilhelm's driver. "He moved through the place like a guy picking up the last odds and ends. The movers were told to clean out everything except the upstairs office, so we let the guy go about his business. No panic, nothing. Nobody paid him any mind until he grabbed the kid. When the kid cried out, Lia ran after him. The guy took them both."

"Where was Peter when all this happened?"

"In his office. Top floor in the back. He couldn't hear nothing until the guys downstairs started yelling."

"He still up there?"

Bianchi waved the gun at me. "You're about to find out."

"Who's with him?" I asked as we crossed the street.

"The police."

"I want to avoid the police," I said. "You're good at keeping out of their way. Can you do it again?"

"We're going around back. They won't see us."

Bianchi led the way to the back entrance. Inside, we climbed the servant's stairs to the top floor where Peter Garcetti spoke to Sergeant Filippo in Peter's office. Bianchi and I waited on the landing near the door. When Filippo finished with his questions, I heard him climb down the main stairway and close the front door behind him. It was then that Nick and I went in to the office. Garcetti looked up from his desk, the strain of the moment etched on his face.

"Where did you find him?"

"Across the street like you thought."

"As I told you, Nick, people with police training are creatures of habit. They're like Pavlov's dogs. He had to show up here."

"Woof."

"Very good, Mr. Perdoux. You'll need a sense of humor before this is over." Garcetti grabbed the paper from his desk, his hand shaking. "Wilhelm left this trash," he said and read, '*Christ in the Storm of Galilee* for the lives of Lia and Marcus. Villa Sciarra in one hour. Park in back. I will find you.'" He threw down the note. "What the hell is this?"

"Rules of the game," I offered as Bianchi's clinched fist rocked my kidney. I wheeled to strike back but his gun stopped me. "I owe you one," I said, swallowing the pain.

"What makes him think I've got the Rembrandt?"

"Katzen, Severino, and Francesco are dead. Who else could have it but you?" I said. "Why kill them?"

"They'd done what was asked of them," Garcetti said. "Besides, Francesco wanted to continue his little smuggling operation. I didn't want that. You might say, I wanted to put a lid on it."

"Civic pride?" I quipped.

"Specialization," Garcetti said. "No phony watches, leather belts or electronics. Zero in on one thing and provide it less expensively and in greater quantity than the competition."

"You didn't exclude narcotics," I said.

"No I didn't, but it doesn't matter. I'm expanding into the delivery business. What's delivered is of no consequence."

"Until customs discovers the contraband. What's the flavor of the day? I understand heroin is making a comeback."

"No comeback possible for you, Mr. Perdoux. Once I have confirmation that Lia and Marcus are safe, you'll be the next victim."

Bianchi pulled my Ruger from his pocket and put it on the desk out of my reach. "Sergeant Filippo is looking for that gun," he said. "Might have been used to kill Katzen, Severino, and Vega."

Garcetti said, "Sergeant Filippo appreciates the easy life. He likes answers given to him, gives him more time to file his reports. He seemed very pleased when I told him you could be involved in the murder of those three men."

"What was my motive?"

"The painting, of course. You saw Severino put it in the truck. Katzen spotted you trailing them back to Rome."

"Where's the painting now? Where have I hidden it?"

"That's why you're here, you see. I need the Rembrandt to save Lia and Marcus. I'm trying to make you tell me where you've hidden it, but you refuse to say. I'm desperate. Time is running out. When I turn my back, you attack. We struggle for the gun on the desk and . . ."

"You end up dead," Bianchi said with a hint of delight.

"Just like you snuffed Katzen, Severino, and Francesco?"

"Just like that," Bianchi said.

"How about JoJo Weems and Angela?"

"More of the same," Bianchi said flatly. "Everyone knew the rules. Look but don't touch. JoJo should have kept his dirty hands off. Sugar knew the rules."

"What rule did Sugar break?"

"Calling you. Bad idea."

"Did you know she and Francesco had once been married?" I asked.

"Of course," Garcetti said. "When I learned about her background and real name, I thought she might be a worthy addition to our team. Someone needed to distract the security guard while Francesco dealt with the Rembrandt. During the actual robbery, she served as a look-out."

"Keeps things in the family," Bianchi said.

"Only she decided to call me."

"Like I said, bad idea. You're all in or you're out. No middle ground."

"I can see that," I said, "only there's one small problem with blaming those murders on me. Sergeant Filippo and I arrived at the leather shop at the same time."

"What better alibi?" Garcetti mocked. "You and the law show up together. Of course, I had to point out to the good sergeant that Silvio overheard the phone conversation in which Reese Ogilvy told you when Francesco and Katzen would be at the shop. You had to hurry, but you had time to go there and kill them before picking up Filippo and returning to find the bodies."

"Surprise, surprise," Bianchi said, pointing his finger at me and pulling the imaginary trigger. "Bang."

"Which one of you pretended to be Severino and called Ogilvy?"

"I did," Garcetti said. "I didn't want Ogilvy waiting around. I wanted the place empty when Nick arrived, so I reminded Ogilvy that Francesco had his own key. That Ogilvy called you was a bonus."

"Glad to be of help," I said. "I assume you've told all this to Sergeant Filippo."

"Of course. He's on his way now to Latina where I suggested he might find evidence that I placed there proving your father stayed in that apartment. And speaking of being on their way, a van full of my men ought to be arriving soon at Villa Sciarra. Once they spot Wilhelm, they have orders to kill him."

"They wouldn't be the first to try," I said.

"Some of *Don* Roberto's loyal men are in that van. They are itching to reclaim past glories. Rescuing Lia and Marcus will be a good start. Killing a Nazi war criminal will be a better one. Too bad he had to crawl out of his hole and come to Rome."

"Too bad you tried to frame him," I said.

"Tried?" Garcetti shot back. "I've yet to fail. His arrival has complicated matters just as your coming here has created problems. But problems can be solved."

"Sure. Call Nick and tell him to start shooting," I said aware of Bianchi's hard glare. "One thing I don't quite understand. You had men in the Gardner for nearly an hour and a half. They carted off thirteen pieces, including *Christ in the Storm of Galilee*. But that was a copy painted by Francesco. Why go to all that trouble?"

"Because of my father," Garcetti said. "His plan was to hit the Gardner, then barter for early release. He tapped two of his top men to work with Wilhelm to pull the job, only Wilhelm wouldn't play ball.

My father was bullshit. He is not accustomed to being turned down. That was a problem crying out for a solution, and I came up with one. I would take over Wilhelm's role with minor variations. Vincent's two men would follow my instructions starting with dressing as Boston police, securing the guards in the basement, and taking the art pieces I identified. In addition, I would recruit Hans Katzen to whip into shape a small team whose only purpose was to copy the Rembrandt, exchange it for the original and get it safely to Rome. My team and Vincent's selected two thieves would have no knowledge of each other."

"But why?"

"Because *Christ in the Storm of Galilee* was the key to the entire enterprise. After *Don* Roberto died and left me this house, I began to explore my options with Lia. Why couldn't I build a life here with her and Marcus? Why couldn't I start a new operation here that was entirely my own? I've had ideas before on how to make the Boston operation modern, more progressive. My father had other ideas. He liked things the way they were. He saw no need for change. After a while, I stopped butting heads with him. I accepted the fact that in Boston, I would always be Vincent Garcetti's son. I would fall in line. I would do what he wanted."

"And what your wife wanted?" I quipped.

"I was not looking for a permanent move. Lia understood I couldn't live here fulltime. We would be discreet. We would start by making this place livable. *Don* Roberto's illness meant that his house and business interest fell into disrepair. I needed a substantial amount of cash to resurrect both. When my father broached the subject of hitting the Gardner, I saw a way to get that cash."

"You would steal the Rembrandt and have Niles Huygens sell it."

"That's right. Every step I took was designed to get that painting safely in my hands. I learned all I could about your father. He was like a case study for me. How would he attack the Gardner? How had he worked in the past? It was then I saw his possible involvement in the Stedelijk Museum robbery. He sent in an imposter to get information about the place. I thought I could make the same ploy work for me."

"Enter Francesco Vega as Aldo Conte."

"That's right. Francesco and Silvio would be my team and Katzen would make sure they followed my every order exactly as I imagined Wilhelm Barr would have demanded. There was only one hurdle to overcome. My father needed the return of all thirteen pieces in order to negotiate early release. I couldn't let it be known that . . ."

". . . that in order to finance your Rome operation, you had to betray your father," I said, watching Garcetti's expression sour. "That's why you needed to blame the theft of the Rembrandt on somebody else."

"Not just anyone. Wilhelm Barr, the best art thief the world has ever known. The man who strikes and then disappears to the shadows." Garcetti's mood darkened. "Only not this time," he said, glancing at his watch.

"Worried?" I asked.

"About what?"

"Your men not calling in. Shouldn't they have arrived by now? I wouldn't think they'd wait to call in good news," I said. "Maybe they don't have any. Maybe Wilhelm had other plans."

"Shut up."

"Just a thought," I said, thinking that Wilhelm would never give away that he waited at Villa Sciarra unless he wanted to lure Garcetti's men there. He didn't stay free all these years by giving away the element of surprise. I wasn't sure what Wilhelm had in mind, but I decided to keep Garcetti occupied. "A clever package," I said.

"I thought so."

"Are the other paintings here in Rome?" I asked.

"No."

"Where did you hide them?"

"They're where no one will find them but me. Don't even try. If I need more cash, I'll sell another. Huygens and I have already talked."

"Who was responsible for leaking news that *Christ in the Storm of Galilee* was available on the black market?"

Garcetti cracked a teasing smile. "I did. I wanted to pressure Huygens to raise his price."

"And, did he?"

"Of course. There's only one Rembrandt seascape, which will be on its way to Nice later tonight. I think you should bring it in," Garcetti said to Nick. "We want to be ready when Huygens gets here."

When Bianchi moved toward the door, Garcetti picked up my Ruger and pointed it toward me. "I don't bluff."

I could see the coldness in Garcetti's eyes and had no doubt he would fire if I tried anything. I decided to keep still and see what happened next. It seemed like time stopped, but eventually I heard voices out in the hall. When the door opened, a slow moving Silvio entered holding the Stradivarius with Nick beside him carrying the Rembrandt. *Christ in the Storm of Galilee* was a dazzling blaze of color and energy that momentarily distracted me from my precarious situation.

"How are the ribs?" I asked as Silvio grimaced. "Not feeling too chatty?"

Silvio put the violin on the desk and helped Nick lean the painting against the far wall. Garcetti put the Ruger beside the Stradivarius when Nick resumed pointing his Berretta in my direction. Garcetti's attention now on the wonders of the painting.

"Beautiful, isn't it?" he said. "Absolutely lovely."

"Ironic a thing of beauty is going to finance something so vile," I said.

"Redoing this wonderful old house?" Garcetti smirked.

I shook my head. "Smuggling narcotics. The Garcetti family's reputation in Boston left the drug trade to genuine lowlifes. I was just thinking that part of the reason you don't want your father looking over your shoulder is that you're about to stoop pretty low in a Rome operation peddling pills."

"And powders and anything else I see fit. Smuggling is a transportation business, Mr. Perdoux. What comes and goes is of little concern."

"Then why shut down Francesco's operation?"

"The same reason I kept Francesco locked up, out of the way. I wanted potential adversaries to see that I meant business. Shutting down Francesco's operation was a warning to others. Thousands of dollars of contraband were left behind in that shop. I wanted my competition to know that that is nothing compared to what I have planned for the future."

"Anything as long as it makes a profit," I said.

"That's what business is all about."

"From what Sergeant Filippo told me, *Don* Roberto and your father would probably disagree."

"I'm sure they would."

"All the more reason to rejoice that one is dead and the other stays in prison."

"All the more reason," Garcetti said.

"How does Vincent feel about your new life in Rome? I take it he's met Lia and Marcus?"

"I haven't asked how he feels. I take care of my wife and children back in Boston. That's all that matters. When I'm there, I'm Vincent Garcetti's son, faithful husband and father. When I'm in Rome, I make my own rules. I plan on dividing my time between the two cities."

"I suppose you keep your wife in the dark?" I said as faint knocking drifted up the stairs.

"What do you think?"

"I think I hear someone at the front door," I said as the knocking grew louder.

Garcetti glanced at his watch. "One admirable trait of Niles Huygens, once you get his attention, is that he's very punctual. Go downstairs, Silvio. Let our guest in and bring him up."

When Silvio left, I asked, "Don't you think you ought to check in with your men? The Villa Sciarra show should be over."

"Don't try to distract me, Mr. Perdoux. I'm about to conduct important business."

"Just thinking."

"And don't think. Or Nick will shoot you right here and now. That's always been his preference and I'm beginning to see his point. You and your father end up shot dead in Rome. Fitting, don't you think? One stole my son, the other a Rembrandt and neither got away."

"Might be fitting, but it'll be hard to explain."

"Not really. After Huygens pays me for the Rembrandt and takes it away, I contact Sergeant Filippo and tell him to hurry back from Latina. Something terrible has happened at Villa Sciarra. A shoot out. When the gun fire ended, you and your father were found mortally wounded. What you did with the painting before I found you, I'll never know."

"Nice and neat," I admitted.

"Nice and neat and utterly believable by the likes of poor, dumb Sergeant Filippo. Who's to prove otherwise?" Garcetti asked as the door flew open.

"That might be me," Sergeant Filippo said using Silvio as a shield and stepping into the room. Filippo's service weapon was pointed straight at the stunned Peter Garcetti who burst out orders.

"Kill them!"

Nick didn't hesitate and fired two rounds toward the door. When Silvio cried out, I dropped to the floor and rolled up on Nick's legs. With all the strength I had, I scissor-kicked at his knees causing one leg to snap. He dropped to the floor like a wet bag, grabbing his broken leg. His Berretta skidded across the room. I clawed my way toward it. Before I reached the gun, another burst of gunfire filled the room.

"Stand still. Everyone."

Filippo stiffened at the sight of Wilhelm and his driver, both carrying Heckler and Koch MP7 submachine guns. Without being told, Filippo dropped his service revolver on the desk.

Wilhelm trained his weapon on Peter Garcetti as his driver shoved Sergeant Filippo hard against the wall. Garcetti stood frozen, beads of sweat popping across his forehead.

"How did you get up here?" Garcetti shouted. "My men . . ."

"Back to the wall. Now," Wilhelm said, cutting him off.

Garcetti stepped away from the desk, his shoulders leaning against the wall. His breathing rapid and shallow. "Where are Lia and Marcus?"

Wilhelm said nothing. The tension in the room built in the silence. Finally, Wilhelm barked at me with an order. "Pick up that weapon," he said pointing to the Berreta on the floor. "Touch the barrel only and set it on the desk next to the Ruger."

I stepped over the writhing Nick Bianchi and did as told.

"You," Wilhelm snapped at Nick. "See if that man is alive."

"I think my fucking kneecap is broken," Bianchi whined.

"Then, crawl out of the way. If you move again, you won't move again." He motioned to me. "You do it. Check."

I hurried to Silvio and knelt beside him. He was in shock, bleeding but breathing.

"Verdict?"

"He's alive," I said. "But he won't be for long."

Wilhelm said nothing. He picked up the Stradivarius and tucked it under one arm while still controlling the Heckler. "Partial payment for my inconvenience," he said and motioned to his driver. Without a word, the driver eased the Rembrandt out into the hall. When he stepped back in the room, Wilhelm said, "Any damage?"

"It looks fine."

"Of course it's fine," Garcetti shouted. "It's fine and it's mine and keep your damn hands off!"

"Take the painting downstairs," Wilhelm said calmly. "Count the money. If it's right, send Huygens on his way."

Wilhelm's driver nodded and left.

"You can't do that!" Garcetti blurted. "That money's mine!" Garcetti stepped away from the wall, the blood vessels knotted on his neck about to burst. "You can't get away with this. I won't have it. All I've worked for . . ."

"Back to the wall," Wilhelm said, his eyes frozen on his advisory. "I told your father I wanted no part of this. You must not have gotten the message. So, I'm delivering it in person."

I could almost hear Garcetti's mind cranking. He was trapped, literally backed against the wall, watching everything he'd worked and hoped for racing down the stairs. He couldn't let that turn to dust. Not without a fight.

He lunged across the desk, groping for one of the guns, any gun when the rapid-fire burst of Wilhelm's machine gun slammed him back to the wall where he slid down to the floor.

Wilhelm's demeanor did not change.

"What are you going to do now?" I asked as Wilhelm backed to the door.

"I'm going to resume my life."

"What about the boy?" I asked. "What about Marcus and Lia?"

Wilhelm stepped over Silvio and out onto the landing. "Occupy yourself with the wounded," he cautioned. "If I see one of you on the stairway, I'll come back and kill you all. Officer?"

"Yes?" a shaken Filippo answered, his voice a whisper.

"No heroics."

Filippo nodded. "No heroics," he said softly as Wilhelm climbed down the stairs.

I grabbed the Ruger and raced to the door.

"*Dottore*. No!"

I stopped.

I heard voices.

I heard a door slam.

I heard the sound of a child echoing in an empty house.

Chapter Twenty-Three

The Hotel Raphael felt eerily quiet as I packed my bag. Before I checked out, I reported in to Clair Bowman. When she answered, I reminded her that she wanted to be kept informed, even if it was bad news.

"How bad is it?" she asked.

"About as bad as it can get," I said. "The paintings are lost. Peter Garcetti hid them without telling anyone where he stashed them. Garcetti's dead."

The only sound on the line was a distant hum.

"I don't know what to say," Clair Bowman finally managed. "Lost?"

"Yes. I'm flying home. I'll stop by. We can talk then," I said and hung up. My second call was to Brody Flynn who sounded eager to hear my voice.

"I've got the details on the Gardner heist," I said. "Peter Garcetti was behind it."

"He was at the top of my list," Brody said. "Is he still in Italy?"

"He's in the morgue. Nick Bianchi is in the hospital recovering from surgery on a broken kneecap. The police have him under wraps here for shooting a local, which may delay getting him back to the US for the murder of Angela Ricci and JoJo Weems. Any word on what happened to Charles Raskin? Did Nick do him in as well?"

"No. Raskin showed up in Maine where he was hiding out in his sister's house. She convinced him to come back and tell all he knows. Francesco Vega gave him five hundred bucks to look the other way. Where did Vega end up?"

"Wrapped in plastic."

"Say again?"

"He's the local Nick took out along with two others. It's a long story. I'm coming home, Brody. I'll tell you then."

"I'll buy lunch," Brody said and hung up.

Sergeant Filippo was busy finishing his report when I stopped by to see him before going to the airport. He seemed happy with what he'd written in triplicate.

"I didn't get to thank you," I said. "When you stepped into that room, things were looking bleak. Why'd you come back?"

"Pietro's insistence that I travel to Latina," Filippo said. "It reminded me of many conversations I shared with *Don* Roberto. He often sent me on wild goose chases so that he could conduct his illegal business. He swore that it was to keep me from harm, but I knew that was not the case. Pietro learned many things well from his grandfather. Sending me off to Latina was one, so I did not go. Instead, I went to the apartment where Severino had been killed. There was something there I wanted to look at again. Do you know what that was, *dottore*? I will tell you. It was a closet filled with a man's clothes. Those clothes were much too small for Severino, but they fit perfectly on the body of Francesco Vega."

"Garcetti said he kept him on ice. Maybe Severino's fulltime job was to make sure Francesco never left that apartment."

"That is my thinking," Filippo said. "Pietro kept him as a prisoner which is why you could not find him."

"It doesn't matter now," I said.

"No," Filippo said. "It doesn't matter. Have you an opinion regarding Ogilvy? Is this man a crook or no?"

"I don't think so," I said.

"Nor do I. He is just an office manager making sure Giuseppe Vega had plenty of work. That reminds me, my men went to work in the storage facility Pietro had rented. Sorry, *dottore*, they found none of the Gardner paintings. None in Giuseppe's shop either. My men went back and opened every crate. Nothing."

"Too bad about Giuseppe's son," I said, not wanting the reminder that the paintings were lost. "Finding Francesco wrapped like that on top of that lovely sofa."

"Too bad about many things," Filippo admitted as I put Francesco's notebook on the sergeant's desk. "What is this, *dottore*?"

"Notes about how to act like Aldo Conte. Paint formulas to help create a masterpiece. Sketches Francesco made of shipping crates and the leather sofa. You might want the notebook for your records."

Filippo flipped through the pages. "A man of many talents," he said and dropped the notebook into his top drawer. "Pietro, too, was a man of many talents. A ruthless man of many talents. He ordered the killings, yes? Nicolas Bianchi pulled the trigger."

"Nick's job was to dole out punishment. He was very good at it."

"The killings bothered me, *dottore*. Almost as much as finding the narcotics. *Don* Roberto would never agree to such a business. And, here, his grandson was about to open such a shop. I would hate for *Don* Roberto to hear me say that Pietro's dying was a good thing, but that is what I believe. A better thing is that Lia and Marcus are both safe. Is a miracle, no? Wilhelm let them go."

"Once Peter fell into the trap of sending his bodyguards to Villa Sciarra, Wilhelm knew there'd be few gunmen left at the house. He got all the mileage he needed out of holding Lia and Marcus, so he released them and came after the spoils of war."

"Two masterpieces," Filippo mused. "A violin and a canvas."

"What will you do now that the Stradivarius has again been stolen?"

"I suppose that depends on you, *dottore*. You could ask that my department look into the original moment the Stradivarius was reported missing. If so, I would be obligated to involve the insurance company and Aldo Conte and his son, Silvio, who at this moment is suffering in the hospital. My superior has spoken to me about the situation, *dottore*. I agree with him in this instance, which is saying something as he and I do not often agree. But here, we think little is to be gained by speaking publically about the theft of either the violin or the painting."

"No? Why shove them under the rug?"

Filippo wagged one finger. "No, no. The question is, why ruin the possibilities of a fine life that may come the way of Marcus Conte? If convicted of fraud, Aldo would likely die in prison. If convicted of robbery, Silvio's already tarnished life will be ruined. How will Marcus survive that, living already with the knowledge that his father was an American gangster shot dead during the theft of the very violin that began the downward spiral of the Conte family?" Filippo let the thought settle, then said, "It is the official position of this department, which will be confirmed in my report, that the Stradivarius and the Rembrandt were stolen by the notorious Wilhelm Barr who has left this country for parts unknown."

"That's it?" I asked. "No involvement of Peter Garcetti?"

"It is enough that the man is dead. *Don* Roberto accomplished many fine things in his life. It is best to remember those and not the lapses of his grandson."

"But he was behind the robbery of the Gardner," I protested.

"All fingers point to your father, *dottore*. That, too, will be in my report." He pushed himself up from his chair. "I hope you find the missing artwork. You will continue your hunt upon your return to America, yes?"

"I have my plane ticket, if that's what you mean."

"Excellent," Filippo boomed and extended his chubby hand.

A feeling of hopelessness rushed through me as I considered walking away. In the end, I reached out and shook Filippo's hand.

"I hope the Contes appreciate all you've done," I said.

Filippo shrugged. "We do what we can, *dottore*. That is all we can do."

The Fiumicino Airport was packed with its usual jostling crowd. I checked in, passed security, and headed to the gate as my cell phone rang.

"Gina," I said. "I was going to call you. We can add the Gardner paintings to all the lost art we're looking for. Peter Garcetti hid them where no one can find them."

"Someone will make him talk."

"He's dead."

"What happened?"

"It's a long story," I said. "And I'll gladly tell you once I collect my thoughts. I think a trip to Spain is in order in the next week or so."

"Splendid," Gina chirped. "We can coordinate your visit with the delivery of the ransom. The London collector is anxious to get his Matisse back as well as news of the other pieces lost in his collection."

"I take it the thieves and you have agreed on a location to transact business?"

"We have, the Catalonia Plaza Hotel. Madrid."

"Excellent. And we're dealing with them directly? Niles Huygens is out of the picture?"

"I guess you haven't heard, Theo. The *Garde Nationale* raided Huygens' Appraisals last week. Niles Huygens has been locked up in France for the past several days."

"That's impossible," I said. "Huygens was here in Rome last night. My father . . ."

I caught myself. My father would never mention the name of the man who bought *Christ in the Storm of Galilee*. Wilhelm's life, his dealings, his whereabouts were a secret. Whoever took delivery of that Rembrandt at the bottom of the stairs, no one will ever know.

"Theo? Your father what?"

"My father cleaned up a mess."

"You're not making much sense."

"No, I'm not. Book me a room at the Catalonia and I'll collect the Matisse. I could deal with a simple, uncomplicated transaction."

"Rome got complicated?"

"Very, but finished."

"You're saying we're out of the missing persons business?"

"Missing person found. Case closed," I said, knowing that was far from the truth.

As I boarded the plane for my flight back to Boston, I wondered if 'case closed' would ever be applied to the Gardner heist.

Somehow, I had my doubts.

About the Author

Larry Maness is the author of two books of plays and four novels. *3 Plays* were introduced by Pulitzer prize-winner, William Inge. His plays "War Rabbit" and "Bailey" both premiered in New York City at The American Theatre of Actors.

His first novel, *Nantucket Revenge*, is called "The best beach read since *Jaws*" according to *Florida Crime Writers* author Steve Glassman. His second novel, *A Once Perfect Place*, is included in the Literature of Social Change collection at Duke University. *Strangler*, his third novel featuring Private Investigator Jake Eaton, is a Detective Book Club selection. *The Voice of God*, his fourth novel, is called by Rosemary Herbert, author of *The Oxford Companion to Crime & Mystery Writing*, "an assured production that snares the reader from start to finish."

Maness lives on the south shore of Massachusetts with his wife, Marianne, known as "The Cookie Lady" in some parts of the world.

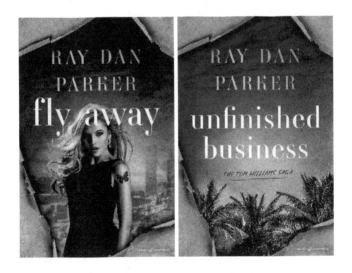

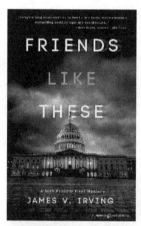

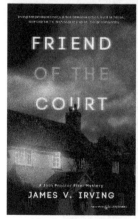

Printed in the USA
CPSIA information can be obtained
at www.ICGtesting.com
LVHW041804110324
774146LV00001B/136